CHRISTMAS IN Crooked Creek

A Crooked Creek Novel

MK McCLINTOCK

Christmas in Crooked Creek

Join the women of Crooked Creek in a heartwarming tale of survival, hope, love, and maybe even a Christmas miracle.

As the holiday season approaches, Michael and Clara must find the courage to let go of the past, survive the present, and embrace a future neither envisioned.

Trappers Peak Publishing
Bigfork, Montana 59911
www.mkmcclintock.com

Christmas in Crooked Creek; novel/MK McClintock
Cover Design by MK McClintock
Cover images: Deposit Photos and Shutterstock

*To all those whose favorite holiday is Christmas,
and especially to those who know it's about more than presents.*

PROLOGUE

"Tragedy and heartache have touched us all, and we'll carry those memories for the rest of our lives, but our adversities have brought us all here and strengthened us."

- Emma Latimer in "Clara of Crooked Creek"

Appomattox Station, Virginia
April 8, 1865

DEATH WOULD NOT TAKE HIM. With his breathing labored, the lieutenant removed his glove and reached for his side. When he held his hand inches from his face, he didn't need to see the red, sticky blood to know he had little time. Michael smelled death everywhere, and it would seem heaven intended for him to meet the grave before this godforsaken war ended.

Gun powder filled his nostrils and his eyes watered,

caused by smoke lingering in the air from cannons and gunfire. He should be used to it after four harrowing years, yet he breathed in the acrid air as though smelling the horrors for the first time.

He saw Lieutenant Colonel Augustus Root falter and lost sight of the commander in the chaos. The 15th New York Cavalry was weary, yet they still secured the Richmond-Lynchburg Stage Road and charged into Appomattox Court House. Michael righted himself atop his horse, as exhausted and battle worn as he was, and followed the others.

He didn't know why one shot out of so many drew his attention.

A bullet struck their colonel's neck and pandemonium ensued.

"Retreat!" His shouts pierced through the din of shots and screams. "Retreat!" The calvary pulled back, taking as many prisoners as they could. He never had the stomach for it. His commanding officer often told him he felt too much sympathy for the enemy. Yet, Michael knew a man who fought on the other side of a battle was not automatically an enemy.

A single cry from the cacophony of discord reached his ears. One of the Union men—a boy of nineteen who dreamt of soldiering and the excitement of action—wanted desperately to fight before the war ended. John was his name. The week before, he'd regaled Michael with tales of the adventures he planned to take when he finished his enlistment. The boy tumbled forward across the body of a fallen Confederate soldier, his face now planted in the blood-soaked earth.

Those few seconds of distraction became Michael's undoing. He lurched, and his strong steed reared back. A bullet to his back joined the one already in his side, and he toppled from his mount. How many men took shots they never saw coming during the war? he wondered as he hovered on the brink of unconsciousness. Michael grieved for those whose job called upon them to keep count of every fallen soldier, adding them to list after list, until the names blurred together and hearts became numb.

Michael never once fired his gun unless he could see the iris of the other man's eyes. The brief moment between recognizing death and extinguishing life was his penance for taking so many. Even if it had been in the name of freedom under the cloak of war, he could not reconcile the needless loss of life.

He knew the taste and longing for freedom well. His family had come to America from Ireland in search of freedom and hope, and he was raised to believe no man should enslave another and no state or industry belonged to only one people. He believed in a united country, though the reality soon overpowered the ideals. Hope for a better future, for their country and families, kept the exhausted and disillusioned soldiers pushing forward in search of the light beyond war's darkness . . . hope that the lost lives had been sacrificed for a purpose greater than one person.

He wanted to believe, but as his body pressed into the ground, beneath the weight of boots running to their salvations, he whispered, "Please, Death, do not take me. Not yet. Not now."

CHAPTER 1

"It is difficult to describe the air here. I suppose the closest I can come to it is the year we summered in Maine and the cool breeze carried the sweet scent of fresh pine everywhere we went."

- Clara Stowe to her parents soon after her arrival in Crooked Creek, May 1866

Crooked Creek, Montana Territory
December 4, 1866

CRYSTALS FROSTED THE WINDOWPANES and snowflakes melted from pine branches beneath a bright afternoon sun. The Stowe Family Inn bustled with life during the long summer days, well into the crisp autumn nights of September.

With winter underway, only the bravest of travelers, seasoned mountain folk, and miners or timber workers from nearby settlements made their way to Crooked Creek, Montana, the quaint mountain town Clara Stowe now called home. Crooked Creek boasted two hundred and twenty-seven souls, tucked away in a valley of meadows and thick woods brimming with fresh-scented pine trees. Many of them she was proud to call friends.

A few reclusive townsfolk kept to themselves, while others relished in the meager social events during the rare times when they stopped working long enough to appreciate their land, freedom, and livelihoods. More than eight months since the war's end, men still trickled through in search of lost families and second chances, or to simply forget.

Clara's extreme excursion west began as a grand adventure and an attempt to escape the painful memories of loss from the war.

"Heroism arises from the unexpected," Gideon once said, "because only out of the unexpected does one discover the true depth of one's courage."

Clara Stowe had recited Gideon's words every day since she left her comfortable, New England life for an adventure she had promised to fulfill in his memory. What an adventure it had thus far been. The slightest tilt of her lips formed a smile, the same as every time she thought of Alice's father. He'd given her more than one precious gift before succumbing to duty's call.

She'd been told the vast, western territories held hope, promise, and opportunity. Clara had found all three, though none came without struggle. She ran her hand over the polished banister of the wide staircase and enjoyed the snowy landscape through one of the sparkling glass windows by the front door. The grand home, originally built, she was told, by an extravagant Connecticut man who thought to turn Crooked Creek into a great mining boomtown, had become a solace for Clara since her arrival in Montana. Luckily for Clara and the townsfolk, Mr. Cromwell's mining scheme did not go as planned. Now the home belonged to her and her daughter.

She walked through the cozy dining room to ensure her guests did not want more beverages or another helping of Susan's delicious food. Clara greeted them with smiles and the charm learned from childhood. Her mother had groomed her for a life of entertaining—a life Clara once thought she desired with its endless comforts—until Gideon.

Through his eyes, she had seen the possibility of a life and purpose beyond ballrooms, grand dinners, and dress fittings. Gideon's dream, then hers, brought Clara and their daughter, Alice, to the boundless expanse of Montana. Before the war, when ambitions held no limit, Gideon thrived on the adventures written and told of frontier explorers: Zebulon Pike and the impressive Pike's Peak named in his honor; Jim Bridger, who was known as the first white man to see the Great Salt Lake; and Kit Carson, the trapper, soldier, and guide who explored the southwest up through Oregon. Their stories, and those of many others who ventured west in search of adventure and the unknown, enthralled the young man from Connecticut until the day he enlisted. Gideon then embarked on a new adventure with an ending none of them expected. He missed his chance to follow the same path as the great mountain men of legends. However, in Crooked Creek, even in a small way, Clara and Alice could experience a little of those adventures for him.

Clara crossed from the dining room into the sitting room and across the foyer, each step over freshly waxed wood floors and thick hooked rugs in floral patterns with shades of ivory, red, and green and furnishings Mr. Cromwell left behind with the house. She longed to open windows and welcome in the fragrance of pine and the sounds of birds enjoying the sunlight, as she did for many months in summer and autumn.

Clara learned quickly after the first, early snow how winter in the majestic Rocky Mountains was unforgiving to the unprepared. Thankfully, she had friends aplenty in her new home who offered guidance and support. While New England winters were harsh, Montana offered a challengingly cold and unexpected season. Clara recalled asking what Hattie meant by "unexpected."

Her friend had delicately responded, "We'll make a list of what you'll need to see you through winter."

With gratitude in her heart for wonderful friends who cared for each other and a secure home to keep her and Alice safe and warm, Clara stepped outside. Wrapped in her plaid shawl of fine wool, she stood on the expansive front porch, protected from most elements, yet a faint breeze ruffled the wisps of hair fallen from their pins.

Clara watched from a distance as the townspeople of Crooked Creek crossed from one side of the frost-covered road to the next, moving through their daily routines. She enjoyed the view from her property and smiled as she imagined how the inn would look for the coming holiday season. Her land—Gideon's dream, now her dream. She held fast to their imagined life every day since her arrival. Knowing the life she was forging in Crooked Creek was what he wanted for her and Alice instilled in Clara the courage to keep faith, regardless of the obstacles, and push forward.

They had always celebrated Christmas at home in Connecticut with festive gatherings of friends and family. Even during the war years, the traditions continued for Alice's sake, and as battles raged on, her mother was careful not to pare down the festivities. Christmas 1861 was the first one in Clara's memory when her mother did not host a lavish holiday celebration. The expense once reserved for such extravagance was given to younger families in a nearby parish who, with husbands away, struggled to feed their families. Clara learned of her parents' generosity and kindness by chance from a parishioner, for her father and mother never spoke of it. The tradition continued each war year after, touching Clara deeply and setting an exemplary example for Alice.

Clara desired to mark their first Christmas in their new home with a celebration like those of Alice's childhood—though not nearly as grand—resplendent with warm hearths, delicious fare, and friends and family around the table.

The sound of a wagon passing over frozen dirt and pebbles drew Clara away from her rambling musings, and she shivered from the full force of the early winter cold. A genuine smile formed on her lips as Peyton Sawyer pulled his wagon to a stop parallel to the porch.

"You shouldn't be outside without a coat," Peyton said, smiling from atop the wagon's bench.

"Your timing is good. I was just about to go inside." Clara's smile brightened as Peyton helped his wife down from the wagon, earning him both a glare from the dark-haired beauty and a soft kiss. Clara laughed, for she remembered being in Briley's condition once.

"You are the picture of a happy, blooming mother-to-be."

Briley patted the top of her extended midsection and spoke in her soft Irish brogue. "I am the picture of a woman eager for the mother part." She pointed to her husband. "This one refuses to let me remain at home without him." Briley smiled up at Clara. "Like I cannot sit and do my needlework next to my own warm fire."

Peyton rolled his eyes. However, Clara caught the undeniable love that burned every time his gaze settled on

his wife. Clara remembered that feeling, as well. Briley was
one of three women she considered the dearest of friends,
and like herself, each had forged a new life in Crooked
Creek. They had each been sincerely blessed to find great
love.

"I am always happy for the company, and my warm fire
comes with Susan's cookies."

Briley grinned. "For Susan's cookies, I'll forgive my
husband his mothering."

Peyton smoothly ignored his wife's teasing. "You have
guests. Three, if I recall."

"It is comforting to know you are always watching over
us, Sheriff. Yes, there are three guests, though one is leaving
today. He is a photographer from South Carolina making his
way across the territories, though he confessed waiting until
spring would have been wiser. I had hoped to have Alice sit
for a photograph before he left."

Peyton's brow furrowed. "I didn't know he was a
photographer."

Clara gave him an indulgent smile. "I do not believe he
intentionally hid his profession from you. You're aware guests
tend to share more information with someone offering a
comfortable room and serving them a hearty meal than with
an intimidating lawman."

Peyton's left brow inched up. "You think I'm
intimidating?"

Briley laughed and held onto her husband's arm as he
helped her up the steps and out of the cold. "You've done it
now, Clara. He'll be strutting around town, terrifying every
man who doesn't properly announce themselves."

Peyton indulged his wife by adding a chuckle to their
joined laughter. Once the door closed behind them, the
warmth from the inn's fireplaces seeped back into Clara's

skin. Peyton kissed his wife soundly, tipped his hat to Clara, and promised to return in a few hours.

Briley waited for her husband to depart before releasing a soft sigh. "Thank goodness."

Clara laughed and invited Briley to sit on the settee. "You sound like a woman needing a respite from her husband."

Briley settled with her back against one of the delicate floral pillows she'd sewn for Clara and accepted a light blanket to cover her legs. "Glad I am to spend every breathing minute with that man, but dear me, he worries over me more than a mother does her newborn babe."

"He is just excited and protective as any husband and father should be."

"He is at that," Briley agreed. "Never did I imagine this moment. I came here to marry a stranger and found Peyton instead. This babe will be lucky to have him for a papa, though I daresay he is less anxious than I am."

"You have both had plenty of practice with Emma and Casey's baby."

"Oh, and the sweetest dear one ever, he is. From how Casey dotes on the boy, I do not believe the worry leaves after the babe is born."

"No, it does not." A twinge poked at Clara's heart, as it always did when she thought of what Gideon missed by never knowing his beautiful daughter.

"Forgive my heartless words."

Clara held out her hand to stop Briley from sitting forward. "You are never heartless."

"You still think of him often."

She did not mean it to be a question.

Clara answered anyway. "Not as often as I once did. I miss Gideon, true, except it is Alice who has lost out not knowing her father." She clasped Briley's hands. "Let Peyton worry and care for you until you have gone mad from his smothering of love."

"I will." Briley wiped away a fallen tear. "It does not take much to set me crying these days."

"Then let us talk of it no more." Clara leaned back and forced herself to relax. "Have you thought of names for the baby?"

"We have. For a girl . . . you have guests," Briley said as she peeked out a window. "Someone is coming."

Clara and Briley waited for the two riders' faces to come into focus when they stopped in front of the inn. Briley waved through the window. "'Tis Hattie and Carson."

"It seems the morning sun has brought everyone out early today." Clara rose with the grace of a seasoned hostess. Though Carson and Hattie White Eagle were two of her closest friends, she ensured that all who arrived at her door was welcomed as a special guest.

With hair fairer than Clara's and bright green eyes that burned with love for her husband, friends, and the land she nurtured, Hattie White Eagle found her new beginning in Crooked Creek with a man whose affection for the land ran as deeply as her own.

Hattie laughed and shook her head at something her husband said as they walked their horses closer. Clara, at rare times, envied Hattie's freedom to ride across the land as though the wind carried horse and rider as one. She once saw Hattie and Carson race across their ranch land, both laughing even when no clear victor could be called. Clara had yet to be comfortable enough on a horse to attempt more than a walk, though living within sight of town did not require much more than her own two legs for transportation.

They reached the front door before Clara. Carson opened it wide enough to enter and quickly ushered his wife inside. A fierce wind blew in behind them before Carson secured the door. "You both look too happy, considering how far you have ridden in this cold."

Hattie smiled and waved away Clara's concern. "This is only a glimpse of what is to come. Carson says we should expect a hard winter to take us several months into early spring at this rate. You've prepared well, Clara, so all should be fine for you, Alice, and your guests."

"Thanks to all of you." Clara hoped she kept her nerves from showing. While New England winters could be fierce, they passed in a few months, and she never had to worry about where necessities such as water and food came from; her family provided all they desired. Even during the war years, her parents' connections helped procure whatever they needed, not only for their family but many others as well.

Not until she arrived in Montana did she realize her new home lacked indoor plumbing, and delivery of goods was not commonplace. She had, of course, expected to face more challenges in the mountains than in Connecticut, yet there were days when the lack of amenities made her a little weary.

"Clara?"

She pushed thoughts of home and her unsettled nerves to the back of her mind. "I am sorry, Carson. What did you say?"

"Elis said you could do with more hay for the stable."

"Yes, thank you. Elis mentioned we were running low." She felt like a fool. After seven months, she still knew so little, but her education on frontier living expanded daily. Elis, who came highly recommended by Petyon, and who she hired two months after her arrival, managed the grounds and kept the house in excellent working order. He also kindly reminded her when something needed purchasing. Clara had arrived in town blessed with the financial resources to see her through several years. However, she soon learned money did not buy warmth during a long, frigid winter when one was unprepared.

"I am sorry. May I offer you tea or coffee? Briley is in the sitting room."

Hattie looked at her husband first, then said, "That would be nice, thank you. We have time for coffee."

Clara entered the warm kitchen where water was always at a near boil, and the fresh scent of rising bread and molasses cake in the oven invited visitors to sit a spell. Soon after Clara gave a few quick instructions to the inn's cook, she carried two cups of coffee back to her guests, followed by Sadie, a young woman who occasionally helped at the inn, who brought out a tray with two cups, a teapot, and a plate of ginger spice cookies.

Carson lifted the tray from Sadie's hands and set it down for her. When the young woman left, Clara shifted into the role of hostess. Tea for her and Briley, coffee for Hattie and Carson. Ginger cookies were passed around, and the small group smiled in appreciation for good food, warm drink, and friendship.

"Susan gave me her recipe for these." Briley took another bite of her cookie and sighed. "There must be a secret she did not reveal, for mine never taste this good."

"Susan guards her kitchen secrets well." Clara sipped her tea and thought back to late spring when she had first met Susan and her children. Half-starved with little hope for their future, they had been the inn's first employees, and quickly became Clara's dear friends. With Susan's children spending the winter in Salt Lake City with cousins, her friend spent more time bustling about the kitchen, constantly experimenting with new recipes. She suspected Elis's affection for the cook had extended beyond the woman's culinary talents. He was never late for a meal or to visit with Susan over a batch of cookies or cinnamon buns fresh from the oven.

Her thoughts returned to the present and what Hattie had said earlier. She peered out the window where the sun's bright glow off the snow-covered ground had diminished in the past hour. "Exactly *how* hard will the winter be, Carson?"

His expression grim, Carson took a few seconds to mull over his words before speaking. "Winter will be what it will be, and no amount of worrying will change that. You're prepared, Clara, with a full larder, plenty of hay for the horse on the way, and enough cut wood to heat every room in your inn."

He did not answer her question, and Clara suspected he would not, at least not directly. "It's the folks at the camp just outside town who aren't prepared that concern me."

A sliver of guilt momentarily overtook Clara. Carson, as usual, was right in his assessment. No matter how hard winter might be, she and those in her employ would not suffer. The camp Carson spoke of comprised half a dozen wooden huts, a few too broken down to be habitable. Four families lived there, by last count. "Carson, you told me once that the first settlers in Crooked Creek lived there before they moved the town to this spot. Are those the same cabins?"

"They are, and we should have torn them down years ago, but hunters occasionally use them."

"Will they not move into town before the worst of winter sets in?"

Briley spoke up first. "Peyton has asked, and they refused. They are a proud group of Irish and won't accept charity, and work this time of year is scarce."

"They don't intend to stay." Hattie set her half-empty cup back on the tray. "Carson was out there a couple of weeks ago, and they mentioned they plan to move on as soon as possible."

"To where?" Clara asked. "I cannot imagine they will get far this time of year."

Carson also set his empty cup down and fingered the leather gloves he held in one hand. "They might find work in Helena, though their destination is California. Tensions between soldiers and tribes right now are tenuous south of here. They certainly would be safer in Crooked Creek until spring, if we can persuade them to stay."

Clara wondered at the look Carson shared with Hattie, and the one Hattie returned. She remembered similar glances with Gideon, often before a difficult decision had to be made. Clara asked Briley, "Has Peyton said if anything can be done to help these families? I cannot imagine how they will brave the winter alone, especially if they have children."

The mother-to-be cradled her teacup in both hands like one would hold a baby bird and sipped before answering. "Could be if they accepted help. We Irish are oftentimes too proud, and every one of them staying in those cabins comes from my homeland. Peyton thought it might help to hear from one of their own." Briley shrugged. "I tried, but my words did nothing to sway them."

"Neither could we." In an automatic gesture, Carson rose and held a hand out for Hattie to hold as they stood together. "We'll try again on our way back to the ranch. Do you need more beef here, Clara?"

"Thank you for always watching over us. We have plenty of salted and dried meat to see us through winter if the cold and snow continue to keep guests away. I'd like to serve roast for Christmas dinner."

"We'll see you have plenty."

Clara stood and walked her friends to the front door. Carson stopped before she could open it.

"Has anyone come to the inn from the lumber mill looking to board with you?"

She shook her head. "No. Is it not about twenty miles north of town? I recall hearing of it a few times, though I do not believe I have met anyone from there. They have a self-sufficient operation at the camp, do they not?"

Carson nodded. "Yes, except spring flooding from the mountain took out a third of the cabins and washed out part of the road between Crooked Creek and the camp. Deliveries have been hindered, and word is some men have left the mill."

Clara glanced over her shoulder at Briley who still nursed her tea. "Does Peyton know?"

"We're headed to his office next to let him know. Two men from the mill camped at the edge of the ranch last night and nearly froze to death. Promise me you won't board any man from the lumber camp, Clara."

Clara studied Carson and wondered at the deep concern she saw in his sky-blue eyes. "If someone needs a place to stay—"

"Promise me, Clara. Or, if not for me, for Hattie, for Emma." He tilted his head to indicate Briley. "For all of you."

"What are you not saying, Carson?"

Hattie touched Clara's arm. "I had the same questions, with no answer, either. Please, trust him on this."

"Of course, you know I do." Clara nodded. "I will refer them to Peyton if any stop by."

"Good."

Carson and Hattie left through the front and quickly shut it behind them to keep the cold air out. Clouds formed beyond the covered porch, darkening the land. Only a few minutes before, the sun had welcomed everyone to bask in its rare winter appearance. She wrapped her arms around her body, hugging tight to ward off the sudden chill.

"Clara?"

She caught Briley pushing herself up from the settee.

"You are to rest, or it will be my head."

Briley grinned. "Not if you don't tell my husband. Come, I want to see what your Alice is up to. She's a pleasant reminder of what awaits."

"You are impossible. You make mischief every time Peyton leaves you for me to watch over. What do you tell him when he picks you up?"

"I smile." To prove that is all it would take, Briley slipped an arm through Clara's, grinned at her friend, and leaned on her a little as they walked into the kitchen where Alice chattered around a scone, while Susan removed a fresh batch from the oven.

For all Briley's good spirits, Clara clearly saw exhaustion etched around her friend's eyes. This would be Briley's second winter in Montana, and another Christmas without her mother, father, and brother. She confessed to Clara only the week before that while too often little more than the essentials were scarce in their home, her family had cherished Christmas.

Clara thought of her family's home, grand and bustling with activity during the holidays, with never a thought where the next meal, trinket, or new dress would come from. Even though this holiday season would be her and Alice's first away from the splendor, and while a gentle twinge pushed against the edges of her heart, Clara had only to think of Gideon and their shared dreams. The dreams that, against the odds, were now hers to carry on.

CHAPTER 2

"You asked what keeps me here, and I hope the enclosed photograph, courtesy of the mercantile, explains the draw of this majestic land. It is more beautiful than I could have ever imagined. I am told the snow-capped mountain peaks are not uncommon in summer."

- Clara Stowe to her parents a month after she arrived in Crooked Creek, June 1867

DAYLIGHT MADE WAY for the moon to gently replace the sun and cast a soft blue hue on the inn's front porch. The heavy wool shawl Briley made for and gifted to her before the weather began its first turn into autumn kept her warm against the cold, early-evening air.

Unwilling to surrender her few moments of solace before retiring to bed, Clara returned to the porch night after night. Only when winds stiff enough to make the porch roof creak or rain substantial enough to reach beneath the eaves, did she watch the sunset from within the comfort of her sitting room.

The night brought a blessed silence save for a slight ruffling of leaves and the smell of promised snow. She thought Carson daft when he first said one could smell the snow long before its soft, white flakes appeared. Though familiar with snow in New England, she had never once noticed if it carried a bouquet strong enough to detect.

She learned from Carson how to predict a snowfall, and from Hattie how to tell when a mare was ready to drop her foal. Emma taught her how to make a salve to treat minor scrapes and burns, and Briley showed her how to stitch a delicate edge on her pristine white handkerchiefs. Her needlework had always been subpar, so she cherished every new piece created under Briley's guidance.

Alice would know as many things, and far more, than the limited lessons of reading, writing, needlework, and dancing Clara had been taught in her youth. Numbers, geography, and history were just as valuable, and between school and Clara's supplemental teaching, Alice's quick mind would be well educated. Clara, however, wanted more for her daughter. To sew as Briley, to learn the way of animals like Hattie, and like Emma, to reach beyond what most women of their age achieve. To become whatever she desired and to see however much of the world she longed to explore.

That was also part of the dream she and Gideon had shared for the children they planned to have together. Alice and Gideon would never meet in this life, yet for their sake, Clara held firm to the belief they would know each other in the next.

She breathed in the night air, noticing only now the temperature had dropped several degrees while her mind wandered between past and future. Pulling the edges of the shawl tighter over her chest, Clara rose from one of the sturdy pine rockers left by the unsuccessful Mr. Cromwell and gazed once more upon the snow-covered trees and ground. The brook nearby continued to flow, and if she listened carefully in the darkness, its burbling music drowned out the sadness of her memories.

More than the water's sound reached her ears. A broken twig? The swish of a branch as someone passed? A whisper or two? Clara braced herself against one of the posts holding up the porch roof and gripped the top of a railing. She did not leave the protection of the sturdy structure but leaned as far over the railing as possible to hear more.

The next sound, a child's soft whimper, was unmistakable.

"Who is out there?" She thought of the rifle hanging safely out of Alice's reach inside, the rifle her dear friends' husbands insisted she learned to use. With only one lesson to her credit, Clara did not trust her aim, nor did she think she could raise the weapon at a human being.

Was it a child or an animal?

The whimper reached her ears again. Undeniably a child. Almost to the second she decided to leave the porch and seek out the young boy or girl, two shadows emerged from the trees, one several feet taller than the other.

Again, she asked, "Who is there?"

As if the adult was unsure about putting a voice to their presence, the response was several seconds in coming.

"Please, we mean no harm." The woman's clear and strong voice fit the form that soon appeared beneath a sliver of moonlight. "My horse came up lame, and I had to let her return home without us. I had heard there was a hotel in Crooked Creek."

Clara clearly saw both woman and girl now and ushered them up the steps. "You have found it." The woman, too delicate in manners and appearance to be without a home of her own, held fast to the young girl's hand. "Come inside and out of the cold."

Once inside, Clara propelled them toward the sitting room, where a fire still burned in the hearth. "Please, sit and warm yourselves. I believe Susan is still in the kitchen preparing for tomorrow's breakfast. You both could use something warm to drink and eat. How long have you been walking?"

"I am not sure. My watch came unclasped at some point. The sun began to set when we were forced to walk." The woman stroked her daughter's hands in her own and encouraged the girl to sit on the floor closer to the fire's warmth.

"Close to an hour," Clara confirmed. "I am not in the habit of expecting or insisting on explanations from people who show up at my door, but for your daughter's sake, I must."

The woman nodded. "My name is Augusta, and this is Grace. It is true; we need a warm place to sleep tonight. We won't be a bother and will leave early tomorrow."

Worry tightened Clara's chest. "And go where, without a horse? There is more snow coming. I can send someone to deliver word to your family that you've arrived. Your husband?"

Augusta shook her head and darted a glance at Grace. "No, please. No one must know we are here."

"Whatever the issue, Sheriff Peyton is a good man. He can be trusted. I can get word to him tonight, and tomorrow—"

"No one." Augusta stood as though readying to leave.

"Wait." Clara coaxed Augusta back onto the chair. Grace had moved closer to her mother, kneeling beside the cushioned seat. "Please, stay. I won't ask any more of you tonight. Tomorrow will be soon enough for such discussions."

As much as she wanted to know more, the pair needed sustenance, sleep, and a place to feel safe. "My name is Clara Stowe, and you are welcome here. My daughter and I live on the top floor, with spare rooms down the hall. Private, where no one will disturb you. There are only two other guests at the inn tonight."

The other woman studied Clara and finally nodded. "Thank you."

"For now, stay by the fire while I speak with the cook." She added before Augusta could object, "She will not ask for details beyond what I will tell her. We have welcomed guests before who found themselves lost."

Augusta rubbed the back of her hand over Grace's cheek. "We are in your debt."

Clara left them alone and made her way through the lower floor of the inn to the kitchen. Susan had already cleaned the counters and put away kitchen tools, dishes, and dry goods for the night. A large bowl sat in the center of the long table, which ran almost the room length. Covered with a tea towel, it no doubt held dough for tomorrow's bread.

After a quick check, Clara found the stove top still hot, and the water inside the kettle warm enough for tea. The door to the pantry opened, and Susan came through the portal between the pantry and kitchen.

"Oh, Clara. I did not hear you. Are you after tea, then? I thought you'd gone to bed already."

"I tarried outside longer than usual and welcomed new guests in the process. They found themselves stranded because of a lame horse and will stay for the night. Is there any soup left from tonight's dinner and a few squares of cornbread?"

Susan set the paper and pencil she'd been holding down. "Of course, there is enough of both to feed two more. Are there more than two new guests?"

"No, a woman and her daughter. I do not want to send them to bed without something to eat." Clara sensed Susan wanted to ask more about the newcomers, but as predicted, she did not.

"I was just taking an inventory of the pantry, and could use another cup of tea myself. Would you care for one?"

Clara did not, then thought better of having nothing to do with her hands while Augusta and Grace ate. "Yes, and a small square of the cornbread, if there is enough. Yours is the best cornbread I've tasted. How are the stores? Do you have all the nonperishables you need?"

Susan nodded and stoked the fire in the stove. "It is getting easier to order supplies, though I noticed a rise in prices on some things, and we canned, pickled, and preserved plenty of fruit and vegetables. There's enough smoked ham, and Carson keeps us well-stocked with beef. I am planning menus that use foodstuffs easier to come by."

"I wonder if it would be possible to build a greenhouse here."

Susan stopped her hand in midair, a wooden spoon pointing toward the soup pot. "Greenhouse?"

Clara smiled. "Glasshouses to grow plants during every season. A real greenhouse, like those I've read about, wouldn't be possible. Perhaps we can build another barn with benches under large, glass windows. We'd have to find a way to warm the space. Imagine fresh vegetables even during winter."

Susan tested the soup and added a dash more of salt. "I've never heard of the like. Should I ask Elis about it?"

"You do that." Grinning, Clara left Susan to see to the

warming of the soup and bread. She brought three sets of plates, cups, and cutlery, plus two bowls, from the dish cupboard to the long table, pulled down a silver tray from where Susan kept them on a nearby shelf, and laid everything out on the tray.

The savory aroma from the hearty vegetable and rice soup wafted through the kitchen. Soon after, and ignoring Susan's curious stare, Clara carried the laden tray into the dining room, spread out the offerings, and fetched mother and child from the sitting room. Not long after Grace sampled a piece of cornbread, she consumed half a square. After gentle admonishment from her mother to slow down, Grace did, and then tried the soup. Augusta was slower to enjoy the meal, ensuring that the repast appeased her daughter's initial hunger first.

"This is kind of you, and rest assured, I can pay. Funds are not an issue."

Clara took in the woman's appearance again, under more light from the extra lantern at the table. Smooth black hair was swept up in a loose knot. Her neutral-hued skin appeared smooth, the kind of softness achieved through either staying inside all day or applying expensive ointments. Mother and daughter shared the same eye shape, except while Augusta's were a light brown, Grace's wide were hazel.

Peyton Sawyer was no one's fool, and come morning, he would know a new guest had arrived at Clara's inn. He often traveled to neighboring towns and even beyond when his work required. Perhaps he had seen the woman before. It was one of many questions Clara checked off in her thoughts while she enjoyed her tea and picked at her piece of cornbread.

It did not take long for everyone to finish the light meal.

Clara almost offered second helpings, but now with hunger sated, young Grace's eyes fluttered close.

"Come, I will show you to your room." Clara did not bring up payment, nor did she intend to charge Augusta for the room or food. Clara recognized a woman in trouble and fully intended to speak with Peyton before Augusta disappeared back into the cold unknown with her young daughter.

After showing them to the room down the hall from the rooms where she and Alice slept, Clara left them alone long enough to return with nightgowns. "These are new. My mother sent them last month, and we have not had use for them." She laid out a gown for Augusta and a shorter one for Grace. "My Alice is only five, and this nightgown is too long for her. It should do well for Grace tonight."

Augusta opened her mouth to speak, then quickly closed it. Clara suspected a lie had almost emerged and applauded the woman for not voicing it.

"Whatever you are running from cannot harm you here. Think of your daughter and reconsider speaking with our sheriff. He is a kind and discreet man." Having voiced her opinion, Clara pointed to the commode. "There is clean water in the basin, and a bathing room through that door. A small service lift allows us to pull pails of hot water up from the kitchens. It is rudimentary but serviceable. You will both have warm baths in the morning. The necessary is left of the house set back a way, but a serviceable hall of sorts was built to keep out the elements." Clara still could not get used to it. Augusta, however, did not seem the least bothered.

"Thank you again for everything."

Clara nodded and started for the door.

"Mrs. Stowe?"

Clara did not correct the woman's address of her.

"I *am* thinking of my daughter."

Each woman measured the other's integrity over the length of a thorough study. Clara could not tell from the woman's expression what she had concluded, but she did not miss the glistening start of tears in Augusta's eyes. Without another word, Clara smiled and left them to their rest and returned to the kitchen. Susan had cleared the dishes from the dining room, and the kitchen was once again tidy.

Clara sat at the long table and stared outside, unable to see past the darkness beyond the glass. Nights such as this, when she was alone without the stars or sounds of nature to occupy her, unable to conjure the sweetest of memories with Gideon, or Alice's effervescence to distract her, Clara understood what it meant to be truly lonely.

CHAPTER 3

"Please do not worry about us, Father. We are happy here. The people are remarkable and many have become dear friends. We even have a woman doctor from Boston who, I believe, would impress you. We are in excellent hands."

- Clara Stowe to her father her first September in Crooked Creek

ONE YEAR, SEVEN MONTHS, and fifteen days since he fell on the battlefield, certain his life was over, Michael sat atop his bay roan on the outskirts of Crooked Creek, Montana Territory. For the first time since he began the journey west, he breathed deeply enough to release some of the strain he had carried with him across the miles. The frigid air stung a little going into his lungs, and he relished the sensation.

"She might not be here."

Michael glanced at his friend, healer, and traveling companion. The look he gave him suggested Michael did not appreciate Isaac had voiced his worry. "Then we keep searching. Crooked Creek is where the letter from Christopher Smith came from, and I just hope that if Briley has moved on, she left a clue for me to follow."

Isaac Worth did not offer further opinion or conversation as they stood and watched the sun rise over the mountain town. Crooked Creek was nestled in a valley surrounded by thick forests covering more land than Michael could have ever imagined exploring.

"I'd best wait here."

Michael's initial reaction, "Don't worry about it," remained in his thoughts. After they had left the eastern states and traveled across the frontier into the western territories and mountains, the number of colored people decreased. While most folks ignored Isaac, others gaped at him as though they hoped he was just passing through. Most probably assumed Isaac was Michael's servant, and neither cared to correct misconceptions.

They passed through one town then on to another, moving as quickly as Isaac's wounded leg allowed. Even traveling by horse, the injured limb required the man to walk for spells or rest. Michael could have made the journey in half the time alone. However, just as Isaac hadn't left Michael on the battlefield to die, Michael would not leave his friend behind.

"It's unnecessary to stay out here. We ran out of food last night and used the last of our bullets hunting yesterday's breakfast. We need provisions, and you need medicine for the pain in your leg."

Isaac darted a look at Michael. "It ain't paining me any more than usual."

Michael managed a smile for his friend's benefit. "I won't

believe that lie now any more than I did last week or the
month before."

"It ain't likely there's a doctor here; if there is, he ain't
going to want to treat a colored man."

"You're a man, Isaac, no better or less than me or any
other man. Remember that, my friend."

Isaac said nothing and Michael did not press the issue. It
was a long-running debate between them, and folks *did* treat
Michael differently, at least until he spoke. No matter how hard
he worked to mask his heritage, the lilting accent of his birth
and family slipped through. Isaac could not be swayed, though.
Previously, he always waited at camp while Michael rode into
towns for supplies, and so it had been since they left Missouri.

"If my sister is here, Isaac, this is where I stay."

"I reckon it's as good a place as any." Isaac sighed, his
breath creating a plume of warm air against the cold. "Let's
get on then."

Michael led the way into town beneath a sky cast in
shades of yellow, orange, and red, as the sun drifted slowly
above the snowy mountain range. The town, still quiet,
boasted more conveniences than he expected for this far into
the territory. A café and large mercantile were prominent on
one side of the wide, dirt thoroughfare, while the other
boasted a livery, jailhouse, and a doctor's office to his surprise
and relief. He wasn't sure about the quality of a frontier
physician, but Isaac's leg needed tending.

A small boarding house that appeared newly built stood
on one corner, and farther down the road, nestled among
trees, a grand white structure more suited to a southern
plantation, stood apart from the town.

The faith a person must possess to make such a personal
and financial investment in a place like Crooked Creek was

beyond Michael's understanding. Smaller buildings, old cabins, and businesses with living spaces on the second level filled in the rest of what passed for Crooked Creek.

After taking in the general layout of the modest town, Michael headed toward the jail where a sign on a post read SHERIFF'S OFFICE. No light shined from within, which meant the jail was likely empty and the sheriff was not yet in. He did not bother to check the door.

His gaze drifted back to the large white house down the road. A light flickered out front, moving slowly back and forth before settling in one spot. Someone was awake, and a voice inside Michael compelled him to start there.

When he noticed the direction of Michael's gaze, Isaac laid a hand on his arm. "Ain't no folks in a place like that is going to welcome me. I think I'll just wait here."

"If you prefer, and while you wait, think on this my friend. If you keep expecting people to treat you differently, they likely will. Besides, you need a warm place to stay as much as I do."

When they had managed to find a boarding house or hotel, Michael paid extra for the proprietor to not care about letting a room to Isaac while others cared more about coin than who let their rooms. Sometimes they found a warm stable to bunk down with their livestock. Tonight, Michael wanted a soft pillow to rest his head and a fire to warm the cold deep within his bones.

Michael left Isaac to join him or not, as Isaac often preferred to keep to himself. He turned up his collar against a gust of wind and raised the scarf his sister knit him before the war to cover the lower half of his face. Together, man and horse trudged through the snow trampled on the road by horses and wagons.

Upon his approach, Michael slowed his horse to a stop

and watched. Though the cold pricked the surface of his skin beneath the layers of clothes, he did not move for fear of disrupting the woman whose serene expression enthralled him. When had he last witnessed such peacefulness? Years of pain and loss had sought to bury Michael beneath sorrow forever, yet desperation to see his family once again kept him fighting demons within and without.

During those years, he would have been tempted to give up his tent and a week's worth of rations for a moment of peace so pure as what he observed now. A smile formed when the woman opened her eyes, and she opened a book and began to read by the soft glow of light from a brass lantern. How she stood the cold with nothing more than the shawl around her shoulders and a blanket on her lap, he could not guess.

Michael urged the horse forward, guiding the animal over a few twigs. The snaps and cracks alerted the woman that she was not alone, and as he hoped, she lifted her head.

"Good morning, ma'am," Michael called out loud enough for her to hear, but not so loud as to sound threatening or disturb anyone who might be asleep inside. Then he noticed the carved sign hanging between two sturdy posts: THE STOWE FAMILY INN. Good luck for him and Isaac if they had rooms available. "I'm sorry to have disturbed you so early. Yours was the only light I saw from town."

The woman rose from her chair, set the book down where she had sat, and hugged the shawl closer as she walked to the railing. Something about her, or perhaps what she wore, niggled a corner of Michael's memory. From her place on the covered porch, her smoky blue eyes were almost level with his brown.

"Most people in town do not open their doors until the

sun rises, and the hour is much later in winter. The sheriff makes rounds before opening his office. He should be here soon."

Michael took her words to mean he did not have much time to allay the woman's concern over his presence at such an early hour. "I apologize again, ma'am. The sheriff is who I need to see. My friend and I also need lodging for a night, maybe longer."

"Friend?"

"He preferred to wait in town."

Clara peered in the direction of town before turning back to Michael. "We have two rooms available, but forgive me, sir, what is your name? You seem so familiar, yet . . ."

"This is my first time in the territory, ma'am. First time west of Kentucky in fact. The name's Michael Donaghue."

CLARA KNEW SHE should say something, any word, yet the shock of what the man revealed had momentarily stolen her good sense. His eyes were what first caused her pause. The eyes told her this man was familiar, though in what way she had not been able to piece together. How could she when Michael Donaghue was supposed to be dead? She told herself it was a common enough name.

"Donaghue?" His accent was faint, and she caught the subtle edges of a brogue beneath the surface of certain words. "Irish."

His smile faltered a fraction and the lines around his eyes tightened at the same time as his voice. "I am."

"Pray, forgive me, sir, it is not . . ." There are other Donaghues out there, Clara thought, and surely some found their way to Montana. What are the chances of another

Michael Donaghue showing up in Crooked Creek? "Do you have family in the area?"

"I hope so, ma'am."

"It is Clara Stowe."

"You're from the East, New England I'd guess."

Surprised into confirming, Clara said, "You have a good ear."

"My family lived in New York."

"I see." And she needed to speak with Peyton and Briley. Clara's heartbeat elevated its beat without prompting, and she fought back the desire to ask if this man was Briley's brother. "You and your friend are welcome here for as long as you need."

"Mrs. Stowe—"

"Clara if you please. Formalities are not as necessary here, but I'm grateful all the same." Nor did Clara enjoy the guilt she suffered every time someone called her "Mrs." She did not wear deception well, and only bore it when necessary for the sake of her daughter. Clara preferred the guests to assume her a widow.

"My traveling companion is a free man. It's only fair to ask you if that will be a problem."

"Well, of course, he is free. I do not know . . . oh." Clara chided herself for not grasping the man's meaning before. "You are both welcome, so long as you abide by my rules."

Michael's lips twitched as though to hide a smile. "Rules?"

"No cursing, no drunkenness, no dragging dirt across my floors, and no disturbing other guests."

Now he did smile in full, and his smile came near to strangling the voice from Clara's throat. He had Briley's smile.

"Sounds reasonable. Does the livery in town board horses?"

"Thomas Doby is the blacksmith and owns the livery. He will board your horses. We also have three empty stalls in the small stable out back if you prefer to keep your horses close. Some guests do. There is feed, and you will have to look after them yourselves."

Michael tipped the edge of his hat. "Suits just fine, ma'am. We'll be along directly."

Clara's eyes did not move from Michael's departing form until she had no choice save to step back and take a deep breath. Picking up her book, she hurried inside.

CHAPTER 4

"I have enclosed three varieties of wildflowers Alice pressed for you so you would have a piece of summer all the year. The yellow flower is arnica, the blue one is appropriately a bluebell, and the red one is called by some prairie-fire. The identifications are courtesy of Dr. Emma Latimer and Carson White Eagle."

- Clara Stowe to her mother her first October in Crooked Creek

CLARA HURRIED THROUGH the quiet house to the kitchen, where she knew Susan would already be working. She followed the scent of baking bread and found her carrying a jar of lard out of the pantry.

"Good morning to you, Clara. Water's not boiled yet——"

"I do not need tea now, Susan, thank you. Will you listen for Alice and our other guests? I should be back before they are moving about, but I must speak with Sheriff Sawyer. Nothing is wrong," she was quick to add.

Susan did not mask her bewildered expression. "Of course. I'll see to them."

"Thank you." Clara walked from the kitchen to the mudroom off the back, replaced her everyday boots with the more durable Wellingtons she had ordered, much to the bemusement of Maeve at the mercantile. They weren't exactly what Hattie had in mind when she suggested boots more suited to their winters, but they kept the snow off her feet.

Clara pulled each one on with a couple of unladylike grunts and then slipped into a long wool coat. Grabbing a thick, blue scarf Briley had knitted, she hurried out the back door and around the house. She righted herself twice when the ice beneath her boots would have toppled her to the frozen ground.

With cold air in her lungs and cheeks stinging from the morning frost, she sent up a silent thank you that Peyton was now in his office. She peered through the window to make sure Briley was not there before she entered and closed the door quickly behind her. "Where is Briley?"

Clara must have looked as harried as she felt if the expression Peyton wore was any indication. "What happened to you, Clara?" He wrapped an arm around her shoulder to guide her to the stove, where a new fire was gaining strength.

"I am well." She welcomed the meager heat and stuffed her hands beneath her arms. "I did not intend to alarm you, and I will explain. Where is Briley?"

"Is something—"

"Nothing is wrong, Peyton. At least I don't see it as wrong. Where is—"

"Briley's with Emma today while Casey is helping Carson

at the ranch. They've had a few more squatters from the mining camp show up." Peyton sat on the edge of his desk, his gaze never once veering from Clara's face. "What's going on?"

"A man arrived this morning in town. He came to the inn in search of lodging, and he's not from the camp. Without explanation, Carson warned me not to board any of them. No, this man is not from around here."

"Clara."

She caught the undertone of impatience. "Goodness, you *are* intimidating. He is also looking for his family. Peyton. He said his name is Michael Donaghue."

The door to Peyton's office swung open and the man under discussion walked through. His eyes narrowed on Clara. "Interesting to see you here, Mrs. Stowe."

Whether he dropped the use of her Christian name already because they were in company or because he did not trust her now, she couldn't say. Clara attempted to rectify his sudden distrust in her, for his eyes now held the truth of his thoughts. "I cannot imagine what you must think, Mr. Donaghue." She placed a hand on Peyton's arm when he stood and faced the newcomer. "I had hoped you might be awhile yet."

"Sorry to disappoint."

Peyton focused on the man who stood a few inches shorter than him. "You'll watch your tone with her, and now someone will explain what the hell is going on. Pardon, Clara."

"It is all right." She took a deep breath. "I had hoped to speak with the sheriff at more length before you arrived, Mr. Donaghue, and there is no easy way to erase any shock. I recognized you, not because we have met, but because I am certain I know your sister. Peyton, this is—"

"I figured it out, Clara, the moment I saw the man." Peyton approached Michael with caution. "No need to state the obvious since you're not dead, except you'd better explain how it is you're alive."

MICHAEL HAD EXPERIENCED enough anger to know when it was about to bubble to the surface. He clamped it down, uncertain if the sheriff deserved it, and not wishing to thrust it upon a woman. "Since you know who I am, it's only fair you tell me your name and why I owe you an explanation. And who told you I was dead?"

"All right." Peyton held up a hand in surrender. "I expect Clara had other plans for how this would play out, and under the circumstances, I'm willing to agree you deserve more answers than I do. However, you won't leave here until I'm assured of your intentions toward your sister."

"Briley Smith *does* live here, then?"

Peyton shook his head. "No, Briley Smith does not. Briley Sawyer does."

Michael stared at the man while digesting the news. Had he not been used to sudden blows, the information may have toppled him. "You're Briley's husband?"

"I am, and there's a lot of explaining to go along with that story."

"*Briley* told you I was dead?"

With sympathy now etched on his face, Peyton nodded. "She'd received word of your death. Killed in battle was the official phrasing, though it wouldn't have been the first time for a notification error."

In half a daze, Michael shook his head. "I came close more than once and nearly did at Appomattox Station. A friend pulled me from the battlefield."

Clara asked, "If you'll pardon me for speaking out of turn, why did it take so long for you to look for her?"

Snow fell again. First, small flakes danced in the frosty air before thicker flakes blocked Michael's view through the window beyond a dozen feet. "I wasn't able to sooner. She told a former neighbor where she was going and about answering Smith's advertisment. Further explanations will wait until I give them to Briley." He regarded Clara with the same admiration he'd given her when she sat on the front porch. "You and my sister must be close if you came here first."

"Yes, she is a dear friend."

"Thank you for thinking of her, for wanting to protect her." He then said to Peyton, "I want to see her. Now."

"The shock will be too much if she's not given a warning first."

"Briley is strong. You above all should know that."

Peyton stood firm. "Everyone who has met her is aware of her strength. Just now, though . . . Briley is with child."

Speechless for several seconds, Michael's voice sounded hoarse to his ears when he finally spoke. "She's well?"

"Yes, perfectly." Clara walked toward him, putting herself closer to him than Peyton. "She speaks of you often, and though it will be a shock, it will give her tremendous joy. However, Peyton is right. Briley needs to be told before she sees you."

"Where is my sister?"

"With another friend, a doctor, Dr. Emma Latimer. It is probably best she is there when Briley learns you are alive."

Michael was grateful Clara was the one who kept talking. Her voice soothed him in a way the sheriff's did not. He peered at the other man again, imposing in stature and expression, with his furrowed brow and ramrod straight back.

He put Michael in mind of a lieutenant he had served under briefly at the start of the war. His brother-in-law, his sister's wife, family. Family was at the root of everything he treasured, even if he didn't choose the family himself. Michael stared at Peyton. Yet his question was for Clara. "Does he treat her well?"

"Every woman should be so blessed with such a husband, Michael. Take comfort knowing she is happy, cared for, and dearly loved."

His focus moved slowly to Clara and in her blue eyes, he saw she spoke the truth. His next question was for the sheriff. "I'm not willing to wait long, Sheriff. When will you tell her?"

"Something tells me if I don't do it now, you'll take the decision out of my hands."

Peyton held out his hand to Michael, and they clasped one hand to another. Michael felt the man's strength and restraint. After over five years of longing to see his family again, Michael didn't want to wait another second to see his sister.

"Clara, if you'll wait here, I'll take you home once I've—"

"Once you have told Briley her brother is alive and in Crooked Creek?"

"No easy way to explain that news." Peyton walked past Michael to the door. "You're welcome to come with me now and stay out of sight or wait here."

"How soon will . . . When will Briley. . ."

"Emma thinks it will be a few weeks," Clara answered Michael's unarticulated questions. "Emma has warned Briley to be cautious, though," she added to support Peyton's concern.

Michael considered the options, and the urge to follow Peyton momentarily took over his common sense. Until he thought of the baby and what was best for his sister. Briley wasn't going anywhere, and neither was he. "I'll see Mrs. Stowe home. Where and when should I find you?"

Peyton regarded him as though reevaluating an earlier opinion. "If I'm not at the medical clinic, you'll find me at the jail."

Michael nodded once in acknowledgment and waited for Peyton to leave.

"You're good to wait, as much as I can see how difficult the decision is for you. Were I in Briley's condition, and such news came, a little warning would ease the shock, because the surprise will most certainly hit before she's overcome with joy."

Many families had little opportunity to surprise their loved ones by returning from the grave . . . or near to it. He counted himself among those lucky enough to have survived the war. How many others like him were still searching for those they'd lost, those who thought their soldiers gone? Michael wanted to ask if she had lived through such an experience, yet something he saw in her countenance kept his question silent.

Had she a husband, father, or brother lost in battle? He pushed the questions aside and returned to Briley. "Is she well? And the baby? I know I've asked already, but I need to be sure."

"She's been tired more of late, which is to be expected. Emma says they are both doing fine." He followed her with his gaze as she moved to the window. Snow continued to fall, its thick curtain becoming more opaque with each passing minute. "Where is your friend? I should have inquired after his welfare sooner."

"Isaac has a nose for sweets." At her questioning look, he smiled and explained. "The café opened before I came over and a woman named Bess invited us in. She didn't seem to mind Isaac's presence."

"Bess owns the café, and most people in Crooked Creek will not give much thought to Isaac's color." She turned from the window to face him. "However, I cannot say the same for everyone he might meet in the territory. I have learned there are sympathizers from both sides in the area."

Michael shrugged, the movement more stiff than casual. "He's used to it, mostly ignores it. He has an old injury that has healed improperly. Will your doctor treat him?"

Clara nodded. "Emma will see a man in need of healing, nothing more. You called me Mrs. Stowe before, rather than Clara. I know it's informal, and if my family heard me offer informality, they would disapprove."

"And still you offered."

"Yes. In a place like this, where people must count on one another to survive, formality matters little among friends."

Michael removed his hat and held it out to Clara, surprising her into taking it. He next handed her his thick leather gloves. She stared at him. "I told the sheriff I'd see you safely home. Can't do that if you freeze."

A look of amusement passed over her face. Clara placed the hat on her head and slipped her delicate hands into the too-large gloves.

"How long have you been in Montana?"

"Only since May. Summer and autumn were more beautiful than I ever imagined. There was even snow on the mountain peaks before the summer heat subsided. I did not expect wintertime to be mild. However, I am assured the worst of winter is yet to come."

A New York winter, in an apartment with walls and windows that barely kept the cold out and the heat in, was worse than what he'd seen so far in the mountainous wilderness of the territory. A winter of harsh winds and so much snow on the ground it rose above his head sounded better than winters on a muddy battlefield, waiting and wondering which of the men in his regiment would fall next.

He smiled and tapped the top of his hat to fit lower on her head. "It will do. Stay inside while I bring my horse around."

"With my head and hands now protected, I can walk. You should wait for Peyton here. I cannot believe it will be long before Briley demands to see you."

"Briley always knew how to get what she wanted, from the time she learned to walk." Michael smiled at the memory. "Still, I promised Peyton."

"Yes, only . . ."

Michael raised a brow and looked pointedly at the snow outside. "I won't be long."

Five minutes later, Michael walked his red dun, Rian, to the front of the sheriff's office. Clara stepped outside before he could open the door and lowered her head so the borrowed hat caught the worst of the wind.

He led her to the horse without asking permission and boosted her into the saddle. Seconds later, he sat behind her, blocking the wind with his body. He held her close and leaned forward so she could hear him. "Is it normal for a storm to come through this quickly?"

She lowered the scarf and offered a mumbled response. "I really do not know. This is the worst I've seen so far."

"Hold on to the horn and you'll be home in a few minutes."

Clara nodded and Michael guided the horse. Despite the fierce winds raging against his body and whipping his dark hair, he heard the scream.

CHAPTER 5

"You suspect I do not share every detail of each day here, which is true. Most of it is quite ordinary."

- Clara Stowe to her parents her first October in Crooked Creek

MICHAEL LISTENED FOR IT AGAIN, in case it had been only the howling wind. The next gust carried another scream, this time closer.

"Clinic! Over there!" Clara shouted and waved him in the right direction.

Michael gripped the reins and held Clara close as he diverted the horse toward the medical office. They didn't have far to go, and once there, Michael swung off the animal. Without waiting for her to ask, his hands spanned Clara's waist and brought her feet to rest on the boardwalk beneath the building's extended overhang. He rubbed his horse's nose briefly, with a silent promise to return quickly.

Clara removed the hat and kicked snow off her boots so it didn't track inside. "Emma and Peyton must have brought Briley here, which means . . ."

"I'll get you home, I promise. I just need to—"

"If Briley is in labor, I'm not going anywhere yet." Clara brushed past him and pushed open the clinic door in time to see Peyton carry his wife into one of the back rooms. Emma halted them from going any farther.

"Michael, I presume?"

He nodded once. "Briley?"

Emma secured an apron in place and pulled a white sleeve over each arm. "She's in labor. I noticed the signs a short while ago and hoped it would pass. Then Peyton came by with news of your rebirth, so to speak."

Michael blanched. "That's what caused—"

"No, no. It's not your fault, Michael." Clara told him, then said to Emma. "How can I help?"

"I have most everything ready, but we'll need hot water for washing, if you will see to it. Casey filled two pots on the stove before he left for White Eagle Ranch." Emma faced Michael. "Clara's right. This isn't your fault. I suspect the baby had plans to make an appearance today, no matter what. Perhaps it sensed your arrival and was eager to meet you."

"The baby is early, though."

"Yes, but it's not unusual, and the timing is not always exact in these things." Emma gripped Michael's arms. "You don't know me, Michael, but please trust me to do what's best for your sister."

Michael saw the trust and calm in Clara's gaze, then said to Emma, "Please, take care of her. I didn't search this long to lose her now."

"She is strong, Michael. You will not lose her." Emma

headed for the back room, only to be stopped by Peyton's sudden appearance. "She's demanding to see her brother. Emma, she's in a lot of pain."

"She'll see Michael later. Peyton, you wait out here until I say otherwise. Clara, will you please brew tea for Briley? If you'll come with me, I'll explain what's needed." Emma disappeared into the back room without another glance at either man and closed the door against Briley's next scream.

Before following Emma, Clara offered Peyton and Michael assurance. "Briley is as strong as a woman can be, and if there is a doctor more skilled than Emma, I have yet to meet him or her, so stay calm for Briley."

Peyton stood close to the door for a full minute before giving Michael his consideration. "We have a lot to talk about, and we'll get to it, but you'll understand it can't be right now."

Michael understood and felt the same way. His chest had clenched with Briley's first scream and had yet to ease its tight hold around his heart. "How angry is she?"

An unexpected half-laugh, half-groan escaped Peyton's lips. "What a question at a time like this. Angry at you for dying, or not, then taking so long to find her, angry at herself for believing you were dead, and cursing me for putting her in this position. The only one that will come out of this unscathed is the baby, who will have my undying love and gratitude for distracting its mother." Peyton exhaled with a heavy sigh. "She can be angry at whomever for however long she wants."

"As long as she pulls through."

Peyton studied Michael for several seconds. "She *will* come through this. Briley's too stubborn to give up."

Another scream fractured the air, leaving silence in its wake. Clara emerged from the birthing room, closing it behind her. She walked to Peyton, her eyes etched with concern and her smile one of support. "Emma said Briley is doing well. You can go in, Peyton, and sit with her now. It will be a while yet, so whatever you do, don't ask how long."

Peyton hurried into the back. Michael waited until he was alone with Clara before voicing his concern. "Those screams—"

"Are normal. Your sister's indignation is merely adding to their strength." Clara took his hand automatically. "Emma said your presence in the room will excite Briley too much, and she needs her strength. I've assured Briley you are real and will be here when the little one arrives."

"And there's no way to know how long?"

Clara's smile eased some of his worries. "An hour, half a day. No clock can predict such things."

Michael peered past her to the closed door. "She's quiet now."

"Peyton has a calming effect on her, and she won't want to distress him."

"I can't do *nothing*. Give me a task, a job."

"All right." Clara tucked a linen cloth in her apron pocket. "Your friend will wonder where you are, and if you are of a mind to keep busy, will you deliver a message to Susan? She is the cook at the inn. It has been long enough for her to worry, and Alice will be awake by now."

"Alice?"

"My daughter."

Michael momentarily forgot about Briley, though how he could, for even a second surprised him, but Clara had a daughter. What about a husband? He thought it, though could not bring himself to ask. This time, a low moan, rather than a scream, filled the air. "I'll deliver the message and explain what's happened."

"Thank you. Alice will want to come if she hears about Briley. However, she must stay home. Please, assure Susan all is well."

"I won't be long."

Clara stopped him with another touch to his arm and passed him the hat he had loaned her earlier. He wondered how her warmth penetrated the thick layers he wore. "No need to rush. Briley won't know you have gone, and she certainly is not going anywhere."

He glanced again at the room Briley was in before walking to the door. Michael was unable to stop himself from allowing his gaze to linger over Clara's face for a few seconds before departing.

Bitter winds, frozen earth, and a wall of snow so thick he could not see beyond his horse. He expected Isaac would remain indoors until the worst of the storm passed. They had traveled through a few once they had reached the northern states, and later across the territories, but nothing like this.

Michael secured the hat on his head, lifted the collar of his coat, and tugged tighter on his scarf. With a few soothing words to his horse, he brushed snow away from Rian's eyes and nose and then off the saddle before pulling himself with ease onto the animal's back.

He kept his gaze down, hoping the hoofprints from earlier were still visible in places. As each tree or small landmark appeared within view, he kept moving forward, recognizing the path to Clara's inn. Once sight of the three-story structure broke through the snow, Michael dismounted and guided his horse around back to where Clara told him the stable was located. Rian needed shelter no matter how long or short of time he might be there.

Impressed by the clean and maintained state of the smaller building, Michael led his horse to one of the empty stalls, removed the saddle and blanket, and wiped down Rian's coat.

"Who might you be?"

Michael faced the man who seemed to have appeared from somewhere in the back. "Michael Donaghue. My friend and I will be staying over. Mrs. Stowe said to make use of the stable for our horses."

"Fair enough. Mrs. Stowe knows you're here, then?"

"Yes. She's held up at the clinic right now, and I'm supposed to speak with Susan, the cook." Michael studied the man as he walked closer. "She didn't mention you."

Michael recognized the distrust in his voice, yet the other man didn't seem to mind. Instead, he grinned and lifted a bucket off a hook hanging between two stalls. "Elis is the name. There's a pump round back in the springhouse and another behind inn. When the snow's fresh, I collect some and let it melt in the barrel over there. Hay around the barrel does a fair job keeping it from freezing at night." Elis walked outside and returned a few minutes later with the pail, now filled with water. He entered the stall, poured the water into a small trough secured against a wall, and then backed out. "There's hay in the last stall. Take what you need."

Surprised by the generosity, Michael thanked him. "Maybe you should come in with me, so I don't scare the cook."

Elis grinned again and scratched a scruffy cheek. "Susan won't beat you about the head with a rolling pin unless you give her cause." He sighed heavily. "Reckon you're right, though. Come on."

Michael led Rian into the stall, removed the horse's bridle, and saw to the feed before following Elis back into the frigid weather. Snow continued to fall, though not with the heaviness as when he had entered the stable.

The back porch was almost as long as the front and protected them when they stepped up to the back door. Michael followed Elis's lead and stomped snow off his boots. He smiled at the reminder of Clara's obvious fastidiousness about keeping her home clean. Thoughts of Clara quickly drifted to his sister. Clara had assured him the screams were normal and Emma was a brilliant doctor, so what choice did he have except to trust them both? Clara must know, having gone through the experience herself.

A daughter. And yet, still no sign of a husband. Michael brushed snow off his coat and hat before stepping over the threshold. The unmistakable scent of freshly baked bread and sizzling bacon hit him at the exact moment as the heat from the kitchen fires. He trailed Elis through a cloakroom, where coats, scarves, and hats hung on pegs, and a low shelf held well-worn footwear in two different sizes—woman's and child's.

"Is that you, Elis?" a woman's voice called out.

"It's me." Elis beckoned Michael to hang up his coat and hat, yet made no move to do the same. "I've got wood to carry in. You go on in there." He pointed toward the kitchen. "Susan!" he called out. "Got a fella here with a message for you." Smiling again, Elis put his hat back on and shuffled right out the door.

Michael was still staring at the closed door when a woman with medium-brown hair tucked in a knot at her nape—he assumed Susan—leaned into the cloakroom. "Good morning, ma'am. My name's Michael Donaghue, and I've come with a message from Cl—Mrs. Stowe."

"She prefers Clara."

Susan narrowed her eyes, a shade lighter than her hair, as she studied him. They slowly widened as recognition unfolded. Despite the four years difference in age, he and

Briley had always been told how alike they looked, especially when they stood unmoving side by side, which wasn't often in their youth.

"Donaghue. I don't expect—"

"Yes, ma'am. Briley's brother. The brief explanation is: Briley's having her baby and Clara is at the clinic. She asked me to tell you so you wouldn't worry." He thought of Clara's daughter, wondering if she possessed the honey-colored hair and blue eyes as her mother. "And to make sure Alice stays inside." He waved a thumb over his shoulder at the door. "The storm is fierce right now."

Susan stared for a few seconds as she digested the information Michael had laid on her at one time. "Thank you, Mr. Donaghue, for the message. I appreciate it. Will you be staying at the inn?"

"Yes, ma'am, my friend and I will stay for a while, I expect. He's probably still at the café and will be along when the snow lets up some."

"I appreciate your manners, but no 'ma'am' for me. Susan or Mrs. Reed will do, but I mostly answer to Susan." She passed a cursory glance over his boots. "Come along and I'll get you some breakfast. It's still early, so I doubt you've eaten yet today. The other guests are in the dining room. They aren't likely to leave today as planned if it's as bad as you say."

With the message now delivered, Michael wanted to return to the clinic to help . . . with what? Wearing down the boards on Emma's waiting room floor, or listening to every painful moan and scream as Briley fought to bring her and Peyton's first child into the world.

A child. Michael's niece or nephew. The muscles in his chest constricted with sudden force at the pain of knowing their parents didn't live long enough to see their first grandchild.

"You coming?"

Michael had to give himself a few seconds to focus his mind on the present before he answered Susan. "I would appreciate breakfast, thank you."

Susan led him into the kitchen and deftly removed the bacon from atop the cookstove. He'd gone a day or two without a meal—if anyone could consider army hardtack food—and remembered clearly the home-cooked fare his mother and sister had once prepared.

He inhaled the mingling scents and beat back a wave of guilt for thinking of his hunger while his sister suffered. She'd tell him to find his good sense—or knock it into him—and then she'd tell him to eat and enjoy it.

Michael let a smile tug at his lips when he asked Susan, "Is there anything I can do to help?"

"You're a guest." She poured steaming coffee into a mug and handed it to him. With a wooden spoon poised over a batter bowl, Susan looked him in the eyes. "Briley is a dear woman and friend. Nothing is more natural than what she's going through, and Dr. Latimer is the best there is."

"So I hear."

She pointed toward a door on the opposite side of the kitchen. "Dining room is through there."

Michael thanked her for the coffee, pushed through the door, and entered a short hallway with a sideboard against one wall and hooks with aprons on the other. He passed through the space and into a dining room with six polished round tables, each with four oak chairs, their padded seats covered in a rich, indigo fabric. Lamps sat in the center of each table, though enough light filtered into the spacious area without needing the extra. Low flames in a stone hearth mixed well enough with the winter weather to create a comfortably warm atmosphere.

A dark-haired woman and girl of about nine or ten sat at the farthest table from where he stood. Their wariness apparent, he merely smiled and looked away lest he make them uncomfortable. If there were other guests besides them, they either hadn't come down yet or were waiting elsewhere.

"Who are you?"

An angelic face peeked through the balusters on what appeared to be a back staircase. Honey-colored hair, the same shade as Clara's, hung in two braids with green ribbon securing each end.

He remained where he stood. "Hello, Alice. I'm Michael."

She tilted her head, first one way, then the other, and dragged herself up until she could peer over the handrail. "You know my name."

"Your mother told me."

Alice walked down two steps and rested her chin on the rail. "She's been gone a long time."

Michael could not remember a time when he thought an hour or two was a long time to wait. "She's helping Briley with the baby."

Alice fairly jumped down the last three steps and skipped to within a few feet of him. "Briley has a baby now?"

He wished it was now. "Not yet, but soon."

She stretched a finger toward his face. "Mama says it's not nice to point. I can't reach that high to touch."

Michael knelt on one knee. "Is this better?"

Alice bobbed her head. "You look like Aunt Briley."

"She's your aunt?"

"Uh-huh. I have lots and lots of aunts and uncles. Mama

said so. Aunt Briley. Aunt Emma. Aunt Hattie. Uncle Casey. Uncle Carson. Uncle Peyton. That's lots and lots."

"It certainly is." He might have been tempted to ask more if Susan hadn't walked in from the kitchen. "Are you hungry?"

In answer, Alice grabbed his hand and tugged to get him to follow. He saw Susan's raised brow from the corner of his vision and followed the young girl to a table. "We can eat here." She grinned up at Susan. "He says Aunt Briley's having her baby."

"Yes, she is, and your ma will want you to be a good girl and wait right here for her to come back. She'll tell you all about the baby when it comes." Susan set plates of food in front of each of them. Alice's a third of the bacon, sausage, fried potatoes, hotcake, and applesauce portions she gave to him. He supposed he must look worse than he thought if she was going to feed him like a bear coming out of hibernation.

"I want to see the baby." Alice picked up and waggled her spoon. "Mama says babies like someone to hold them."

"They do." Susan poured water into a short glass for Alice. "Eat up or you won't be strong enough to hold Briley's baby."

Alice tucked into her applesauce.

"What about you?" Michael asked Susan. "Won't you eat with us?"

"You go on ahead. I've plenty to do still." Susan left their table and walked to the dark-haired woman and child. Michael met her gaze briefly before she ducked her head away and answered whatever question Susan had asked. He pulled out the silver pocket watch, scratched from years of joining him in battle, and noted the time. Thirty-five minutes had passed since he left the clinic. It felt so much longer.

When Susan passed back by their table, Michael was

tempted to tell her he needed to leave, find his friend, and
check in on Briley. He couldn't bring himself to leave Alice,
though, for Clara's sake. He speared two of the fried potatoes
and savored the first bite. Two bites of egg and a wedge cut
from the stack of hotcakes followed next. He hoped Isaac's
meal at the café proved as appetizing.

Michael rechecked the time. Fifteen more minutes and
half a plate of food marked the time. He glanced up briefly
when the woman and girl left the dining room without a
word. Alice waved, though, and the girl shyly waved in return
before disappearing around a corner.

Something about the girl teased a recent memory, but he
could not pinpoint the "when" or "why."

CHAPTER 6

"... yellow, gold, and red mixed with the deep green of the pine trees. Alice and I are still learning the names of the many genus *Pinus* trees and shrubs and the deciduous trees in the area. Alice is, as always, an excellent pupil. I have enclosed Alice's letter with a drawing of her favorite pine tree, a ponderosa. She likes the cones."

- Clara Stowe to her parents her first October in Crooked Creek

CONVINCING ALICE TO remain at the inn when he left proved a challenge until Susan stepped in and asked the girl to help her make oatmeal cookies. It was enough of a distraction for at least a short while to allow Michael to slip out the back door.

A down-to-the-bones chill hit him as soon as he stepped off the protected porch. The snow had stopped, leaving a hostile wind behind. He'd waited what felt like half the day.

Only a mere hour and twelve minutes had passed. Michael was not optimistic enough to believe Briley's laboring was over. His sister, he reasoned, remained in good care with her husband, Dr. Latimer, and Clara by her side. Isaac, however, should have found him by now.

Michael refused to pull Rian from his warm stall, only to have the horse wait outside when Michael returned to the clinic. If a man survived a war, he could manage a walk in a winter storm. Bracing himself against the wind's onslaught, he lowered his head a fraction and trudged the distance from the inn to the center of town. At least this time the view of the buildings and the lines of the dirt road were visible.

Once at his first destination, Michael pushed into the sheriff's office and shoved the door closed behind him. It took two shakes of the handle to hear the click.

"Reckon you'd come back sometime."

Michael knew the voice without seeing the face, so he discarded his hat and brushed away the snow. Too cold to remove his outer clothing, he merely lowered the scarf so he could speak.

"Glad I am you're here, Isaac. I fretted walking all over town to find you."

The large man sat on the edge of Peyton's desk to keep weight off his injured leg. "I kept at the café for a bit in case Miss Bess—she owns the place—wanted help gettin' home. She said this'll pass and folks'll come out soon enough."

Michael thought of the bitter wind and two feet of snow he'd just waded through and wondered where Miss Bess got her powers of premonition. "Where'd you put Cannon? I didn't see him out front."

"Boarded him at the livery for now, just 'til the storm lets up some."

Michael moved closer to the wood stove and fed another

cut log to the flames. "The stable at the inn has a good stall for him. Mrs. Stowe, the owner, is expecting us to stay for a spell." He glanced at Isaac's leg. "She also said the doctor will look at your leg once she's available."

"I reckon that'll change when she sees me."

Even suffering the prejudices shown to him and every one of his countrymen at home and in war, Michael never claimed to understand what Isaac and his people had been through. "Give folks here a chance to accept you. Mrs. Stowe already knows and claims no one else in town will treat you differently."

Isaac offered a nod but no further words to refute Michael's words. "Any news on your sister?"

Michael smiled, the unexpected swiftness of it surprising him. "Briley's here, and the one currently occupying Dr. Latimer. She's having a baby."

"Well, don't that beat all." Isaac shared in his friend's joy, before the good cheer in his countenance faltered. "She gonna be okay?"

"She is." Michael now believed it with his whole heart simply because he trusted Clara's optimism. "I'll be going back to the clinic soon. I needed to make sure the snow hadn't swallowed you up."

Isaac hugged his arms around his chest. "It sure is mighty cold here."

Michael did not disagree with the obvious. "My sister is here, so, like I said before, here is where I stay. You should go to the inn and settle into a room. I think it will be hours yet before I do the same." He quickly added, "Mrs. Reed, the cook, is expecting you." Michael had explained about Isaac before he left, uncertain if Clara had informed the cook.

He left the warmth of the wood stove and crossed the room to the door. He stopped with his hand on the door handle and asked Isaac, "Do you remember where we ran into the lumber mill owner who was looking for workers? It was just after we passed around the Crow Nation."

"Dawson's Trading Post. Don't recall it was much of a town, though."

"No, it wasn't." Michael thought of his sister following the same journey west and could not figure out what had possessed her to make the expedition. They'd been lucky, traveling quickly and light, sometimes making camp with wagon trains, other times pressing on when families stopped along the Bozeman Trail to rest their stock and weary bodies.

He wondered why anyone bothered with such a small settlement, miles away from the nearest hub, in a land still suffering clashes with tribes, bandits, and raiders. The people he'd met so far were as refined and well-mannered as any he'd known back East. Finer even, when he counted Clara among the few who by all accounts did not belong beyond the borders of country estates and well-supplied cities.

"Why'd you ask?"

Michael pushed his questions to the back of his thoughts and answered Isaac. "A puzzling recollection I'm still working out." He secured his hat low on his head. "If you're not going to the hotel, you can come with me to the clinic. It'll be a long wait."

Isaac shifted his body from the desk and tested his leg before putting weight on it. "Reckon it'd suit me fine to wait with you."

CLARA REMEMBERED THE day Alice was born, at least the hours after. The birthing she barely recalled, and watching Briley suffer, was grateful the finer details remained forgotten. She escaped the birthing room every so often to get fresh linens and water, prepare more tea, or stare out the waiting room window for sign of Michael's return.

Alice's birth was an almost grand affair, attended by the finest doctor in the county, two nurses, and a hospital nearby should the birthing go wrong. She took for granted the amenities so readily available back East, and not for the first time, pondered on her choice to leave home.

"Women of good birth do not live on the frontier, Clara." Her mother's words repeatedly played, often at night or early mornings when little else occupied her mind.

She returned to the room with a fresh bowl of cool water and replaced it with the bowl at Peyton's side. Wiping Briley's brow had become his task, one to keep his hands occupied since he refused to leave his wife's side.

"All right, Briley, the baby is coming." Emma positioned herself.

"It's too fast."

Emma's laugh somehow sounded encouraging. "It's right on time."

Clara stood close to Briley's head until Emma glanced up at her and indicated the fresh linen in Clara's hands. In a flurry of minutes, she nestled the baby in the large linen and seconds later the baby squalled while Emma tended to Briley.

She beamed at Peyton and Briley. "You have a beautiful daughter." Clara watched the tiny face screw into various expressions, each one conveying annoyance at disrupting her deep sleep.

Once Emma finished tending to both Briley and the baby, Clara gently passed the little one into Peyton's outstretched hands.

"Mariah Rose," Peyton whispered when he cradled his daughter. Clara watched as the new father lowered to the chair beside the bed and, with Briley's hands covering his, they held the newest member of their family.

Clara quietly left the room to give the new family privacy. She'd never witnessed a birth beyond Alice's, and though not eager to do so again, she was in awe of the miracle. Her heart ached for Gideon, who had never had the chance to hold Alice. She ignored the momentary sadness in favor of joy for her friends.

Clara closed the door softly behind her, closed her eyes, and leaned against the door. Michael spoke after several seconds of silence.

"I heard . . . Briley?"

"She is well, and so is your niece."

"Niece?"

"Yes. I will leave it to Briley to share her daughter's name with you. She will insist on seeing you soon, though I daresay right now her thoughts are focused on the baby." Clara washed her hands at a basin in the front room. When she turned back to Michael again, she noticed the other man, for the first time, standing near the door.

"Mrs. Stowe, this is Isaac Worth."

Clara bowed her head briefly toward Michael's friend. "It is a pleasure to meet you, Mr. Worth."

Isaac sent Michael a look of bemusement before returning the greeting. "Pleased to meet you, ma'am. He's been worrying something fierce since we came here."

Since it had not been so long since Clara came out for fresh water, she guessed they arrived at the point when Briley was screaming her loudest. "Worry no more. I have never seen a happier new mother or more beautiful baby."

Michael indulged her with a lopsided smile. "Considering I've now met your daughter, I doubt the veracity of your claim." His face softened, the reverence of his expression interrupted when Emma entered the room.

"Well, good you're here, Michael. Briley is already asking for you again. She and the baby will stay here for a few days, and then they'll return home."

"Where's home?" Michael asked.

"Not far," Emma assured him. "Briley lived in a small cabin when she first arrived, a good distance out of town, but Peyton built a place for them this past summer, an easy half a mile away."

The sudden force of the clinic's front door interrupted Michael's walk to the back room opening. Clara rushed past him and pulled an anxious young woman inside while Isaac closed the door. "Sadie, whatever are you doing here, and in this horrid weather?"

The young woman unwrapped her wind-reddened face just enough to speak. Each heavy breath released in a quick intake and deep exhalation as she tried to calm. "Men—the inn." She almost doubled over before straightening her shoulders. "Susan said to come straightaway. Mr. Elis is—" she took another deep breath "—he's not letting the men inside, but Miss Clara, they have guns!"

"Shh." Clara darted a look at the door, hoping the girl's voice hadn't penetrated Peyton's fog of happiness. "All right, Sadie, it will be all right." Clara guided the young woman to Emma's side. "Watch her, please."

"Clara, Peyton needs—"

"Leave him." Michael, too, cast a glance at the door and lowered his voice. "Peyton is where he needs to be right now. Is there a deputy?"

"My husband," Emma said. "Except he's at White Eagle Ranch. There's no way to get word to him quickly enough in this weather. There are other men in town who—"

"I'll go." Michael shrugged back into his heavy duster. "Isaac, I may need your help." In response, Isaac placed a worn, wide-brimmed hat on his head.

Torn between telling Michael to stay for Briley and thanking him for going, Clara said nothing. She lifted her outer clothes from nearby hooks instead.

"What do you think you're doing?" Michael asked.

"Going with you."

"No." Michael started for the door.

"Yes." Clara followed and when he stopped, she ran into his back.

"We don't know the situation yet. It's too dangerous."

She raised herself to her full height, which still left Michael with four inches to his advantage. "My daughter is at the inn, and no one is going to stop me from going to her."

"You won't do her any good if you get yourself hurt or killed, and there's a good chance of that when we don't know the situation. I promise, nothing will happen to Alice."

Clara wanted to believe him, *did* believe him, yet until she saw with her own eyes that Alice was safe, she would not stay behind and wait. "I'm going."

Michael held back an oath, though everyone in the room except Sadie recognized what he almost said. "I didn't bring my horse. Are you able to walk through this snow?"

"Yes." She would, for Alice. "Yes, I can."

"Fine. Isaac, fetch your horse from the livery and ask the owner—"

"Thomas Doby," Clara said.

"Mr. Doby to join you if he's able." Michael looked at Emma. "Not a word to Peyton while he's with Briley."

"Peyton will know something is wrong when you don't go in there, Michael."

"Then tell him, but not around my sister. She'll worry,

and I'd just as soon not have her think I'm off to face my maker once again." Michael placed a gloved hand on the small of Clara's back and followed her outside. Isaac moved past them, and with a slight limp, half walked, half ran toward the livery.

"Who is the girl who came into the clinic?"

"Sadie Walker. She sometimes helps at the inn when she's not working at the café or helping her aunt and uncle at the general store." Clara raised part of her thick wool shawl to cover her head. "Susan would not have sent her unless the situation . . . Alice. The guests. Michael, I need—"

"I know. Stay close and don't stop moving."

Clara nodded, huddled close to his side, and almost as one unit they plodded through the snow. The wind had built waist-high drifts and created a path covered with only a few inches of snow, making the trek from town to inn easier. A shiver creeped along every surface of her skin, and she longed to close her eyes. Michael held some of her weight against him yet never faltered. Within minutes, they were between the protective covering of two mighty pine trees and the side of the building.

"Is there a way upstairs without being noticed?"

"Yes. A staircase off the kitchen."

"Good. Head upstairs. Be as quiet as possible." Michael surprised her by grabbing her hands and clasping them between his. He rubbed them, and until then she hadn't realized her fingers were numb. "I'm going in through the front, like nothing's wrong."

"What about Isaac?"

"He'll know what to do when he gets here."

When Michael started past her, Clara looped her arm through his. "Mariah Rose is her name."

Understanding showed in Michael's eyes as a gentle smile played across his mouth. "Thank you for telling me, Clara."

"Please, be careful." They stared at each other for five seconds, each beat of time counted in Clara's head, before Michael left her to enter through the front door.

CHAPTER 7

"The house is grand enough for Connecticut and quite beautiful, but the front porch is my favorite place to spend a peaceful morning."

Clara Stowe to her mother in early November, the year she arrived in Crooked Creek

CLARA WORKED HER boots off on the back porch and curled her toes under when the cold penetrated her feet. She left them next to the door before turning the knob by slow degree and inching the portal open.

She identified only one voice speaking, though Elis's tone was not raised enough for her to make out the words. Clara recognized the undercurrent of anger and worry, both of which she'd had the misfortune of hearing before, though never directed at her. Elis could be fierce when needed, despite his seemingly harmless appearance.

The other man's voice belonged to a stranger, someone she'd never heard, even in passing. Clara made a game of remembering the faces and voices of her guests, so if they ever passed through again, she could greet them on sight. However, right now, she didn't want to meet this stranger, let alone welcome him to her inn.

She shut the door and thanked the sudden shout from the other room for masking the soft click. On padded feet, and without taking the time to remove her outer clothing, Clara crossed into the kitchen and pushed aside a lightweight curtain to reveal a narrow passageway.

The stairs led her to each landing, and the first two she passed, praying Alice had stayed hidden on the third floor. Hear-a-pin-drop quiet greeted her on the top landing. The two floors muffled even the voices below. Clara padded down the hall, noting the open door to the suite of rooms she and her daughter shared.

Her chest tightened as she continued down the hall, passing a wall of built-in cupboards before reaching the room Augusta and Grace shared. The door lay open, but she felt compelled to enter this time. Drawn across the room, Clara opened the adjoining bathing room door. Huddled between the wall and a large copper tub, she could see only Augusta's back hunched over, her arms spread.

"It's Clara."

"Mama?"

With what sounded like a half-sob, Augusta fell backward in a rush to let Alice get past her. Clara took her daughter up in her arms and hugged her close before setting her back on her own feet. She pressed a finger to her lips at Alice and Grace's wide-eyed expressions, and helped Augusta to her feet.

In a whisper, she asked, "Has anyone else come upstairs?"

Augusta shook her head and drew Grace close. "We were going downstairs when the men first came. They didn't see us, or they would have followed."

The terror in Augusta's voice when she spoke of the men's arrival triggered Clara's next question. "Did you recognize them?"

Instead of answering, Augusta glanced down at her daughter, who kept her eyes downward. Clara couldn't worry about what Augusta might know, but she had to ask one more thing. "How far will they go? Will they hurt the others?" Augusta's grip on the fabric of her skirt caused her knuckles to whiten. "All right. Will you stay here and keep Alice with you?"

"No, Mama!" Alice tugged on Clara's sleeve.

She knelt in front of her daughter. "I promise to come back for you. Will you be brave and strong for me, like you were on the stagecoach when we first came to Montana? Remember how fast it moved, and how it fell over? You were the bravest girl I've ever seen. Can you be brave again?"

Tears hovered just on the edge of Alice's lashes. "That wasn't fun."

Clara smiled for her daughter's sake. "No, it wasn't, but it was its own kind of adventure, and so is this. Besides, Grace could use someone to hold her hand."

As if already planning to do so, Alice clasped her small hand with Grace's and smiled up at the other girl. "We can be brave together."

Grace peered up first at Clara, then at Alice, and nodded.

"Good. Very good." Clara stood and spoke to Augusta. "I will close the doors this time behind me and lock the outer one. There is a spare key in the drawer of the stand next to the bed. The key won't fit under the door, so you will be locked in until I return."

"I understand. You should stay, though, with us."

Clara longed to stay with Alice, but she had other responsibilities. "Alice is safe here, with or without me. I trust you with her." Augusta was a mother protecting her own child, and Alice would benefit from the woman's motherly instincts.

Augusta grasped Clara's arm as she turned to leave.

Clara read fear in the woman's eyes. "What is it?"

"You asked before . . . If the men know we are here, their attempts to reach us won't stop."

Which is precisely what Clara feared. "Then they are here for you." It wasn't posed as a question. "Stay here." She smoothed back Alice's silky flaxen hair once before leaving the room. She retrieved the spare key and locked the door between the bedroom and hall. When she reached the top of the main staircase, an unfamiliar voice had joined the others. Clara removed her coat and muffler and draped them over the railing. Stepping as softly as possible, she descended the first two carpeted stairways until she stood halfway down the last one leading into the dining room.

Voices carried easily, and this time, there was no mistaking the tension in Elis's voice with his next words. "No one here like that. There was a woman yesterday, but she left when the sheriff came around."

"Sheriff Peyton, isn't it?" one man asked.

"That's right," Elis said. "The lady said she didn't like him asking so many questions 'bout where she'd been and where she was going."

"Where'd she go?" Another man's voice joined the mix.

"Can't rightly say for sure where she reckoned going with the storm coming. She headed east, though. Widow Stowe let her take a horse."

Silence filled the house for several seconds before the first man asked, "You won't mind us takin' a look around first, just to be sure. Could use breakfast."

Susan's voice reached Clara next. "We serve meals to guests only, sir. There's a nice café just down the road a spell. Bess will be open."

"I like what I'm smelling, so here'll be fine." A few footsteps and then they stopped. Clara heard the front door open and knew it to be Michael, though she worried over why he was coming in only now. She eased down the last stairs and pressed her body against the wall as she moved closer to the foyer where she could peek around a hutch.

"Elis. Susan." Michael removed his hat and stomped a remaining bit of snow from his boots onto her front rug. He shrugged when the men eyed him with more than a passing curiosity. "The widow might have mentioned she doesn't like the outside tracked in on her floors. Sure smells good in the kitchen. You folks checking in?"

"What business is it of yours, mister?"

Clara caught sight of a tall, yet lean man with a dark, thin mustache. The words, like his expression, exuded impatience with Michael.

Michael shrugged again. "Just being friendly. Sounds to me like they asked you to leave."

The shorter of the two men eyed the front door, no doubt wondering how long Michael had been out there or how much he'd heard. "You work here, mister?"

"More like I'm new in town, and I've already noticed how people around here look after one another." Michael hung his hat on a peg by the door and kept his duster on.

The stance of the two strangers tightened and the tensity cut through the air to touch every person within reach. Clara prayed for Michael to look her way, but if he knew she was there, he gave no indication. She put one foot out of her hiding place, froze at Michael's next words, and pulled herself back.

"I had breakfast here earlier, and no one else was around. Even the old Widow is with the sheriff and his wife right now, though I reckon they'll be bringing the widow Stowe back soon. Might be wise to leave before they arrive."

The taller man eased the edge of his long duster back to reveal a pistol snug in its holster. "I reckon you ought to stay out of this, mister."

Niceties gone, Michael stepped around the two men and put himself between the strangers and Elis and Susan. Clara covered her mouth to stifle a gasp. With every possible ramification rising to the top of her thoughts, she stepped out from behind the hutch, smoothed her skirt, and called out before she walked into the foyer. "Where is everyone? Susan?"

She halted and fully took in the scene. Susan stood close to Elis, doing an admirable job of trying to mask her fear. Elis's expression remained unflappable, while Michael kept his back to her.

"Thought you said no one else was here," the taller of the strangers said to Michael before he faced Clara. "Anyone else hiding with you, lady?"

"My name is Miss Simmons and I have only now come from the general store. If you are here for a room, I regret to say the widow has already rented out the last one. I recommend you look in the next town. I am told there is a lumber camp twenty miles north. Perhaps they will have a spare cabin."

The strangers shared an unreadable look before the shorter one spoke. "You speak mighty fine, Miss Simmons, so might be you'll listen better than these folks." He pulled his gun from its holster and leveled it at each of them, one by one, settling on Michael. "We're looking for a woman and child. The girl is about ten years old. We followed their tracks to Crooked Creek."

"I do not know of who you speak, and I assure you if a woman and child had arrived in town alone, everyone would most likely know about it. Widow Stowe will not appreciate your poor manners in her home or toward her staff, so again, I can only recommend you continue your search elsewhere."

MICHAEL SHARED HIS imagination with two images. One of him throwing the two men out the front door and the other wringing Clara's pretty neck. What had she been thinking? She hadn't been, he decided, or she would have remained hidden.

He edged closer to her and saw the men noticed his movement. He didn't care. Michael sidled close enough to push her out of the way if necessary, and far enough from her so she wouldn't catch a bullet meant for him.

Michael had expected Clara to stay upstairs with her daughter, and now there was nothing left to wager in the conversation. Someone needed to make the next move, and he preferred it to be him. "I swore my killing days were done when I left the battlefields behind. Seems a shame to break a promise to myself."

"There are two of us, mister," the shorter one said.

"Two fall dead as easy as one." Michael was mentally transported back to a soggy morning in Tennessee, days after the Union's victory at Vaught's Hill. It had been difficult to keep a line between scouting and sniping, except the day he came across the ramshackle farmhouse outside Milton. The screams reached him soon after he caught the rank scent of burning wood smothered in dampness from the early morning rain. They hadn't bothered to drag the young woman inside before having their way with her.

One man North, the other South, by their uniforms, though where they belonged didn't concern him. He readied his Whitworth rifle without taking his eyes off the two men. The screams had quieted, and they left her in the dirt temporarily to share whatever liquid they'd smuggled in a flask. With the muzzleloader primed, he focused through the telescopic sight, waited for the men to line up, and aimed. No shot during the war had ever filled him with as much disgust or satisfaction.

Before he reached the young girl, she stabbed the man who hadn't yet died with his own knife. She had saved the bullet from the man's Colt for herself.

Yes, two fall dead as easy as one. His words, and the promise they held, proved the last tolerance for the strangers before him, in search of a defenseless woman and child. His move first or theirs, the choice required little thought. Michael yanked Clara around and pushed her toward Elis and Susan, trusting Elis to do what was needed.

The first bullet fired skimmed Michael's leg. He'd suffered worse, and it did no more than sting his flesh. Michael charged forth like a bull, his arms spread wide, and launched the men toward the door, when one of them fell away. He heard a fist connect with bone and saw the dark skin of Isaac's hand before the taller man beneath him fell out the door. Icy air burned his face and ruffled the hair on his uncovered head before someone also pulled his quarry from his grasp.

Michael's back met one of the porch beams before he stepped on the wet edge of a step and stumbled backward to the snow. The breath of air he attempted to suck into his lungs was forced out when a body fell over him, unmoving.

Seconds later, the body lifted and Michael focused his vision.

Isaac helped him stand, then stared at the red stain his wound had left in the snow. "The shot hit you."

"Barely." Michael focused on the steady beat of his heart and matched each breath until both slowed. "Your timing, as always, is perfect, Isaac. Thank you."

Isaac shook his head and Michael's poor sense of humor. "Brought help as soon as I found some. Never seen so much snow in my life. Ain't no one with sense out in this."

"Then we are all without sense." Michael straightened to his full height and met the eyes of a man he didn't recognize. "I take it you're the help."

"Casey Latimer. Your friend found me heading into the sheriff's office." He yanked the taller man Michael had tangled with by the collar and shook him hard. "Bad luck for you because I know your name, Jim, and worse luck that I dealt with two more of your friends last night squatting at White Eagle Ranch." Casey indicated the man Isaac had knocked down. "He's Johnny. Both are from the lumber camp." Casey assessed the closed front doors. Someone had shut them without Michael realizing. "Everyone in there okay?"

Michael nodded. He glimpsed the badge pinned to Casey's chest and narrowed his eyes when he caught sight of the full etchings. "Guess I heard wrong about you being a deputy."

Jim slightly twisted his head to ask, "What the devil does he mean? You ain't no deputy?"

"You're not that lucky, Jim." Casey yanked on the man's collar again. "Now shut up and save your energy for the walk to the jail." Casey looked at Michael. "I'll need to speak with you."

"After I see to things here."

"And your wound." Isaac indicated the blood seeping into the fabric covering Michael's upper leg.

"Fine," Casey said. "My wife will see to your leg. Isaac, if you'll get the rope from my saddle, we'll tie these two up before we walk them over."

Seeing they had the situation under control, Michael limped up the porch steps, stopping long enough at the top to pull the torn edges of his pant leg apart and look at the wound. The bullet had gone deeper than he initially thought, and needle pricks of pain slowly replaced his waning adrenaline.

He pushed the pain aside as much as possible and entered the inn. What he saw nearly had him falling to his knees and praying for the first time since he lay near death on the last battlefield.

CHAPTER 8

"The people here would do anything for each other. Truly, I could not have asked for dearer friends."

- Clara Stowe to her father her first November in Crooked Creek

"CLARA!"

Michael ran, dropped to his knees, and skid the last foot to reach Clara's side. She lay unmoving, her body face down and head twisted to the side. His cursory inspection revealed no blood or obviously broken bones. "There's no blood."

Elis knelt on the other side of Clara while Susan stood above them, her fingers lost color from gripping her apron.

"What happened, Elis?" Michael eased Clara over until she faced up. Her head lulled to the side and rested on Michael's lap.

"I pushed them out of the way when the gun fired, but she wouldn't . . ." Elis shook his head. "She wouldn't go down. She grabbed me and tried to push me under her. I ended up falling on top."

Michael hovered his hand over Clara's mouth. "She's breathing, barely." He lowered her flat on the ground.

"What the hell happened?" Casey's boots pounded across the foyer rug until he, too, knelt by Clara's side.

"She'll be fine." Michael knew it down to the depth of whatever soul he still had. He leaned over Clara and gave her his breath. Once. Twice. The third time he felt her stir, and she returned the breath with her own. He helped her into a sitting position and rested her back against his chest. "Slow breaths, Clara. Take it slow."

Clara focused on each face. "Casey? Whatever are you doing here?" She twisted a little and peered at Michael. "What happened?"

"Short of it is, you fell and lost your breath for a spell."

"I fell on you," Elis confessed, his cheeks still pale from worry. "I'm real sorry. You sure you're all right?"

Clara sat quietly for several seconds before nodding. "I think so."

Casey held onto her arms and helped her stand when he got to his feet, leaving Michael no choice except to release her.

"Steady now," Casey said. "Tell me now if any part of you is in pain, Clara. Emma will have both our hides otherwise."

"I promise, Casey." She leaned into him for a moment before her head cleared and she stood straight. "I will let Emma examine me later, so ease your worry."

"Nothing about this is easy. Have you met Isaac yet?"

Clara nodded. "Yes, once at the clinic. Is he here?"

"He took those two men on ahead to the jail for me and

seemed pleased to lead them tied together with a rough rope. He didn't have time to tell me much, so I'd like the whole of it now. If not from you, then . . ." Casey glanced at Michael, "from you."

"Peyton is with Briley," Clara said. "She gave birth not long ago, and when——"

"That's enough for now." Michael stepped up beside Clara and stared at Casey. "I'll tell you what I know. Clara needs to see to her daughter."

"Where is Alice?"

Clara clasped Casey's arm. "She is safe with a friend upstairs. Michael is right, Casey. I need to go to her. They will be terrified after hearing the gunshots."

Clara's hand twined with Michael's. "Thank you." She tightened her grip before releasing him. "Thank you. Susan, please come with me."

Michael breathed a little easier after Susan wrapped her arm around Clara's waist and they ascended the stairs together. "Elis. I'd consider it a kindness if you'd go to the jailhouse and sit with Isaac while I speak with the marshal."

"Sure will. You aren't goin'?"

"Not until I speak with Mrs. Stowe again."

Only when Michael heard Elis's footsteps fade did he face Casey. "You don't go out of your way to advertise you're wearing a U.S. Marshal badge. Unusual for a town this size. I heard you were the deputy."

"If you want to get specific about it, I'm both. The marshal appointment is as-needed, and with the trouble going on around here the past few months, it's been necessary to wear this badge."

"Are those two men who came here part of the trouble you've been having around here?"

Casey scratched his jaw and rubbed his fingers briefly

over his eyes. "Those two work for Lucas Harrigan. He owns a large lumber operation twenty miles north of here."

"Any reason this Lucas Harrigan might have business at Dawson's Trading Post?"

"He recruits new workers from there. A lot of men pass through. Some stay hoping to find work." Casey waved over his shoulder in the direction of the town. "A lot of those men are no goods like Jim and Johnny over at the jail. They work cheap, sometimes for only room and board, and do whatever Harrigan tells them, just happy to have food in their bellies."

Michael thought of the tall, dark-haired man he'd seen at the post dressed too fine for the area. The earlier recollection he'd been struggling to clear up did so now. "Does Harrigan have a wife and daughter?"

Casey's eyes narrowed. "Both. The fellas we ran off White Eagle Ranch say they've gone missing. It's why I came back when I did, instead of waiting out the storm at Hattie and Carson's place."

Michael sorted through the names, placing each one he'd heard so far. From what he'd gleaned, Hattie, Briley, and Emma, along with their husbands, were close. Friends, yet something more besides. He noticed it in the familiar way Casey handled and spoke to Clara. "Good thing you did."

Casey pointed to Michael's duster. "I can see you're carrying a pistol under there. You didn't draw."

He would have. If the choice had come to killing those men to keep the others safe, he would have drawn, shot, and not regretted the act for a single moment. "Wasn't necessary."

"Huh. The paperwork is easier when they're alive, though I suspect you didn't consider the extra workload at the time." Casey held out his hand, palm up. "If you'll forgive the impertinence, I'd like to see the gun."

Michael withdrew his pistol and passed it, handle first, to Casey.

"Remington. Not a Colt. Interesting choice."

"It was a gift from my first captain."

Casey inspected the pistol before handing it back. "The only guns I saw that well cared for during the war belonged to sharpshooters."

"Is that right?"

"You don't want to talk about it. Fair enough. Most of us don't, but I wonder why a Union sharpshooter kept his gun holstered when confronted with life or death. It's just curious."

A faint smile touched the edge of Michael's mouth. "Could be I'm lousy with a pistol."

"Huh. Why'd you ask if Harrigan had a wife and daughter?"

Not his secret to tell, Michael told himself, and yet, if Clara trusted Casey as much as he believed, then he'd have to trust the man as well. "There's a woman and a young girl here. Likely they're who Alice hid with upstairs. Clara saw fit to keep their secret, so—"

"You don't know us yet." Casey dropped the hand he'd raised to quiet Michael. "If Clara is hiding them here, she has her reasons. Isaac only gave me your first name. What about the last?"

Michael smiled then. It wasn't the kind of smile that filled a body with joy, but it was a smile. "It's time I tell you the 'everything' you wanted to know." He gave Casey the abridged version of what had transpired since he and Isaac had ridden into Crooked Creek. "Your wife helped bring my niece into the world today, and she has my undying gratitude. A woman like her claims a man like you, well, you must have a fair number of redeeming qualities to recommend you.

Until you give me reason otherwise, I'll trust you as Clara does."

Casey's lips twitched as he held back a grin. "You're Briley's brother, which makes you family and a friend, so I'll place my trust in you. Since we've exhausted pleasantries, I need to get to the jail."

"What are the chances Peyton hasn't heard about any of this?"

"After the gunshot? He's probably at the jail waiting for me."

Michael nodded. "Isaac will have filled him in."

"Good." Casey rubbed a hand over the top of his head and looked around. His hat rested upside down a foot from the front door. "Come by the sheriff's office later. We'll need an official statement."

"I will. And Marshal?"

"It's Casey."

"What are the chances more of those men will show up?"

"Good, I think. There's unrest, and it's about more than some washed-out cabins and the lumber camp. Whatever Clara's good intentions, Mrs. Harrigan, if it's her, and her daughter aren't safe here until we figure out what's going on."

Michael watched Casey Latimer's departing figure and continued to stare out the front window for several minutes. The landscape glistened with snow crystals beneath the emerging sunlight.

"I will not toss them out. They sought shelter here, and this will remain their haven for as long as they need one."

He remained facing the window when he asked, "How much did you hear?"

"Not enough, though I daresay more than you and Casey would like."

Sunlight filtered far enough into the house to reach where

Clara stood half a dozen feet behind Michael. Her flaxen hair glowed beneath the midday rays and the eyes staring back at him, studying his face as intently as he studied hers, offered no encouragement to argue.

CLARA ONCE GAVE the same close examination to Gideon from across a ballroom, when the throng of dancers and merrymakers vanished, leaving only them and unspoken promises.

Now, half a decade later and many experiences wiser, Clara dared not examine the tender prickling on her skin or her accelerated heartbeat beneath Michael's perusal.

"How is Alice?"

"She is resting now beside Grace. I envy them the ability to sleep at such a time." Clara closed the space between them by half. The most pressing question on her mind related to his time in the war. Casey had called Michael a sharpshooter. She eyed the place beneath his duster where the pistol rested at his hip, then met Michael's gaze again, and she put off asking him anything. "Thank you for what you did for us. Briley will insist you stay with her. However, I would invite you and Isaac to lodge at the inn for as long as you like."

"My sister and her husband should be alone with their new daughter. I've no plans to leave, so we have time. Clara, no one said you need to toss the woman and her daughter out. I expect Augusta and Grace are this Lucas Harrigan's wife and child. For reasons she cares not to discuss, she left, and Harrigan seems to want them back. She's hiding and he's hunting, and if he wants them badly enough, he'll send more armed men, which puts all of you in danger."

Clara's chin lifted a fraction. "Then we will have to be extra careful."

"Yes, we will. And yes, Isaac and I will stay here. We appreciate the invite, and of course, if it's okay with Miss Simmons and the old Widow Stowe?"

Clara's cheeks blossomed with a light-rose hue. "Miss Simmons was my governess during my formative years and the first name to come to mind. The 'old Widow Stowe' was not my idea." The explanation gave her time to release a touch of her earlier annoyance. "Of course, you and Isaac are welcome to stay."

Frigid air entered with Peyton through the front door and dispelled the warmth accumulated during the ruckus. He hurried inside and stopped a foot short of Clara's side. He lifted her hand in his and visually examined her for any sign of injury. "I'd give you a dressing down if I thought it would do any good. Then again, you might wish it after Briley and Emma have at you. Heaven knows what'll happen when they tell Hattie." He let out a deep breath. "You're all right?"

"I promise, all is well now, and a restorative cup of tea with some of Susan's apple cake will set it more than all right." Clara gently squeezed Peyton's hand before releasing it. "We have Michael to thank for seeing us through the worst of it. How did you find out?"

His raised brow told her he thought the question insane. "Gunshots and Emma wearing a look of guilt when I came out of Briley's room. Casey told me the rest. I would have been here sooner if Isaac hadn't arrived at the jail with trussed-up men." Peyton faced Michael. "And Briley——"

Michael cut him with a quick shake of his head. "I imagine her admonishments were not so different from before I enlisted."

"You'd better go and see your sister." At Michael's hesitation, Peyton relented. "Fine, but I'll have my say. Clara, I . . ."

The sun shined brightly now, deceiving anyone who had not weathered the recent storm. Clara longed to let the sun's warmth caress her skin and listen to the lilting birdsong she'd grown familiar with during summer and autumn. Her eyes fluttered closed, blocking from sight Michael, Peyton, and all except the remembrance of warm days and the abundance of foliage.

"Clara?"

She dusted away the longing and returned her thoughts to winter and the cruelty of some men's actions. "Forgive me, Sheriff."

"You only call me Sheriff when you're angry, something you have in common with my wife." That brought out her smile. "Good. Remember you don't dislike me when I ask you to close the inn for the time being."

"I will do no such thing. There are guests under this roof, and I will repeat what I told Mr. Donaghue: I will not turn them out."

"Whoa."

Clara's eyes narrowed.

Peyton lowered the arms he had raised in defense. "I'm not asking you to turn anyone out, and frankly, I'll feel better knowing Michael and his friend are under your roof." He asked Michael, "You are staying?"

After Michael nodded, Peyton continued. "Briley will want her brother to stay with us, but when I explain you'll be safer with him here, she'll relent. I'm only asking you to close the inn to new guests. We can't know who they are or what their intentions will be. Not everyone Mr. Harrigan sends in his stead will look and behave like vagabonds and criminals. The next ones—"

"I never know the strangers who come here in want of a room, Sheriff. It is the nature of running an inn, an establishment I might add that is the only decent hotel within two days' journey. I cannot turn people away with winter already heavy upon us. However, we will be cautious. I have already given Sadie time off. She's at an age where . . . well, a tempting age for men like those Harrigan might send back. No one else is of a mind to accept the same offer." Clara peered upward and lowered her voice to a mere whisper. "Do you know who is upstairs then?"

"Casey gave me the short of your conversation with him. If you won't close down for your sake, please consider the option for her and the girl."

"Will it not appear more suspicious? With the doors open to guests—no matter how few there are at present—anyone looking for her might think they have moved on."

"You don't understand. Were it in my power to send you and every other woman here west of the Mississippi until spring, I would do it. It's an empty sentiment since none of you will leave and I—me, Carson, and Casey—have a duty to stay right now."

An inkling of defeat and frustration in Peyton's voice mellowed Clara's energy to argue with him. "How bad is the situation, really?"

"If ever there was a time to not have come to this territory, it is now. Lawlessness has increased and vigilante justice is thwarting efforts by the U.S. Marshals. We've been lucky in our valley so far, beyond the reach of most skirmishes and battles, and the tribes are content to leave us be as we leave them alone, but the unrest is real, and Harrigan is a man who thinks he's a law unto himself."

"How many times have you had this same conversation with Briley?"

"Too many." His heavy sigh broke through the last of Clara's defenses. She walked to a window and studied the untouched snow beyond the glass. "It is inconceivable for so much discontent to exist in a place of such remarkable beauty. When he conceived of the idea to come west, Alice's father spoke of its splendor, never having seen it, and yet he was right." She looked between Peyton and Michael rather than directly at either one.

"The war broke many of us, not only the men who fought. We escaped not the physical world in which we lived, we escaped the ghosts haunting every house, hill, and city." A heavy tear fluttered on her lash before gliding down her cheek. She swiped it away with the painful memories. "Each of us purchased freedom when we came here, and such a sacrifice is worth holding onto. When I left home, some called me a fool, and my mother and father begged me to remain with them. My father's wealth made my crossing easier and life here more bearable. Not everyone is so blessed. I intend to help as many as possible with what my father has given me and with what Gideon left his daughter."

Shoulders back and chin high, Clara stared each of them down. "The inn remains open, and heaven help anyone who attempts to destroy the peace we are struggling to build."

CHAPTER 9

"The colder days are made warm by the beautiful scarves Briley Sawyer has knit for us. Mother, you should see her intricate lacework and the woolen blankets she weaves. They would, I think, be well received by Connecticut society. I have enclosed a handkerchief she made for you."

- Clara Stowe to her parents after her first Thanksgiving in Crooked Creek

WOMEN, NO MATTER how many he met, lived with, loved, or fought for, remained God's greatest mystery. Death, he understood. The cycle from birth to end made sense, even if the struggle to get from one to the next was more than a person could bear at times. Nature and its vagaries offered beauty and variety, and if a body didn't want to be rained on, snowed on, frozen to the bone, or roasted on the inside, they could huddle in the shade or beneath a shelter until it passed.

Women, however, bewildered and humbled him. Briley and their mother's strength when he and his father enlisted left him in awe. More than once during his service, a farmer's wife or city widow offered hospitality in the face of an encroaching army. He now added Clara to the ranks of women who left him amazed.

Peyton stood beside him, less dumbfounded than Michael, yet equally impressed. After an almost indiscernible curse, he pulled on his gloves. "By everyone, she meant us, too."

"I figured that one out for myself." Michael offered Peyton a wry smirk. His mouth then thinned into a tight line before he asked, "What is it about this Harrigan fellow has you and everyone else so worried? Not the soft-touch version you gave Clara. The real reason."

Peyton motioned to the steps. "Walk with me to town, would you?"

Peyton took for granted Michael would follow, and so Michael humored him.

Michael said, "In the normal way of things, we'd get to know each other as brothers first, but we have other pressing matters right now. Tell me about Harrigan."

"Are you sticking around?"

Michael nodded. "This is home for as long as Briley's here." *Not only Briley.*

"Then you'll need to know more than just about Lucas Harrigan, but we'll start with him." Peyton stopped halfway between the inn and town, used to the cold for it not to bother him. "Truth is, there's more we *don't* know about Harrigan. Casey rides farther afield and has pieced more together. Harrigan arrived about two years before war broke out, when this was still part of Idaho Territory. His name meant little in those days. We know he left for Georgia three years ago, then two months after the war ended, he returned, bought a lot of land, and built the lumber mill."

"What has he done since then, besides running the mill?"

"He kept mostly to himself until this past summer, the Monday of the last week of June. I remember the day because it's the first time one of Harrigan's men came down from the camp in need of a doctor."

Not as impervious to the cold as Peyton, Michael tucked his gloved hands deep into his pockets. "They don't have one of their own?"

"They did. The man who asked for the 'lady doctor' said the doctor at the lumber camp left. Casey and Carson rode with Emma to the camp, but arrived too late. Three died that day in what Harrigan claimed was an accident."

"They didn't believe him?"

Peyton shook his head. "No one from the mill stepped forward to say otherwise."

"I'm missing part of the story."

"One of the dead was a woman, another a boy, thirteen years old. They and the boy's father were under a pile of fallen logs."

They left two sets of deep boot prints in the snow when they started to walk again. Michael swore the heat from the sun managed to break through the cold long enough to warm his skin. He tipped his head back and breathed as deeply as his lungs allowed. "What about since? I'm ready to despise the man on principle, but one incident doesn't make him a criminal."

"Rumors are all we have at this point, which is why Casey hasn't been able to arrest him. He has friends among the vigilantes, so they leave him and his men alone." Peyton stopped once more and faced Michael. "How did we know if a man was a good general?"

Michael thought back to his company captain and each commanding officer above him. "By the way his men spoke of him . . . their loyalty to him."

Peyton nodded. "Harrigan's men speak of him in one of two ways: with fear or ambivalence."

"All right, point taken. So his Augusta and Grace shouldn't continue to stay at the inn."

"I don't intend to be near the place when you tell Clara."

Michael blew out a breath and gauged the rest of the distance between where they stood and the clinic. "I'll give your warning some thought on the way to see my new niece."

He entered the clinic alone. Peyton needed ten minutes with Casey to square away their prisoners, then he'd be back. Michael would take those ten minutes to be with his sister and niece. Emma smiled at him from behind her desk and raised a finger to her lips.

"They're asleep again."

"Should have been here earlier." Michael stared at the closed door where he knew Briley and baby slept. "They're well?"

"Once Peyton assured Briley he'd make sure you were safe after we heard the gunshots, she calmed down." Emma stood and walked around the desk. "Casey was here and explained. Only after she knew you were safe did she drift off to sleep again."

"Then let's not tell her about this." Michael pulled the edge of his duster back to reveal the bandage around his thigh. "Clara wrapped it, but it might need stitches."

Emma shifted from a concerned friend to a no-nonsense doctor in the space of a second. "Come, lay down up here." She patted the fresh linen covering a long, padded examination table.

"I don't think it's serious, just——"

"Up on the table and lay down." She left him to obey her directive while she gathered supplies.

Michael smiled at her back and removed his coat and hat before he thought of what came next. "You can reach the wound without me stripping down, right?"

Emma carried strips of cloth, a pair of shiny scissors, and two amber bottles on a tray, and lowered them to a wheeled cart that reached two inches above the table. "If you're shy about removing your pants, I'll cut away what I need." She fingered the shredded edges Michael had already torn. "Briley sews Peyton's clothes, Casey's, and a few others, too. I'm sure she can manage some new pants for you."

"Our mother taught her." Michael levered himself onto the table, carefully dangling his booted feet off the edge to spare the linen from soiling.

"Talented women," Emma murmured as she focused on cutting a larger area from Michael's pant leg. "My skill with combining fabrics is middling, though I manage a hem well enough. There's a reason Casey pays Briley rather than asking me when he needs a new shirt." She hissed on a low breath and glanced at his face. "This went in and out. Are you in any pain?"

"No pain. The cold must have numbed it enough." His leg twitched when Emma pressed at the edge of the entrance wound. "Well, *that* doesn't feel good."

Emma wet one of the cloths from the tray and cleaned around the wound. "You are lucky the bullet passed through the outer leg, only two inches in. It missed your arteries. The entry will need two stitches, and the exit three. Did you feel it go through?"

"I didn't feel it at all." Michael closed his eyes and replayed the confrontation in his mind. He'd had it under control until Clara entered from behind. What had she been thinking, to put herself in danger?

Emma brought him out of his own head when she pressed another cloth, this time covered in some kind of fire-induced torture liquid, to his wounds. He clenched his mouth closed.

"Why is it men always think they cannot show pain?" Emma asked without a glance his way. "It is prudent you are such a person, otherwise your sister would hear."

He believed himself capable of talking again when the pain subsided. "You don't talk like any doctor I've met before."

She smiled. "Have you ever been to a female doctor?"

"First time."

Emma threaded her surgical needle and studied him. "It doesn't bother you."

"No, ma'am."

"It's Emma." She made quick work of the first two stitches. "You will need to turn on your side, facing away, so I can reach the exit wound."

Michael did as she instructed and gave her a wry smile. "You have a gentler touch than the Union Army docs."

"Their wounded numbered in the hundreds and thousands. I have time for gentle."

"I'm grateful they were there to save the men they could. Still, I'll take a delicate touch any day." He barely felt the gentle threading of her stitches. "Except whatever you put on the wound bites."

"You can lay flat again. The mixture contains a few things, and you're smelling onion, but it's the cayenne in an alcohol base that leaves a person feeling like their eye has been punched."

"I recall the docs using onion juice for gunshot wounds. Cayenne's new."

"There's more in the honey paste, though not as much. Tribes have used pepper in wounds for centuries, and it's perfectly safe." Emma smoothed a thick paste over each set of stitches and carefully wrapped the leg over and over until she was satisfied with the covering. She sliced the edge of the strip and used the two new strips to secure the bandage.

The paste soothed instead of stung. "Where'd you go to school?"

Emma laughed. "I assure you, my medical degree is real. The New England Female Medical College is not Harvard, but anatomy does not change because it is taught to women."

Michael's face heated, though not in embarrassment. "I didn't mean my words to sound as if I doubted your abilities."

"I know. Proper healing requires use of what both science and nature can provide. Modern medicines aren't always available here or get used up before a new shipment arrives, so I've learned to adapt and use what nature provides when other medicines aren't available. Isaac fared a little better than you under my ministrations."

Rather than take offense, Michael stared at the top of her dark hair until she looked up. "Isaac's been tended?"

"Of course." Emma wiped her hands on a clean flannel. "It's a long festering wound he's suffered, and he wasn't forthcoming with details."

"Will he mend?"

"Depends on him. I need to see inside the leg to determine if my suspicions are correct." At his blank look, she asked. "He never told you?"

Michael shook his head. "Only that it happened long before I met him and it's getting worse with age."

"Well, it's neither my right nor place to tell you if he hasn't, though it is unlikely a lack of trust on his part."

"What makes you think so?"

Emma gathered up the implements she'd used to treat him and dropped them into a large wooden bowl to be cleaned. "The injury is part of his past, and nothing to do with knowing you. If you want to help him, convince him to let me help. The medicine I gave him is only a temporary relief."

"I'll find a time to speak with him." When Emma indicated he could sit up, Michael pushed himself to a sitting position and lifted his leg an inch off the table. A slight throbbing remained. Without the reminder, he might not have remembered he'd been shot. He eased off the table and tested the leg with his full weight. "You do good work, doc."

"See it stays good. Keep off the leg as much as possible for a day. I doubt you'll last longer. Keep the wound covered and dry for the next two days. I'll come by the inn to change the bandage and use more salve. The stitches can come out in a week."

Michael wanted to argue about keeping off the leg for a full day. His leg didn't seem to have a problem with the weight he put on it. As though Emma knew he was about to argue, she added, "A full day, Michael, and it begins as soon as you leave here. I'll ask Casey to take you over in a wagon. It's not far enough to the inn to warrant him hitching up the sleigh. No riding for at least three days or you'll undo my beautiful needlework."

He wanted to hug her. No explanation accompanied the urge, and he refrained. Instead, Michael gave her a smile. "Thank you, Dr. Latimer, for everything."

Moisture rimmed Emma's eyes. "You never leave her again, and we'll call it even."

"Yes, ma'am." He glanced at the door to Briley's room. "How long do you think they'll sleep?"

"Haven't you ever been around a woman who has just had a baby? It's a lot of exhausting work for both of them."

Sheepishly, Michael shook his head. "Self-preservation and the weakness of my gender compelled me to stay away the first few days. No woman I knew to give birth before was family, though."

Emma smiled in appreciation of his admission. "Would you like to hold your niece?"

He nodded and followed Emma when she motioned him to join her. Burrowed beneath the covers, with only the top of her head and one arm visible, Briley did not stir as they entered. Emma bade him stay while she gathered the baby from its cradle. The baby rested comfortably in a knitted blanket of soft wool that Michael recognized as Briley's handiwork.

"Have you ever held a baby?"

"Yes. It's been a while, though." Michael's voice and touch were filled with reverence when he accepted the small bundle into his arms. He remained still, careful not to breathe too hard lest he wake the baby. "Mariah Rose." His gaze fell on Briley's covered form then back to the baby. After a few minutes, and with great reluctance, he returned the baby to Emma and backed out of the room.

Emma closed the door softly. "You are welcome to wait and stay off your leg here, but it could be hours before Briley wakes again. I will tell her you were here and that you'll return tomorrow. Your first day in Crooked Creek has been more eventful than you expected. You need to rest up."

Eventful enough to make Michael wonder what tomorrow would bring. He hoped Emma could see in his eyes the genuine gratitude for all she'd done. With a half-smile, he pointed to Briley's door. "Do me a favor, please, and leave out the part about me getting shot."

SUNSET AND SUNRISE had been his favorite times of day since boyhood. One meant most of the world would soon be tucked away at home or falling asleep after a hard day's work. The other meant an awakening, a daily opportunity to get it right if you messed up the day before. Both moments in the day were quieter than all the rest.

Michael used to love the quiet . . . before the war, before quiet meant death, before it meant sitting in muck during the cold of winter or the blazing heat of summer waiting for the next gunfire to destroy body, spirit, and hope.

He slept when his mind gave him no choice, when his limbs refused to perform even the most basic of functions. He slept because the limits of man's control over his flesh and blood gave him no other choice. Most nights, Michael floated on the edge of exhaustion, rather than close his eyes and welcome the nightmares.

Clara had put him and Isaac in separate rooms—a rare occurrence during their travels, either due to cost or lack of space—on the guest floor. No one else occupied the other rooms on the floor, and given the recent storm, it was unlikely Clara would play hostess to new guests in the immediate future.

She'd quoted a price Michael knew to be far less than anyone else would have been charged for one of her well-appointed suites, yet he did not argue. He did not wish to embarrass her by offering more, which would have implied she asked for so little because she thought they couldn't afford it. Or, it might have been her way of thanking them, but giving them rooms for free would have been an insult.

What a mess. He stared at the long shadow of a tree cast by the moon's light through the open bedroom window. His body sank just enough into the thick mattress for him to believe it was the most comfortable he'd ever laid upon, and the iron bed frame barely creaked when he rolled to the left and dropped his stockinged feet to the hooked rug on the floor.

The flame burned out hours ago in the lamp on the narrow table next to the bed, and his eyes adjusted well enough, with help from the moonlight, for him to believe he could walk about without striking flame to a fresh length of wick.

Michael slipped on the only clean pair of pants from his traveling bag and left his shirt untucked and the braces hanging down the sides of his legs. He tested his weight on his feet after hours of inactivity and decided what Emma didn't know could only hurt him if his wound took longer to heal.

On padded feet, he left the room and waited for a minute in the hallway to ensure his quiet exit had not awakened Isaac in the room next door. When he heard nothing more than the gentle creak brought about by the wind outside, he walked with a slight limp down the hall, used the handrail to hold most of his weight down the main staircase, and in the dark, found his way to the kitchen.

The dinner of thick beefsteak with onions, fried potatoes, canned peaches, and the softest biscuits he'd ever eaten had sated his hunger well. If Susan cooked with such abundance at every meal, the empty stomachs he and Isaac suffered more than once in their travels would never be empty again.

If they remained at Clara's inn.

Halfway through Missouri, Isaac had mentioned his desire to return home to Georgia, yet he continued west with

Michael. When Michael asked why he remained, Isaac told him that when the time was right for him to leave, there'd be a good reason to go back. He planned to stick with Michael until a good reason came along.

Michael appreciated the company, but now that he found Briley, they both needed to make plans. He intended to stay in Crooked Creek as long as his sister lived here, which, considering her husband and new baby, meant Michael was now home.

His hand hovered for a second over the cloth covering Susan's apple pie. Home. A concept, a place, an idea he imagined every day of the war. How often had he thought about what awaited him in New York? Did his family live, and if so, were they still in the apartment where he had hugged and kissed them goodbye? The answers to those questions waited for him on the other side of every battle and kept him from succumbing to defeat.

Hope had not abandoned him, even when he believed the emotion far beyond his reach. Hope led him across the continent and eventually to Crooked Creek and his sister.

To Clara.

He helped himself to a slice of the pie, with only a small helping of guilt on the side for sneaking into someone else's kitchen. He found a fork in a sideboard drawer and sat on one of three stools placed around the long worktable in the center of the kitchen.

His mouth gave little notice to the first bite since his thoughts still floated around his honey-haired hostess. One day into his new life in Crooked Creek and he already thought of her as someone to come home to. Michael stabbed a second helping of apples and crust, and this time the cinnamon and a hint of pepper flavored his tongue. He released a sigh with the third taste and wondered how he'd ever lived without Susan's apple pie.

He wanted to ask Clara if she baked, then he thought better of it. Even if she had not confessed how her father's wealth made life on the frontier easier, he would have known she'd been born to affluence and opportunity. She consumed dainty portions of food, as he'd seen at supper, like someone who never thought about where the next meal would come from. Her skin glowed like a woman used to having pots of moisturizers sitting on a dressing table. And her scent. Michael closed his eyes and recalled the scent—something with roses and lavender—that gave her the essence of summer gardens. Only a woman born to privilege had access to such finery and mannerisms.

Michael always regretted he'd been unable to give the same luxuries to his mother and sister. They had arrived in America with just enough to start anew and struggled alongside too many others like them who desired to build a life in the new country. Prejudice and oppression cut down more of his countrymen. And yet, his family had been luckier than most.

"We are of the same mind."

Clara's melodic voice sliced through his musings and brought him to his feet, nearly knocking the stool over when he stood. He steadied the stool, not intending to meet her eyes, but meet them he did. For a space of time, they said nothing until a slow smile on her lips put his brain in working order again. Her wrinkled skirt and wisps of loose curls that fell softly from their pins, made him think she had fallen asleep fully clothed. The lamp she held cast a warm glow over her beautiful face.

He found his voice and swallowed a bit of crust before speaking. "I hope Susan won't mind."

"She'll be flattered to know her pie brought you to the kitchen at such a late hour." She set the lamp down on the table. Clara passed him to reach the back door and returned seconds later carrying a pitcher, the top secured with a cloth. "We keep an icebox on the back porch. Susan assures me it is normal during the winter months, and I am still learning how things are done here," she offered as an explanation for going outside.

"I find a cup of warm milk with honey and cinnamon helps when I cannot sleep." She set the pitcher near the lamp and unwound the tie holding the cloth in place. "It might help more than pie."

Michael glanced down and realized he'd consumed the whole slice. "I shouldn't have made freely with your kitchen or the food."

"Why ever not? You are not only a guest here. You are a friend and Briley's brother. Besides, you have earned every slice of pie we can provide after your gallantry and much-needed protection today." Clara took down a mug for herself and held a second one in the air. "Would you care for a cup of milk?"

"It can't hurt." And he didn't want to meet whatever awaited him in sleep. Michael carried his plate and fork to the sink and searched for a pot to warm water from the reserve bucket placed on the counter.

"Leave those dishes for the morning," Clara instructed.

Michael admired her efficiency as she stoked the embers in the cookstove, checked the dampers, and warmed a generous helping of creamy milk in a small pot. "I didn't figure you for someone who knows their way about a stove." At her over-the-shoulder glance and raised brow, he added, "An error in thinking."

She smiled. "You are not incorrect in your assumption. I

can manage tea, scrambled eggs, and warming milk. The kitchen is Susan's domain; I gladly leave it to her expertise." Her smile faltered. "I hope today's events haven't kept you awake. You appeared quite engrossed in your thoughts when I came in."

He must have been deep in his thoughts not to have heard her entrance or sensed her presence. Memories of war overtook and consumed him, and he despised their hold on him. "No, nothing so recent as today. You didn't say much at supper."

"Alice was more inclined to conversation tonight, and it was easier to listen—and think."

"She recovered fast." Michael closed his eyes briefly and savored the aroma of cinnamon warming in the milk.

"Alice usually does. On our journey here, men overtook our coach, and I awakened later in Emma's clinic." Clara added a little honey to the pot, stirred, and ladled the liquid between two mugs. "She has me to worry for her." Clara placed one cup in front of him. "Children deserve to remain free of the world's troubles, and to have their innocence protected for as long as possible."

Michael sipped, blew on the surface, and sipped once more. He took up the stool again when Clara sat down across from him. A gentleman of her social circles would have left her company the moment she arrived. To be alone with an unmarried woman, especially when not properly dressed, was frowned upon in any polite society. Yet Clara seemed unbothered, and so Michael said nothing, nor did he want to leave her company or the kitchen's warmth.

He thought about it, though, and her, since their early morning meeting in the cold. Such a contradiction she'd already proven herself to be. If she wanted only to escape the reminders of war, a thousand other destinations offered comforts beyond the conveniences this territory was likely to see for decades. The clock on the wall told him it was half an hour before midnight.

"You are woolgathering again."

From where she perched, Michael easily met her steady gaze. "A habit I can't seem to break. Thank you for your kindness with Isaac."

"I wish he had not seemed surprised by a little kindness."

"It hasn't been a simple journey."

"More than a year and a half has passed since the war's end. How long do you suppose it takes, for someone to expect kindness from strangers?"

"How long does it take anyone?" Michael drank deeply, relishing the smoothness of milk and honey as it warmed his insides. "My family immigrated in 1854. We were better off than most, with a farm to sell in Ireland and enough funds to see us through the first winter." He shook his head and retreated once more into his memory. "Hatred burned deep for my people long before we reached America's shores. I never imagined the like, though, as what we've tolerated here. They despised us for daring to come here, for those who came diseased and poor, and those they thought would take work from them. And if you were Catholic, the prejudice deepened. Not everyone despised the Irish, and plenty of generous people wanted to help."

A trace of the old Irish drifted into his voice as he spoke of home. "Trying times came upon us all, but I never wanted to leave Ireland. Neither did Briley." He glanced at her. "Did she ever tell you?"

Clara warmed her hands with the mug. "No, she never did, though she spoke as though she loved her homeland."

"A verdant paradise, with one hill rolling into the next.

Farms of vast acres, some covered with so many sheep you couldn't always see the green beneath them."

"Why leave, then?"

Michael stared beyond her into the past. "Our mother wished it, and our father never hesitated to make her happy. Her brothers and their families came ten years before the famine plagued our lands, and she saw the troubles as a sign it was time to follow them to America."

"Did you consider staying behind?"

"Yes, up until the minute I stepped onto the ship." He finished his milk, now tepid. "Thousands upon thousands of Irish came here as indentured servants for generations. Some willingly, many forced. Our family arrived free, with skills to contribute and a little coin in our coffers, but it mattered little. The animosity my people suffered differs from what Isaac and his people experienced, yet it is still difficult for the Irish. I think Isaac allows his history to dictate his choices too much, but the point is, I can't know what he endured any more than he can know what discrimination and hate my people bore. Pain is pain, no matter how it touches us. How long will it take for Isaac? I expect until the day he leaves this earth, or he finds something or someone to take away his pain, ease his nightmares, and make him feel truly free."

Michael rubbed a hand over his closed eyes, the strain of not sleeping a full night in many months weighing heavily. When he looked at her again, the moisture in her eyes undid him. "I should not have spoken so freely."

"You speak with the heart of a poet."

"And you sound surprised."

Clara's color rose, giving a delicate bloom to her cheeks even in the kitchen's dim light. "It is my turn to apologize."

"My father insisted on an education. It wasn't from the likes of Oxford or Cambridge, but we managed a year at

Trinity College. The foundation proved strong enough to keep me interested in continuing my studies privately." Michael smiled and carried his mug to the sink. He leaned back with his hips against the sideboard next to the basin, his arms crossed as he studied her. "Did you receive an education?"

"Nothing formal. My grandfather was a self-proclaimed scholar who tutored me until his passing. By then, I had developed a fondness and thirst for learning, though less from books and more from using my head and hands."

Michael had seen little of the town, and a school had not been among the buildings he noticed upon his arrival. "What about Alice?"

"What Crooked Creek lacks in formal teaching, it makes up for in life experiences. School takes place in the church, but the town is without a dedicated teacher at the moment. Alice and I have lessons four days a week, and she spends time with Emma or Briley once a week, learning what they can teach. She's fond of horses and would love to visit Hattie and Carson's ranch more often, but it is too far to go with winter."

He continued to study her, noting how the room's warmth added a rosy flush of color to her ivory-hued skin and how wisps of hair curled around her face every time she glanced up. *What makes a woman like her come to such a wild and desolate place?*

"Of all the places across the continent you could have gone, why Crooked Creek?"

CHAPTER 10

"With December upon us, my mind drifts often to Christmases before the war. We have nothing so grand here, so I am grateful for the crate of ornaments you sent. It is impossible to find such trinkets out here. I am saving them for Alice to look through when we put up the tree."

- Clara Stowe to her parents in a letter not yet sent

CLARA HAD SPENT the whole of her upbringing doing what was proper and acceptable. She attended affairs at country homes, appeared at church every Sunday because her grandmother dictated everyone in the family should attend, and she had planned for a life of quiet rectitude, married to a man who would further her family's empire.

Then she met Gideon Yost.

"You left Ireland, a home you loved, because of your mother. Did her dreams never become yours?"

"I wanted them to be, but no."

"Well, Alice's father possessed an incredible capacity for dreaming, addictive even, and his dreams became mine. We heard whispered tales about the great western mountains at dinners and teas. None of our acquaintances seemed interested beyond speculation, and certainly, none desired to give up their refinements and comforts to explore this vast land."

"Except Alice's father."

Clara nodded. "Yes. As for why Crooked Creek?" She smiled, a bit sheepishly. "This house. It seemed to be the most comfortable to be found in the wildest of places. The man who built it was from the East, and little spreads so quickly in my circles as gossip. His financial struggles were unfortunate for him, yet a blessing for me."

"Your father let you come," Michael said with reverent surprise.

"My father wanted to appear supportive. He located grand homes in Atlanta, Denver, Salt Lake City, even San Francisco, though not one of those places offered what I pictured every time Gideon spoke of going west. And so, he indulged me my adventure. Albeit reluctantly. I sent my maid and her brother back when we reached St. Louis. The poor woman nearly fainted at the thought of me traveling unescorted. When I did not return home after a few days, then weeks and months, he realized I did not intend to return. I found a new place to call home. We write and telegram regularly, and he promises to visit next summer. There are times when I know a measure of guilt for taking their granddaughter so far away."

"Would Alice's father want this life of uncertainty for you?"

Clara almost told him he spoke out of turn. What did he

know of Gideon, of her, of the life she wanted to build in Gideon's name for her daughter's sake? She held back the harsh retort and carried her cup to the sink to sit beside Michael's.

"I'm sorry." His fingers brushed the sleeve on her arm briefly before dropping. "It is not my business."

He walked past her and nearly reached the doorway.

"Wait."

Michael turned.

"God forgive me for asking this, but if *you* had not returned home from the war and left behind a child, would you not want your child to experience the life you envisioned for him or her? The life and adventures you might have had together?" Clara remained still beneath his exacting perusal. Every inch of her warmed under his regard, leaving her to wonder at his thoughts. She failed to say, "*wife and* child," and wondered if Michael noticed the omission.

"Were I as blessed as Alice's father, my only wish would have been for my child to grow up in a better world."

Michael's parting words left Clara questioning every choice she'd made since learning of Gideon's death. She had always thought she knew exactly what Gideon would have done, what he would have wanted her to do in his stead. Had she been wrong? Were they not happier for the life they were building in the place Alice's father longed to see? When Clara finally returned to the quiet of the rooms she shared with Alice, and after ensuring her daughter slept in peace, she stripped from her clothes and donned a long, white, flannel nightgown.

She had not bothered with a bed warmer and her knees involuntarily pulled upward until she huddled beneath the covers. Her body warmed the linens by slow degrees as memories kept her hovering on the brink of sleep. When faint, blue morning light shined through a slit between two curtain panels, Clara longed to cover herself with heavy quilts and sleep through the day.

Alas, seconds into her fantasy, she pushed the bundle of blankets aside, rolled her legs over the edge, and settled bare feet on the thick rug covering the wood floor. Her head still throbbed over the late-night conversation with Michael, and his parting words blocked her usual joy at rising before everyone else.

With regret at leaving the comfort of bed and mindful of guests under her roof, Clara readied herself for the day. The cold splash of water on her face revived her flagging spirit somewhat, and by the time she wrapped a thick blanket around her shoulders and carried her book to the front porch, she had fully awakened.

She sucked in a breath and during the time it took for the icy air to burn her lungs, Clara realized she was not alone on the porch.

"Seems I have a bad habit of invading your space." Michael pushed himself up from the rocker—her rocker— and took one step toward her. Unlike her, he had thought to put on a full complement of outer clothes in addition to a heavy woven blanket. "It's cold enough out here to freeze a few limbs."

"Colder than I expected. The shining sun is deceptive when standing on the warm side of a window." She tightened her hold on the blanket wrapped around her shoulders and decided to rethink her morning solitudes on the porch until spring.

Michael opened the blanket he held and dropped it over the one she already clutched closely. Before she objected, he opened the front door, urged her inside, and cupped her cheeks in his gloved hand to turn her face one way then the other. "Elis was building the fires up when I came down earlier. You need to warm up."

"I am capable of—"

Michael took her hand, pulled her into the parlor, and guided her to the chair closest to the hearth. "Put your hands under your arms for a few minutes so they don't warm up too fast."

"My hands are . . ." Clara wiggled her fingers and found them stiff. "Fine." She stretched them open a fraction before burrowing them beneath her arms as Michael suggested. "I was outside less than a minute."

"You'll be fine." Michael fed another log on the fire and set the screen back in place. "I expect it's well below freezing out there right now."

Already warmth inched back into her fingers and toes. "You seem unaffected."

Michael remained standing by the fire. "I'm wearing more clothes."

Clara flushed at his both suggestive and accusing words, though she somehow doubted he meant them to be either. "I didn't think. It has been my routine since we moved into the house." At least she hadn't thought beyond the three layers she already wore beneath the wool dress. A single petticoat more made moving about indoors unbearable. "It is more than clothing, I think. You appear impervious to the cold." She avoided asking him how someone became resistant to the weather, then wondered how weather had become the only topic she could think of to talk about with him.

Their shared confessions the night before left them both awkward without the protection of lamplight to mask their faces and warm milk to occupy their hands. Michael spoke before Clara had a chance to push beyond the discomfort.

"I had no cause to speak to you the way I did last night.

Where you live and how you choose to raise your daughter is no one's business, especially not mine. I expect you get enough unsolicited advice from your family." Michael met her eyes. "It won't happen again, I promise."

Clara scooted closer to the edge of the wingback chair, ignoring the fire's warmth for a moment. "You weren't wrong." The aroma of coffee wafted from the kitchen, telling Clara Susan was already awake and would soon prepare for breakfast. A slight ache pulsated in her head from lack of restful sleep, and she fought the urge to rub the dry weariness from her eyes. "I need to see to Alice."

"Clara."

She stood but waited.

"Your kindness alone isn't going to keep Mrs. Harrigan and her daughter safe, but it's admirable."

"My standing on the matter has not changed from yesterday. I will not ask them to leave. They need a haven, and the inn can offer them comfort and safety for as long as they need."

Michael left the fireside and edged closer, his voice as soft as the crackle of flame to wood. "It's not about asking them to leave, but finding them a safer place to stay until Casey and Peyton learn more about what's going on."

"I don't understand. There is no—"

Clara's words stopped when she caught the movement of Michael's eyes over her shoulder.

"You know who I am?" Augusta stood in the passageway, her dark hair coiled at her nape, and her fine dress held a few wrinkles in the skirt. Smudges shadowed the soft skin beneath her eyes, making her fair complexion paler.

Clara thought to put a little distance between her and Michael before nodding. "Good morning, Augusta. How is Grace?"

"Alice invited her to play in your rooms. I hope you do not mind. It has helped her to have another child around, even with the years separating them."

"Of course, I do not mind." Clara stepped closer to the other woman. "It is good for Alice as well."

Augusta's hands clenched at her side. "For today at least. If we can buy a horse in town, we will leave as soon——"

"You'll do no such thing." Clara whirled on Michael. "Absolutely no such thing. Regardless of what you may have just heard, I will not ask you to leave, certainly not on horseback. I will, however, beg your forgiveness for speaking about you out of turn."

"I heard it as concern and nothing more." Augusta looked to Michael. "Mr. Donaghue, isn't it?" At Michael's nod, she said to Clara, "Mr. Donaghue is right. My husband will not stop until he gets what he wants, and our presence here puts you in more danger the longer we stay. After yesterday——"

"Pardon, Mrs. Harrigan——"

"Ford. I prefer Mrs. Ford or Augusta." Neither Michael nor Clara asked why.

"Mrs. Ford, what I intended to suggest to Mrs. Stowe was an alternative to the inn, not an expulsion from town."

Clara blushed from her own foolishness. "Augusta, will you do me the favor of seeing Alice is ready for breakfast? Susan will have it started soon and if my nose does not mistake me, there are cinnamon buns baking."

Understandably wary, Augusta glanced at each of them before nodding. "I appreciate your concern, but do not mistake my present fear for weakness. I will do what is best for my daughter and will not allow anyone else to dictate what happens next."

Fiercely protective of her own daughter, Clara knew

Augusta meant every word. Clara waited until she was once again alone with Michael. "She's going to leave."

"You can't know that."

"Yes, I can. Augusta is a mother, Michael, and she will do whatever is necessary to keep her daughter safe. If saving her daughter means bargaining with the Devil himself, she will consider it."

"Then we will have to make sure she doesn't have to face her husband, because from how she's behaving, Lucas Harrigan and the Devil may be one and the same."

"Alice."

"She's safe, Clara."

"If you had not been here yesterday . . ."

"Someone else would have been."

"The situation with Augusta, my invitation and insistence that she remain here, are not your responsibility."

In a move that startled Clara enough for her to sway backward, Michael held her arms in the gentle grasp of his hands. "It is now." How much time passed, Clara wondered, between the moment Michael's touch seared through her dress to warm her skin and when he eased her closer. Her body swayed toward him even as her mind tried to come up with at least one reason why this sudden closeness was too much.

His long fingers twisted in a stray curl, skimming the back of her neck. Michael bent his head until they were close enough for their breaths to meld into one, each taking in the other. The slight tilt of her head was all she needed to meet him halfway.

"We can't."

Michael's whispered words took a few seconds to penetrate her haze. He steadied her as he drifted away. Not so far away that she ceased to feel his heat, but far enough so their breath no longer mingled. Not since Gideon had anyone ever touched her so profoundly.

"Alice."

When she finally met his gaze, his eyes were steady. He concealed more than she could ever hope to unearth within the depths, and yet what she glimpsed told her it was more than Alice who stopped him.

Clara adjusted her stance, and Michael's arms fell to his sides. "Breakfast will be ready soon. Please tell Isaac he will be welcome in the dining room."

He reached for her again. "Clara, wait."

"You were right to stop this." She waved her hand in a circle to encompass him and whatever lingered between them.

"Don't confuse *need* and *want*. If I'm not mistaken, I hear Alice and Grace coming down the stairs."

Clara listened for the familiar sounds of her daughter's footsteps, not surprised she had missed them, consumed as she had been in Michael. "So they are." She managed a faint smile. "Please inform Isaac breakfast will be ready soon." She left him for the sanctuary of the kitchen, her hands and heart as unsteady as her steps.

CHAPTER 11

"There is more snow than I imagined ever falling in one place. It blankets the landscape and glistens when the sun shines from a clear, blue sky."

- Clara Stowe to her parents in a letter not yet sent

MICHAEL FOUND HIS sanctuary out of doors, far enough away from the inn's front entry to keep him from going back inside. How easy it would have been to kiss her, no matter how many minute justifications not to kiss her raced through his mind. He recalled Shakespeare's wise words: "Make use of time, let not advantage slip."

He'd let the advantage slip by this time, and while his body regretted it, the wisest, deepest part of his conscience believed there was a time and place for everything. His mother used to quote scripture to explain every challenge life gave them and never had a circumstance arisen that bested her faith.

Since timing mattered, Michael remained outside breathing in the frigid air until it cooled both ardor and ungentlemanly thoughts. He regarded the snowy landscape and the morning sun peeking through dissipating clouds. Michael imagined the rays delivered warmth for a few seconds rather than just blinding light, brighter than any sun over Ireland's green fields.

Since the only way to warm his now-shivering body was to seek shelter indoors, he glanced over his shoulder at the sprawling inn before trudging through calf-deep snow toward the clinic. Isaac, he reasoned, would find his own way to breakfast. He counted on Clara to ensure his friend did not leave the dining room hungry.

He kicked snow off his boots and took extra time to brush excess from his trouser legs. Despite the cold and early hour, Michael heard a door open and close, smelled smoke rising from chimneys, and if he wasn't mistaken, something tantalizing and achingly familiar, already wafting from the café.

His late-night visit to the kitchen for a large helping of Susan's apple pie kept his knowing hunger at bay, and would until he'd had a chance to finally, and properly, accomplish what he came to Montana to do.

Michael entered the clinic and was met with the sweetest sound he'd heard since leaving home. He crossed the room as quietly as his boots allowed, so as not to disturb the soft melody of Briley's voice coming through the opening in the slightly ajar door.

Oh! make her a grave where the sunbeams rest,
When they promise a glorious morrow;
They'll shine o'er her sleep, like a smile from the West,

From her own loved island of sorrow.

She spoke the last verse more than sang it, adding her lilting cadence to Thomas Moore's words. Michael pushed the door inward, allowing the faint creak to announce his presence.

Alone in the center of the bed, surrounded with white linens trimmed in lace and two thick quilts, Briley held the mirror image of herself. Mariah Rose, with her dark tuft of hair and skin as fair as the snow beyond the frost-kissed windows, yawned with eyes closed and returned to her slumber.

"Why is it," Michael asked as he approached the bed, "that so many of our songs are about sadness and war?"

Briley smiled and like Michael, kept her voice low. "We'll be rebels, warriors, and grievers till we die, and even then, our fighting spirits won't know better than to make trouble in the beyond." Fresh tears made gentle runnels down Briley's cheek. "By the saints, Michael Connelly Donaghue, 'tis good to see you at last."

"Not nearly as good as it is to see you." With the gentlest care, he sat on the right side of the bed and leaned against the wood headboard. Michael wrapped his arms around mother and baby, and as though each carried no more weight than one of Briley's lace kerchiefs, he brought them close to his side. "You're alive." He breathed her in as though not believing it, even though she was flesh and blood in his arms.

"I thought I lost you forever, gone the way of Da and Ma." Briley kept the baby safely cradled while she leaned into her brother. "You always took your time about things, never one to rush." She tilted her head enough to look at him. "Except when you left for the war. Tell me this is real and you'll never leave me—us—again."

"I promise you, Mariah Rose, and any other nieces and

·nephews you and Peyton give me, will know their Uncle Michael."

"Will you be content here?"

"My family is here, so yes, I *will* be content."

"I know you wished to return one day to Ireland."

A vivid image of Clara immediately drifted to the front of Michael's thoughts. If he closed his eyes, it was as if she sat beside him. He would stay even if Clara were not in Crooked Creek to tug at him. He pressed his face against Briley's hair and held her fast. "In this moment, I am happier than I have ever been."

Briley seemed content with his response and adjusted the bundle in her arms.

"Do you want me to hold her?"

Briley shook her head. "I'll be willing to share her soon enough, but for now it is difficult enough giving her up to Peyton." The curious look she gave him next matched her tone when she asked, "How is it you sound less Irish than I do now? Never was there a one in our family whose tongue carried the homeland as much as yours."

"A consequence of war." To please her, Michael reached inside for the language of his past. "*Is tusa mo theaghlach.* You are my family." He kissed the side of her head. "Home is where family lives and hearts are free."

"Ma used to say that."

"She did, and she was right, as always." He squeezed his eyes closed. "Did Ma go peacefully?"

Briley remained silent for several seconds. "In the end. You and Da were always in her prayers and her heart. 'Tis where family lives. What about Da? Where does he rest?"

Michael recalled her calling their father "Da" only as a young girl, and again when they said goodbye. He remembered the day of their departure and immediately wiped the recollection from his mind. No amount of pleading had convinced his father to return home, to leave the fighting to foolish young men. He saw his father once after the war began and had not learned of his fate until the end. "When I healed well enough to travel, I found where he'd been buried. Isaac helped me see Da home. I had him buried next to Ma, in the pretty church cemetery outside the city."

"Oh, Michael. The expense of it." She held him in a fierce hug before relaxing her arms. "It's good they're together, even if not in Ireland."

Michael let the image of what Crooked Creek might look like not wrapped in snow, with rich, green pines soaring to the sky, and mountains so tall a person could see them from wherever they stood. A valley covered in enough grass to feed livestock and wildlife alike, and a sky so big and blue that even when filled with clouds, one could not help but stare upon it in awe. Had he known such a place existed, he would have brought their parents here. It was time, though, he thought, to let them rest in peace.

"We'll remember them as they were. What a pair, and both in love with Ireland and family. Da loved you until his last breath."

"How did you find me, Michael?"

He smiled. "You told Mrs. Logan."

Lyrical laughter escaped from Briley's lips. "Oh, what a dear woman. I'd forgotten. She tried to convince me not to leave."

"She said as much. Looks like she was wrong. Da and Ma would be happy for you."

Michael sensed the others in the clinic first, and when the steps beyond the bedroom door stopped, he looked up.

Emma, wiping at the dampness on her cheek, stood beside Peyton. Each wore a smile on their face and love in their eyes. Michael gave Briley's shoulders a gentle squeeze until she, too, noticed their company.

"Look," she said to Emma and her husband. "'Tis truly him."

Everyone laughed, and the vibrations of Briley's body brought little Mariah Rose awake. She opened her eyes, and though Michael did not think a new baby could tell one smile from the next, he would swear from that day to forever his niece recognized him as family. She yawned next, then squalled, bringing a smile to everyone.

"She's telling everyone it's time to clear the room." Emma moved to the bed and held out her arms for the baby. "I'll see to changing her, and then she'll be after another meal."

Michael helped transfer Mariah Rose to Emma's arms before standing.

"I'd think you'd be hungry, too," Michael said to Briley.

"I won't say no to a bowl of porridge with a spot of jam and a thick slice of Bess's soda bread. Bess makes Ma's recipe regularly after I gave it to her last summer.

Peyton grinned at his wife. "It's already in here, staying warm on Emma's stove. Bess took the bread from her oven not twenty minutes ago."

Michael remembered the familiar scent when he stood outside the clinic and smiled at the memories. "Then I'll leave you to your breakfast and return soon."

"Please do. It will be a long time before my heart can believe you are here and never to leave again." Briley peered at Emma. "And a long time before the good doctor says I can go home, so it is here you will find me."

His smile vanished. "Why? Did something happen with the birthing?"

Emma *tsked* and shook her head at Briley. "You ought to know better than worry menfolk about such matters." To Michael she said, "Briley is well and healthy and fought like one of your ancient Celtic warriors to give us Mariah Rose. Every warrior needs time to recover."

"That's quite an image," Peyton murmured as he carried the food-laden tray to the bed and secured it on a pillow over Briley's lap. "And true." Mindful they weren't alone, Peyton brushed his lips over hers before pulling back.

Michael started for the door, then turned at Briley's request for him to stop.

"Promise you'll come back soon. Today."

"Nothing will keep me away." Michael exited the room with an elation so unfamiliar as to give him pause and evaluate how his heart could be so whole, so quickly. When he stepped outside, sunlight burst from the sky and glared off the snowy landscape, forcing Michael to blink a few times until his vision adjusted to the brightness coming from all directions.

No amount of effort by the sun could ease away the intense cold seeping beneath Michael's outer clothes, making him long for a return to the warmth of the clinic. His gaze drifted down the road, beyond snow-leaden pines, to the grand inn Clara called home. Or better yet, the warmth of Clara's parlor where a fire likely still crackled, or Susan's kitchen where he might talk the cook into parting with a plate of whatever she served up for breakfast.

His horse needed tending first, so Michel trudged back through the snow, surprised at the number of fresh hoofprints and wagon tracks already in evidence. The morning travelers on the road made his walking easier. He stepped to the side, intending to let two horses and their riders pass, but the pair atop the impressive spotted steeds stopped.

The woman sat tall in the saddle with a straight back. Two long, flaxen braids hung over her shoulders, half covered with a thick knit scarf similar to his own. Briley's work, he guessed. She studied him from beneath a wide-brimmed felt hat and then smiled brilliantly. "You'd be Briley's brother."

Michael studied her back. "I am."

The man held out a hand to Michael. "Name's Carson. My wife, Hattie."

Michael ran through the names he'd heard. Rancher and horseman, married to Hattie, one of Briley's close friends. "White Eagle Ranch."

Carson's nod was slow. "Some call it that. Most folks in these parts still call it McBride Ranch. We preserve both."

"Those are fine animals you're riding." Michael held a hand six inches from the first horse's nostrils and waited for it to nod before petting the bridge of its nose. "Very fine."

"He descends from a pair of mustangs as magnificent as this territory has ever seen," Carson told him. "Come, I'll walk with you to the inn. Hattie was on her way to see Briley and her new daughter."

"She's the most beautiful baby I've ever seen." Michael spoke the words with pride, knowing they were true. "Briley will be glad to see you, Hattie. Emma won't let her go home yet."

Hattie laughed, a strong yet feminine sound that held nothing back. "This ought to be interesting. Briley will wear Emma down soon enough. I'll be seeing you again, Michael Donaghue." Hattie set her horse back in motion and guided the animal toward the clinic.

"They're close," Michael murmured.

"As close as sisters." Carson swung a leg over the horse's head and dismounted with ease, his feet landing on the ground as though he'd floated to earth.

"I'd fall on my back dismounting that way." Michael got a better look at Carson when they were standing almost eye to eye. With hair a few shades lighter than his own, and eyes as blue and wild as a stormy sky, Michael would have guessed Carson's heritage to be like his own, except his name. "Have you always lived here?"

Carson took a loose hold of the horse's reins and pointed back the way he'd come. "Let's walk."

When Carson started walking in that direction, Michael stepped in beside him, with occasional glances at the powerful horse.

"I've always lived here," Carson said. "Until I met Hattie, I lived most of my adult life on the mountain behind her ranch."

"Do you breed the mustangs or just gentle them?"

Carson's quick smile told Michael he found the question amusing. "Never have I heard a white man put it that way. Break, sometimes tame. Gentle is right, though. No one can break a wild creature, and taming them is beyond my skill. They have souls, as we do." Carson smoothed a hand over the animal's neck. "And are tougher than we are. They deserve respect."

They came upon the inn, but Michael wasn't ready to go inside. "I have to see to my horse." Instead of going his own way, Carson changed direction and led his mount along the side of the inn, following Michael to the barn.

"You also raise cattle?"

"Yes, and horses. The mustangs are free to roam the same land, share the grass with the cattle, and share the land well enough. We keep the horses Hattie began breeding before I arrived separate." Carson and his horse entered the barn behind Michael. He guided the spotted steed to a heavy iron ring hanging at waist height and looped the reins loosely around the ring once. "Are you interested in ranching?"

Michael's red dun stuck his head over the top of the stall door and nickered at Michael's approach. "Never been on a ranch, not like what you and Hattie have."

Carson fed his horse a handful of oats before approaching the stalls. "Your horse respects you. What do you call him?"

"He is Rian. It means 'Little King.'"

"Suits him." Carson slowly stroked Rian's neck. "I've known Briley almost as long as Hattie has, and I think of her —and Clara and Emma—like sisters. You'll find the others feel the same."

Peyton and Casey rounded out the close-knit group of seven friends who thought of each like family. Michael envied the bond and hoped to find his place among them. "How did they come to be so close?"

"The women?" Carson stepped away to speak quietly to Isaac's horse and give the animal a little attention. "Most everyone who ends up here has a story to tell, but those women, well, it's more than a common bond. Loss, strength, determination, and the sheer will to survive. Emma and Hattie knew each other first, then Briley came along and I guess they recognized something in her they saw in themselves. Same with Clara. There's nothing they won't do for each other."

And nothing the men wouldn't do for them, Michael silently added as he checked Rian's feed and water. Both had been seen to, so he had either Isaac or Elis to thank. Friends and connections, he mused, were something he didn't take for granted, and Briley had both here. He knew well enough how strong his sister was, and yet he hadn't known the extent of her fortitude until he learned she'd come west alone. "There are other women here—friends—but it's not the same, is it, as it is with the four of them?"

"It's to your credit you see that." Carson retrieved a wooden bucket hanging from a nail, worked a well pump in the corner a few times until water came out, and filled the pail. As he held the bucket for his horse, he asked Michael, "Are you staying?"

"I am. I'll be at the inn a week, maybe longer, until I find something permanent."

Carson nodded. "Good. It will ease some of the worry to know you'll be there."

"Casey—Marshal Latimer—said you've had some trouble at your ranch, with men from the logging camp."

His horse tended, Carson hung the bucket back on the nail and wiped his hands on his trousers before slipping them back into gloves. "We questioned them. Ran them off. We might have hired them on until spring, but they mistook that horses were free for the taking."

"Casey and Peyton seem to think there's going to be more trouble."

"Expect so. I've dealt with men like Lucas Harrigan all my life. They don't take much to my kind and would just as soon run my people off our land or put us under it. My mother's people have been in these mountains and on these plains for more generations than I can trace. Harrigan wants the riches these mountains offer, regardless of who he has to go through."

"Is White Eagle your other name?"

"It was the name my mother gave me. She was Mountain Crow."

"And your father?"

"As Irish as you and Briley."

Michael grinned. "Suspected there was some of the old blood in you. I'd guess the same of Hattie."

"Many Irish have settled in the area, but don't mistake every one of them for friends."

Michael regretted the truth behind Carson's advice. His homeland's history was built on rebellion. Before he left New York in search of Briley, he learned of another uprising in Ireland by the Fenians to overthrow British rule. Would it ever end? How much blood can one country shed before they learn from their mistakes? "I'll know who my friends are when I meet them, just as I will know my enemies."

Carson moved back to his horse. "Hattie calls him Wanderer. She names every horse on the ranch, some of the cattle, too." He smiled and pressed his forehead to Wanderer's. "I didn't go fight in the war, so I can't know the suffering you, Casey, and Peyton bore or witnessed. I'm familiar with death, though, and recognize the signs of someone who has faced it or caused it."

In a swift and unexpected move, Carson swung up and into the saddle. "I'll be going to see your new niece now." Wanderer perked his ears at the prospect of a ride, but Carson kept him still with a gentle word spoken in a language Michael didn't understand. "There are three Irish families in old cabins not too far from here. We've tried to reason with them, bring them out of the cold. Emma offered a couple rooms at her clinic, and there are two empty cabins right now at the edge of town. They won't accept our help and won't survive the winter without it. Perhaps you can speak sense to them where none of us could, Briley included. She calls them stubborn and proud."

"We Irish are." Michael pet Wanderer's neck and considered. "They don't trust you or anyone."

"We've given them no cause to mistrust us."

"Is it difficult to reach them?"

"I took the sleigh out last time and left food at the door. The recent snow is soft enough to not be a problem for the horses. Why?"

Michael stroked the horse's neck once more and stepped back. "Right now, I'm going inside to talk Susan out of a hot meal. When you're ready, I'll go with you to the camp."

CHAPTER 12

"Susan is so patient with me. I try to help in the kitchen, and you would be impressed with what I have learned, but I accept my culinary ineptitude. I have enclosed Susan's receipt for apple cake. Please tell Mrs. Downey I will miss her plum pudding this Christmas."

- Clara Stowe to her parents in a letter not yet sent

CLARA STARED AT the dozen or more shards of yellow ware bowl scattered among what was once apple cake batter. The mess covered a three-foot area of Susan's freshly scrubbed kitchen floor. She glanced back at the long wooden spoon still in her hand, then at the debris, and tried to figure out how it had slipped from the table.

"I am so sorry, Susan."

The cook raised a brow and smiled before fetching a few

linens. "It's your kitchen, Clara. If you've a mind to break a bowl now and then, I'll not be one to argue."

"We both know that's not true." Clara took two linens from Susan's stack on the table and slowly knelt next to the batter and shards. "And I deserve a rebuke. We're well stocked, but since I've learned fresh foodstuffs are not easy to come by in winter, it's prudent to be careful with what we have." She picked pieces of stoneware from the batter and dropped them into a wooden bucket Susan set close by. "You spent a lot of time preserving those apples."

"There's plenty more to see us through, so don't you worry." Susan scooped up the last shard before tackling the batter. "Perhaps we should wait on cooking lessons. You've been a bit faraway since breakfast."

Clara wiped up the last of her mess, stood, and carried the bucket to the sink basin. She dunked a fresh linen in water and returned to kneeling on the floor.

"I'll clean that." Susan reached for the wet cloth.

"It's my mess."

Susan stood with her own dirty linens and said nothing. Clara wiped with renewed vigor at the floor, worried the mess would somehow stain the boards or soak into them. She knew nothing about cooking—obviously—and even less about cleaning. Her time thus far away from comforts and conveniences had been an education, and one she was grateful for. Yet, still so much remained to be learned. Confident she cleaned as best she could Clara decided she owed her friend another apology.

"Please forgive me."

"It was an accident."

Clara skirted the table and met Susan at the sink. "I do not mean my mishap."

"I know." Susan rinsed off the soiled linens. "Something

has you fretting even more than those men who came for Augusta and Grace. Care to talk about it?"

Clara thought of Michael, more specifically the kiss that did not happen . . . or almost happened . . . she had not yet reasoned which. Alice had spent breakfast time talking with Grace or asking when she could see Briley's baby. After Clara promised the latter to be soon, Alice was satisfied enough to finish her meal and settle into the parlor with Grace to play with two of Alice's dolls. Augusta remained watchful, fearful to let Grace be out of her sight.

As Clara's thoughts drifted into vivid images of Michael's face, the man himself stomped snow off his boots on the back porch and entered through the rear door. She already recognized his stomping.

He hung his outer clothes on pegs as if those two pegs were his alone. Michael stopped under the threshold and stared at Clara. When she realized she was staring back, Clara's gaze darted back to Susan, though not before catching Michael's smile.

"Good morning to you, Mr. Donaghue."

Susan's warm welcome cut through the tension long enough for Clara to regain her bearings. "Yes, good morning." Considering it a safe topic and because she wanted to inquire about her friend, she asked, "How are Briley and the baby this morning?"

"Briley's wearing Emma down about going home soon, and the baby is the prettiest I've ever seen." Michael accepted the mug of steaming coffee Susan handed him. "Thank you, ma'am."

"Please, call me Susan." The cook scooped up the rinsed linens and bucket of broken stoneware. "When I return, I'll see to your breakfast. I've plenty left and have been keeping it warm."

When Susan left the room, Michael tested the heat of the coffee and drank deeply. "I'd worked out an entire conversation on how to beg a hot meal from her."

Some of the tension in Clara's body dissipated at his humor. "No begging necessary. Besides, you were on an important errand. Everyone I've met in town likes Briley, and Susan dotes on every new baby." She tapped the handle of a basket covered in with a thick cloth. "Susan almost swatted my hand away when I dared to look. Biscuits, jam, and pound cake."

Michael appeared to consider. "Do you think she counted them all?"

"Oh, most certainly." Clara laughed and moved to the stove where Susan had kept a plate of food warm under a cloth. "Fresh eggs and porridge will need to wait for Susan, but she has sausage and two biscuits still warm. You won't have to sneak any from Briley's basket."

Continuing with their fun, Michael crossed the kitchen and lifted a corner of the cloth covering the basket. "All this food can't possibly be for my sister."

Clara remembered well enough her hearty appetite after Alice's birth. "It is amazing what she can eat now, though I am sure Peyton will enjoy his share."

"I'm surprised Susan lets you work in her kitchen."

At her questioning look, he pointed to her apron. The hem of the once-clean garment bore evidence of apple cake batter. "I proved to her and myself that the kitchen is better left to those who understand its oddities."

"Your warm milk and honey drink is good."

His smile took her back to the night before when they had shared confidences in the kitchen. Flustered again and annoyed at herself for it, Clara untied the apron and folded it over. "I don't know what's keeping Susan, but please don't wait to eat on my account." She set the warm plate on the table and beckoned him to sit before thinking the dining room would be more proper for a guest.

"This'll do if you and Susan don't mind," he said, as if reading her mind. Michael finished his coffee and sat on one of the stools. "Appreciate it."

She contemplated his breakfast. "I should be able to manage eggs."

Michael chuckled, then covered it with a quick cough. "I can fry one up myself, but this is plenty."

Clara refilled his cup from the kettle on the stove. "Will you return to the clinic after breakfast?"

"Carson's taking me out to a cabin camp or just cabins temporarily housing Irish families, I suppose. He thought I might take a turn at speaking with the folks out there." Michael speared a sausage and savored the first bite before speaking again. "Have you met any of them?"

"No." Clara sat opposite him, putting them in the same places as their late-night visit. "But many others have. They won't accept help, and I cannot understand their motive to suffer through the winter out there. If it is work they want, we can help find it."

Michael spread jam on an airy biscuit and offered Clara half.

"Thank you, no. I ate my fill at breakfast. Enjoy it."

Michael did, and Clara leaned closer to rest her hands on the table. "I have work here if they want it."

"Do you really?"

Clara looked around the tidy kitchen, thought of the house under control, and the grounds covered with snow for many months yet.

"They'll know you don't, which to them means charity.

We Irish are happy enough to give charity and accept help from neighbors when needed."

"Then I cannot comprehend why they turn away the town's help. We are neighbors, even if temporarily."

"Perhaps there is another reason for their wariness. I'd guess the others are wondering the same thing." Michael finished off his sausage and peered at the doorway through which Susan had left earlier. "Think she got lost?"

Clara willed a stop to the rising warmth in her skin and refused to answer his question. She suspected precisely why her friend had yet to reappear and would chide her for it later. "She is particular about the laundry." The excuse sounded weak to her, and by the twitch of Michael's lips, he knew it.

"No matter." He held up the empty plate. "This was perfect and much appreciated, thank you." After cleaning the plate himself, ignoring Clara's protest, he pointed to the basket. "It's a lot to ask of you and Susan, but can I persuade you to part with that basket?"

"For the families at the cabins?"

He nodded. "Worth trying."

Clara hefted the basket, surprised at its weight, and handed it over. "It is not a lot to ask of us. I should have thought to offer. We'll make more for Briley." Seeing Michael's raised brow, she amended with, "*Susan* will make more for Briley, and I will endeavor to help without breaking bowls or burning biscuits."

Their shared smiles trickled to soft laughter, until Michael set the basket on the table, cradled Clara's face gently between his large hands, and brushed his lips over hers. Once, twice, three times before he dropped his hands and stepped away. "That answers one of my questions."

Clara watched as he donned his winter accessories. He

took his time slipping his hands into gloves before once more picking up the basket of baked goods and exiting through the back door. At any time, she could have asked him what he meant. Which question? She had too many now, all without answers.

The impression of his mouth on hers remained long after his steady stride carried him across the back porch and into the cold.

Sunlight burst through the trees when Michael entered the small barn to fetch Rian, giving him hope that some of the sun's rays would deliver enough warmth for them not to freeze on the ride to the cabins.

His funds would last him a few months, but since Crooked Creek was where he intended to stay, finding work —or creating it—flitted in and out of the forefront of his thoughts. Briley and the questions he wanted to ask and stories he wanted to hear, traded time with thoughts of Clara.

He had survived on necessity and practicalities for four miserable years, and it was a tough habit to break.

Wake up, find sustenance, then do what needed to be done.

Right now, what needed doing had nothing to do with Briley, Clara, or a job. Michael buried his face in Rian's coal-colored mane and breathed in the animal's scent. No single man, at least no man he'd ever met, possessed the strength, nobility, and wisdom that coursed through the noblest of steeds. Their loyalty and trust were hard earned and hard won, and he respected the animals more for it.

There were times he believed himself capable of shucking off fellow humans solely for the company of nature and beast. The war, however, taught him human suffering and love attached themselves to one's heart in equal force, and to rid oneself of the former, one must relinquish the latter. He wasn't prepared to do either.

Michael saddled Rian, then held onto the basket while awkwardly pulling himself into the saddle. He kept the basket in his lap to avoid dropping Susan's hard work and rode Rian from the comforts of the barn.

When he rounded the front of the house, Carson was waiting with, to Michael's surprise, Hattie. Carson sat atop his horse, seemingly impervious to the frosty air. Hattie had traded in her mount for a wagon-style box atop two large runners to create a cargo sleigh. A sturdy, flaxen-haired chestnut wore a harness connected to the sleigh. She held her head high, ears forward, and pawed twice at the ground as though eager to keep moving.

"What's in the basket?"

Michael rode up beside Hattie before answering her question. "A gift from Clara and Susan. What happened to your horse?"

"Enjoying the warmth of the blacksmith's barn." Hattie pulled up one side of a canvas tarp to reveal a crate of dried meat and another with jars of preserved vegetables and fruit, which looked more palatable than the desiccated vegetables soldiers ate when fresh could not be obtained. "We can't let them starve. No matter how stubborn they are, we figure they'll eat what we leave behind."

Michael understood the cost of parting with food, especially meat. The war had taught him and too many of his fellow soldiers that food held more value than a bag of gold. "Stubborn yes, foolish, no. Have the folks we're going to see ever accepted your offerings?"

Hattie shook her head. "No reason not to keep trying. We'll offer jobs again today if they'll accept." She glanced at her husband, then back at Michael. "Why don't you think they trust us when we've done nothing except offer help?"

"Guess we'll find out soon enough."

"Fair enough. Do you want to pass me the basket? Riding will be easier without it."

Michael passed her the basket, grateful to have his hands free. He walked his horse along one side of the wagon while Carson rode on the other. The sun appeared and disappeared behind heavy white clouds puffed on top with a gathering of light gray below. Carson said another storm was coming, and the evidence hovered above the spacious valley as a warning.

Twenty-five minutes later, unimpeded thanks to fresh, powder-like snow rather than hardpack, the small party crested a gradual hill where, a few hundred feet away, seven semiderelict cabins stood beneath a thick covering of snow.

No one can survive a winter in these shelters. Stove pipes jutted from each cabin, and smoke streamed from two. From this distance, the most recent snow appeared undisturbed, which meant no one had left to even hunt.

"I count four horses in the corral."

Carson settled his eager mount with a quiet word spoken in the language Michael didn't recognize. He planned to ask Carson about it later.

"There were seven horses last time we were here."

The sun peeked through puffs of white clouds, teasing and beckoning Michael's gaze to look up above the expanse of snow and into the rugged wildwood of sweet-scented ponderosa. "Are my eyes playing tricks on me, or do either of you see the fire beyond the edge of the nearest trees?"

"No trick." Carson withdrew a pair of field glasses from a saddlebag and peered through the lenses. "Two small piles, both burning. They're fresh and just starting to create smoke.

I see the shadow of one man, but there could be others." Carson passed the glasses to Michael.

After several seconds, Michael lowered the glasses. "I don't see anyone else, but you're right, there could be others. Have there been problems with horse thieves in the area?"

Hattie nodded. "We ran three off our land last month. They've stayed away since we brought the horses into the pasture closest to the house. We usually rotate them through the lower pastures during winter, but we aren't risking it right now."

Michael looked her way. "The unrest at the lumber mill?"

"Yes."

"Seems like more than unrest. I think it'd be easier for them to move on rather than deal with all of you and a U.S. Marshal in the mix. Why risk getting shot or arrested?"

Carson and Hattie remained silent for several seconds before Carson spoke. "Casey and Peyton said about the same. Come on, let's get down there, then we'll find out who's camped in those trees.

They rode through the snow at a brisk pace. Sprays of snow dusted the surrounding air until they slowed to a stop a few yards from the first cabin. Hattie maneuvered the wagon sleigh around them and stopped in front of the cabin. Each breath Michael released felt like a vise catching and releasing his lungs, and he marveled at how unaffected Carson appeared. Hattie breathed almost as heavily as him, and not for the first time, Michael found himself in awe of the women he'd met since his arrival.

The door of the first cabin creaked open enough for the barrel of a Springfield rifle to slip through. Michael recognized the gun he'd used during the first two years of the war before he parted with some of his hard-earned money to purchase the Henry repeating rifle he still carried with him.

Michael kept his hands in front of him and made no move toward his rifle or the gun at his hip. "We mean no harm to anyone here."

"Open the door a little more and you'll see it's Carson and Hattie White Eagle. Last time we were here, we spoke with a Patrick Doyle and his wife, Orla."

Michael stared at Carson when he said the names. "Patrick and Orla Doyle. You're sure?"

"I'm sure. They were in this cabin last time we came out."

He exhaled a slow breath and called out, "Patrick Doyle of the Irish Brigade? It's Michael Donaghue."

Seconds passed before the door opened, and a man a few inches short of six feet stepped out. Eyes as green as the hills of Kerry wavered between them, then settled on Michael. In a voice heavy with a West County accent, he whispered, "By the saints, I thought ye were dead."

CHAPTER 13

"You mentioned your bafflement that I should still want to be an innkeeper when it is unnecessary, and yet I meet the most interesting people."

- Clara Stowe to her parents in a letter not yet sent

CLARA UNDERSTOOD HER LIMITATIONS. She could not control a world in chaos, and staying home to feel helpless benefited no one, so she sought the comfort of nature with an awareness that like the weather, change in all things remained constant, and the only way was onward.

With Grace and Alice happily playing with dolls in the parlor, Clara encouraged Augusta out of doors. "On this side of the porch, you can see inside to the parlor." Clara invited her into one of the rocking chairs. "It's too cold to be out here for long, but with the sun bright, it is too beautiful to stay inside. The fresh air will do both our spirits good."

Augusta watched her daughter through the glass and heard her giggle at something Alice said. "All right. Just for a few minutes, and so long as no one comes along."

Clara wished she could offer the woman more than platitudes of comfort and reassurances that she and her daughter were safe at the inn. Augusta had said little behind general niceties or answering questions with friendly, yet brief responses. Clara's mother raised her not to interfere with others' lives, believing that doing so led to misunderstandings, gossip, and losing friends.

While Clara respected her upbringing, she did not always agree with her mother. Gingerly, she asked, "Where do you plan to go if you leave here?"

Augusta averted her gaze from the landscape and tilted her head, listening through the window and walls for her daughter's voice. When the girls' laughter once more reached them, she relaxed a little more. "I met my husband when he came to my cousin's house outside of Charlotte, with plans to join in a lumber scheme of some such."

"It has always been lumber, then?"

Augusta nodded. "We married after a month of courtship, and Grace came a year later. Life was pleasant enough, the business did well, and I had family close by."

"Will you return to them?"

"I will not return to Charlotte. Charleston, perhaps, or north to Boston or New York." Augusta glanced at Clara. "Where is your family?"

"Connecticut. I traveled to Boston once, and once to New York."

"How did you find them. The cities, I mean?"

"Noisy." Clara smiled. "There is an excitement to a bustling metropolis when one has never been, but I was always more suited for a quieter life."

"You cannot find a quieter life than in Crooked Creek."

Maybe, were it not for Lucas Harrigan. Clara kept the unkind thought to herself. "Do you long for city life?"

"I do, and I miss the warmth of home." As if to mock Augusta, a flurry of snow danced across the road and sprayed the air with miniscule droplets. They dissipated before reaching the women, yet the cold the flurry carried remained. "I sometimes cursed the heat during July and August." Augusta shivered and drew the blanket closer. "But I'd welcome it right now."

Clara considered all she had left behind, and though she missed the convenience of someone bringing her a glass of cold lemonade on a hot summer day or a cup of creamy hot chocolate on a cold morning without having to ask, she appreciated those tasks more now, after doing for herself. Home remained where she left it, should she ever wish to return. Not having that security would have made her journey, and her stay in the territory, more challenging to endure.

"You cannot travel safely until spring, Augusta. Surely you can imagine the dangers of such an attempt."

"I know," Augusta murmured in a soft, frustrated voice. "We can't wait, though. For the right price, someone will be willing to take us."

"When you first made the journey, how many men traveled with you and your husband to Montana?"

"Seventeen."

Clara considered what Lucas Harrigan might have been transporting to require so many men but let the musing pass for now. "Seventeen armed and trusted men offer a good deal of protection. Undertaking such an expedition again, with someone you do not know . . ."

"You did it." Augusta sat forward in the rocker and faced

away from the road as a young couple drove their wagon past, waving and saying hello to Clara.

"The Teagues arrived not long after I did. Came from Minnesota and are expecting their first child in the spring. You do not have to fear them."

Augusta barely relaxed again, yet continued to say, "You came here alone, did you not?"

"In a way, yes, but not entirely. We traveled with my maid and two companions to St. Louis, and then we joined a group of Christians, forty-three in all, making the journey to Bozeman. From there, we took the stage. Mine was a trek of adventure, not necessity. It changes the landscape from desperation to one of anticipation and excitement." Clara gripped the edges of the blanket she wore over her shoulders and leaned a little toward Augusta. "What if your husband sent men to find you on the road?"

"He would." Augusta rocked twice, then stood. "You're right, of course. He won't stop."

Clara also stood, stepped closer to Augusta, and lowered her voice lest it should carry beyond them. "What precipitated your departure from the camp?"

Augusta shook her head.

"You should tell someone. Sheriff Sawyer and Marshal Latimer can better help if they know what they are up against."

"I said no." Augusta planted her feet, and with her back as straight as an iron post, she stood resolute in her conviction . . . except the trepidation in her eyes spoke the truth. "There is no one who can help. Not now."

A subtle throat clearing from around the corner put both women on alert. Without forethought, Augusta reached for Clara's hand and squeezed.

"Pardon, Mrs. Stowe. I jest wanted you to know I was

comin' round the house."

Clara's shoulder softened, and Augusta released her hand. "Thank you, Isaac. We haven't seen you since breakfast. Michael is out now, though I expect he'll return soon."

Isaac rubbed up and down his arms as if to warm his skin. "Mr. Carson told me Michael'd be goin' with them." He gently slapped the side of his injured leg. "The doc, she says I can't ride far for a week or more."

"I recall Emma saying Michael shouldn't, either. Are you all right to be out walking in the cold?"

"Michael's had worse injuries, so I reckon he knows what he can handle. The doc says a little walking is good for me, to keep blood flowin'. I was just checkin' on my horse."

Clara waved him up to the porch. "Then you should be inside by the fire. Susan can make you a cup of tea. She keeps herbs on hand recommended by Dr. Latimer for minor ailments—and then you can rest."

Isaac nodded after some hesitation, then climbed the steps, careful to keep several feet between himself and the women.

Clara said to Augusta, "Will you check on the girls?"

Augusta's slow nod followed before she huddled beneath her blanket and entered the house.

With the door closed, Clara spoke to Isaac. "I won't keep us out here long, for we are both bound to freeze. Isaac, I do not wish to make you uncomfortable or question whether my offers of kindness and friendship are genuine. I will not pretend to understand the circumstances of your life because I cannot. What I can do is assure you such offers are genuine, and you will be treated with the same respect we afford a friend while under my roof."

He stared at her for several seconds before she smiled and added, "I sounded rather pretentious just then."

When he returned her smile, Isaac revealed two rows of white teeth, with only a few slightly crooked ones on the bottom. "Michael gets to talking like that sometimes, so I'm used to it. I'll take your word, Mrs. Stowe, but right now, if it's all the same to you, I jest as soon find a place by the fire you offered."

Clara's light chuckle followed them into the inn. Isaac held open the door and made sure it was closed before removing his hat. The coat he kept on. He'd already seen some of the main level, yet his eyes still widened at the rich, woolen curtains, the polished floors beneath thick rugs, and furnishings worthy of fine eastern homes.

She almost invited him into the parlor but thought better of putting him in an awkward position around Augusta and the girls. Clara did not mistake their small step toward trust to be the same as Isaac's ease with his surroundings. "There is a fire in the library, if you'd be comfortable there. I'll ask Susan to make one of her teas." She thought of the basket Michael took with him to the camp. Breakfast had been hours ago, yet Isaac needed several extra meals to fill the gauntness of his face. "And perhaps a few biscuits with jam."

Isaac glanced past her to the parlor, then to the library, which was more of an alcove off the main living area. He visibly relaxed. "I'd appreciate both, Mrs. Stowe."

"If it's all the same to you, please call me Clara."

Michael Donaghue and Patrick Doyle had met on a fateful day in December 1862, far enough into the war for people to have lost hope for a quick end. The Battle of Fredericksburg took 545 of the Irish Brigade's courageous men over five days, a number unlikely changed by the presence of members of the 1st United States Sharpshooters.

They both survived the defeat, and before departing for the next engagement, they had sat by a fire, each with a small piece of their spirit shrouded in darkness, as they spoke of home, family, and plans beyond smoke, hunger, and death. They would see each other again on the battlefield, each time more bruised, filthy, and exhausted than the time before.

Michael sat across from Patrick at a scarred wooden table set with only two chairs. Chinks between some logs allowed cold air to seep into the small space and battle with the meager heat from the small pot-bellied stove. The year and a half since the war's end had not been kind to Patrick. He boasted a long curved scar stretching from his left cheek to under his chin, and even though he'd yet to touch any offering in the basket Michael had placed on the table, he and his family needed the sustenance.

"I heard you were dead."

"I expect we both came close a few times. A friend dragged me from the field and got me fixed up by his employer, a doctor. It was months before I could travel." Michael slapped his old friend's shoulder. "It's good to see you made it through."

Patrick smiled at his wife and son. "They kept me going. Your friends out there have been here before."

Michael nodded. "They want to help. It's not handouts their offering, Patrick, but work and shelter. A few suspicions why you might refuse crossed my mind, but now that I know you're here, I'll wager my first suspicion is right."

"Others have claimed to want to help."

Trust was a currency on its own. No amount of coin, food, or goods equaled in value to the well-earned trust between people. "What happened, Patrick, to make you doubt them?"

Patrick's wife moved to stand beside him and rested a

hand on her husband's shoulder. Patrick covered it with his own and sighed heavily with a nod toward the closed door. "We were after work at the lumber camp. A man at a trading post a day's ride from here said it was the best place to find work for so many of us."

"Working for Lucas Harrigan?"

Patrick nodded.

"Was it all of you who left, or did some stay behind?"

"Three men without families stayed at the lumber mill. The rest of ourselves traveled as far as we could before the storm blew through." Patrick stopped long enough to watch his wife add more twigs to the small stove. "Three weeks back, half a dozen men came, brought food, and offered shelter."

Michael sat forward and rested his arms on the table. "You've been here three weeks?"

Patrick shook his head. "Four, maybe five weeks now. The men used the offerings to get close. In the night, they stole half the horses and a wagon. Almost got my niece, Catie."

Gaunt, pale faces, limbs too weak to fight if needed, yet still a will to survive. *How much longer will they last?* "I've not been in Crooked Creek long, Patrick, but on my honor, you can trust these people. I'm thinking the sheriff—"

"No."

"Sheriff Peyton's a good man, and as it happens, my brother-in-law. Briley said she came out once to see if she could help talk you around."

"We met her. Ye see, Michael, the men who came, well, one wore a badge, and he was as Irish as you and me, and to be sure, he was no friend."

"Sheriff Sawyer—Peyton—can be trusted. There's a marshal in town as well, Casey Latimer. I think you've met him."

Patrick nodded again and pushed himself up to stand tall. Michael joined him and stood still as Patrick took his measure. "We fought together and lost friends together. If ever I set meself to trustin' another man, it'll be you." Gaining his wife's nod of agreement, Patrick said, "All right, then. We'll trust ye, Michael Donaghue, and God help us."

Michael thought of where else on the earth his sister could have settled and what living in Crooked Creek had brought her . . . and now him. "He already is, Patrick."

Cold bit through his outer layers and tightened the skin on his face when Michael stepped out of the cabin. Though meager, the tiny stove within had at least offered some warmth. He shoved his hands into gloves while he walked to Hattie's side. "Where's Carson?"

Hattie smacked her gloved hands together to warm her fingers. "Farther cabin keeping a watch on those men we saw in the trees. How did it go inside?"

"They'll return to Crooked Creek with us, or at least they will after Patrick has a few words with them."

"You fought beside each other?"

"Different regiments, same purpose. We came to know each other as well as men do when they talk of nothing except getting back to their families." Like many other returning soldiers, Michael had little more than his clothes and the coin in his pockets. Every day he thanked God that he still had Briley and his health. "They won't have much. Patrick said one of their wagons and some of their horses were stolen."

"This sleigh can handle more weight in the snow than their remaining wagon. The horses will have a tough enough time pulling it through. Whoever drives best will need to handle the team. They can follow in the sleigh's tracks. It will be easier, if not easy." Hattie returned the hello Patrick offered when he stepped outside and headed for the next cabin. "You and Carson can't give up your horses, in case there's trouble. At least one other man will need to be free on a horse. The youngest children can ride in the wagon and sleigh, or double up, but the rest will have to walk."

Michael studied her with her greater admiration. "You've seen a lot, haven't you?"

Hattie gave him a grim smile. "More than I would have liked, far less than you. The landscape is beautifully deceiving. People see it, hear of it—especially city people—and don't realize life here is harder than they could ever anticipate."

"Yet you stay."

"I stay. Emma, Clara, Briley. We all stay because this is home. You'll learn soon enough that this place calls to those who belong. Carson says the spirit alive in the land recognizes those destined to be here, and to those few it burrows deep in the soul and there it stays forever."

Michael wanted to ask more, but Hattie sat straighter and her body stiffened. He followed her eyeline to where Carson rounded the last cabin. He did not hasten the horse's pace, neither did he slow to speak to any of the people emerging from the cabins. When he reached Hattie and Michael's side, he spoke in an unhurried tone that belied his words.

"They know we're here."

"How many?" Hattie asked.

"I saw three, but they haven't put out the fires, so there is at least one more staying behind."

Michael waved Patrick over. His friend puffed out cold air in a rush to reach them. "Patrick, you need to hurry everyone along. Who here is best with a rifle?"

"That'd be me."

"All right. Tell the others to move as quickly as possible.

Hattie here can instruct them on what to do. Get your rifle and a horse now. Go, and hurry."

Michael walked to his horse, shook his fingers a little to ease the stiffness caused by the cold, and pulled himself into the saddle. "This is your home, Carson. We'll follow your lead."

"How are you with the Henry?"

Michael returned a glance that told Carson what he needed to know.

"The second cabin to the last has a ladder. You'll need to be careful on the roof."

His breathing changed, slowed, as it used to before he readied himself for a shot. Michael hated how automatic his reaction was to an impending job. It always meant death because he never missed.

"Are you okay, Michael?"

Hattie's voice drew him away from the memories veiled in misery. After the war ended, he had promised himself and God that never again would he take a life in the name of duty or even honor. Five children helped their parents carry what remained of their belongings to the single wagon. Five children, two of whom about Alice's age. He gazed at the children, and regardless of his promise, he believed God would want him to protect these people.

"Get them ready." Michael rode Rian to the cabin and dismounted halfway up a ladder sturdy enough to hold his weight. He climbed up with one hand, the other holding fast to the Henry. Michael hid on one side of the sloped rooftop, blocked out the voices below, and ignored the chill as he prepared.

CHAPTER 14

"Alice has written you a Christmas poem about the deer she saw wandering across the meadow near the inn. You'll agree it is quite good for one so young."

- Clara Stowe to her parents in a letter not yet sent

"Mama?"

"Yes, darling?"

"How far away is Christmas?"

The quiet clicking of knitting needles continued as Clara looked up from her project. She had yet to master a particular stitch Briley had shown her, and Clara's frustration at her lack of skill helped keep her mind off Michael's late return. Lunch had been served and enjoyed in relative quiet. Grace and Alice napped while Augusta insisted on helping with preparations for dinner. Clara did not again broach what comes next for Augusta, and she hoped she gave the woman something to consider.

"Christmas is only a few weeks away." Clara set aside her knitting and smiled at her daughter. "Shall we draw a calendar so you can mark off each day to Christmas?"

Alice's enthusiastic nod broadened Clara's smile, until her daughter asked, "Will Grandma and Grandpa be here?"

Their first Christmas away from her family, away from familiar comforts, tightened Clara's heart. And yet, beyond the gentle constriction lay a peace knowing they had found home. "Do you remember the map Grandpa showed you before we left Connecticut?"

Alice bobbed her head. "He said it was really big."

Clara chuckled softly. "Yes, it is enormous. And do you remember how long it took us to journey here?"

She gave an audible sigh and nod in answer.

"We wouldn't want Grandma and Grandpa to get lost between there and here, would we? And with so many feet of snow to make their journey more difficult."

"No, Mama, but why can't we go there and see them?"

Clara eased herself back so the chair supported her. It was the first time Alice had asked or hinted her preference to be in Connecticut. Yet, her precious daughter did not understand that in Connecticut, people in her grandparents' circle knew the truth about her birth. She stood and held out her hand for Alice. "Let us fetch some paper, and my quill and ink, and we shall write a Christmas letter to Grandma and Grandpa. Then we can draw your calendar to mark the days."

Alice bounded up and grasped Clara's hand. "Can Grace help? She likes Christmas."

"Did she tell you so?"

"Uh-huh. Do you think Briley's baby will like Christmas?"

For the moment at least, Alice's excitement to see the baby replaced the crisis of faraway grandparents. "I am sure Briley's baby will love it."

"Can we go see the baby? You promised." Alice stopped in the hallway and crossed her arms. The look she gave her mother, though, was one of a dutiful child near the point of begging.

"I did promise." Clara leaned down and tweaked Alice's little nose. "We can write the letter before bed. There is still time before dinner, so we will bundle up nice and warm and walk over to Dr. Latimer's clinic."

A voice cleared nearby, and Clara saw Isaac standing half a dozen feet away. "Hello, Isaac. I do not believe you have officially met my daughter. Alice, this is Mr. Worth. He is a friend of Mr. Donaghue's."

Alice peered askance at her mother. "He said I could call him Michael, and he told me Isaac is my friend, too, Mama." She waved at the tall man. "Hello, Mr. Isaac."

Isaac bowed his head. "Hello, Miss Alice." He then asked Clara, "Pardon, ma'am, but I heard you say you're goin' to the clinic?"

"We are going to see Mrs. Sawyer." She saw him wince. "Would you care to come with us? I can have Elis ready the wagon."

"Uh, no ma'am. I mean, yes, ma'am, I was thinkin' of lookin' in with the doc." Isaac twisted a wool cap in his hands. "I don't need no wagon, though."

"You are welcome to join us, Isaac. We'll go around from the back and meet you there shortly."

"Yes, ma'am."

"Please, it is Clara."

"Yes, Clara ma'am."

Giving him an indulgent smile in parting, Clara led her daughter upstairs to her bedroom, where she selected a second pair of stockings and thicker pantaloons.

"It's too hot, Mama."

"Not for outside, dearest. You may take them off when we return home." Considering herself suitably dressed for the short walk to town, Clara did not bother with additional underclothing. A few minutes later found them in the back hall off the kitchen where Clara draped a short wool cloak over Alice's shoulders, wrapped a thick scarf of deep rose around her neck twice, and tucked the edges beneath the cloak before buttoning it. Hat, gloves, and sturdy boots followed. Satisfied that Alice would not freeze, Clara donned her own cloak and accoutrements.

"Susan?"

The cook rolled a heavy ball of dough from a bowl onto the floured table.

"Have you seen Mr. Worth?"

"Not since I took him a tray of food in the library. Didn't think you'd mind, what with him resting his leg."

"Of course not." Clara stepped farther into the kitchen. "Where is Augusta?"

"Gone to look in on Grace." Susan returned to her kneading. "Knows her way around a kitchen."

"Augusta?"

Susan nodded. "Didn't even need showing how to make a crust for the meat pies tonight."

From what she had learned thus far about Lucas Harrigan, he did not sound like a man to go without a proper cook.

"Mama." Alice tugged on her arm. "Mr. Isaac is out there."

Drawn away from her musings, Clara said to Susan, "We won't be long. I've promised Alice a visit to see Briley."

Susan grinned. "A new baby is what we need to brighten this winter. I'll have the kettle on for when you return."

Clara and Alice left the house by way of the back door, and sure enough, Isaac was already on the covered porch. Clara held her own counsel when she might have offered him warmer clothing. They walked in silence over a pathway someone had cleared in the snow around the house. Enough wagons, horses, and sleighs had traveled over the road to make the walking easier than it might have been otherwise.

Alice took a few steps, then stopped to shake the snow off her feet, finding delight in the process. Like her father, Alice always enjoyed the winter months, short as they were back home. The young girl interjected a question here and there for Isaac, and he always responded, though with yes or no responses rather than revealing much about himself. As tempted as she was to discover more about Michael and his traveling companion, Clara listened rather than ask her own questions.

Casey Latimer stepped out of the sheriff's office, dressed for the cold weather. Peyton joined him sans coat and hat, and the two were in deep conversation, neither pleased with the discussion. Peyton saw them first and stopped talking. Casey tipped his hat to Clara before hunching down and tweaking Alice's nose. "I can guess there's only one thing that would get a pretty little girl out of her warm house on a day like this. Are you going to see the baby?"

Alice nodded. "Mama promised I get to see her."

Peyton grinned at the young girl. "Mariah Rose is her name, and she'll be happy to meet you. She can't talk to you and mostly sleeps, but she'll like to meet you all the same." To Clara, he said, "I'll head over with you."

"The leg still bothering you, Isaac?" Casey asked. "Emma's at the clinic, and thankfully, no one has come down with an ailment or injury today."

"Yes, sir. She said to come on over any time."

"She meant it." Casey leaned down closer to Alice's eye level. "Will you let Sheriff Sawyer take you over to see his new daughter while I talk with your ma?"

Peyton held out his hand to Alice, red now from the cold. She easily accepted it. "Mama says babies are like fairies. Is Mar . . . Mari—"

"Mariah."

"Uh-huh. Is she a fairy?"

"Let's go have a look and you can see for yourself." Peyton nodded to Clara, then listened to Alice's delightful chatter as they walked to the clinic, with Isaac following.

Casey's hand rested briefly on the small of Clara's back as he opened the office door again and ushered her inside. "There's still some warmth coming from the stove if you'd like to warm yourself."

Clara did, though she didn't look away from Casey as she held her gloved hands in front of the hot cast iron. "What were you and Peyton discussing a few minutes ago? Neither of you seemed pleased."

"Have you seen Michael?"

"He left several hours ago with Carson and Hattie." Clara knew she couldn't keep the trace of concern from her voice. "Have you?"

"No, and I don't mean to worry you." Casey sat on the edge of Peyton's desk, his stance not relaxed. "I ran two more of Harrigan's men off the Peterson land today, not two hours ago."

"The Peterson farm is half a mile away. They're moving closer to town."

"They are. I don't believe these two were up to any trouble, just stopping and planning where to go next. Peterson's wife is about to have another baby, so he was nervous about having strangers around. Thing is, one man mentioned Michael and Isaac. Not by name, but as far as I know, they're the only Irishman and former slave who have traveled through these parts recently, possibly ever."

"An uncommon alliance," Clara murmured.

"It is, but it seems Michael might have had more of a run-in with Harrigan than he realizes."

Clara's whole body stiffened. "You are not accusing him of wrongdoing, are you, Casey?"

With raised brows and folded arms, Casey simply stared at her.

"Of course, you are not. I am sorry." Her stance relaxed a fraction. "Why did you not speak to Isaac about this? He would know what happened."

"From what I was told, Isaac was the reason the altercation happened." Casey held up a hand. "Not his fault, either. Harrigan's man was at the trading post when it happened and heard what Harrigan called Isaac. Michael took exception. I'd have done the same thing."

"Then I don't understand."

"The man thought Michael ought to watch his back." Casey stood straight and watched the snow swirl outside. "I'll walk you over to the clinic now."

Clara remained near the stove. "Why have you told me this?"

A heavy sigh escaped before Casey said, "You know why, Clara."

"My mind is sharp enough to slice through the fog of what you are *not* telling me, so I will rephrase. Why would you think I'd ever ask them to leave the inn? You and Peyton thought it good they were there for our protection."

"That's before I knew they had a run-in with Harrigan. This is getting more dangerous, and—"

"No!" They both quieted, each surprised at her firm outburst. Clara covered the short distance between them and released a sigh of her own before tilting her head back to look up at him. "You, Peyton, Carson, and so many others in town have been good to me since I arrived. You've always made me feel welcome, even when you could not hide your hope that I return to the safety of my family and home back east. I love you all dearly for it, truly I do. However, there are times when annoyance and love are at war within me when it comes to your well-intentioned advice."

"Have you been talking to Emma?"

Clara smiled. "Always, much to your chagrin."

Casey failed to muster a smile of his own. "This is serious, Clara."

"My daughter sleeps like an angel, without a care for what happens beyond the walls of her small world. Even after those men came for Augusta and Grace, Alice quickly overcame whatever fear she might have suffered. I am well aware of how serious the situation is and can become. Do you truly believe we are safer without Michael and Isaac under my roof?"

"Which is the same argument Peyton made to me. Do you have any idea of Emma's suffering should any disaster befall you?"

"The same as mine should the unthinkable ever happen to her." Her proper upbringing did not allow for impulsive shows of affection, and yet, Clara ignored her mother's voice in her head, leaned up, and kissed Casey's stubbled cheek. "It is because of how much you love your wife that I will not tell her about this conversation. When Michael returns—"

Without warning, the air hummed, and not in a melodic way. Even as her mind fumbled with thoughts and words, uncertain as to what had just happened, they drifted unwittingly to war . . . and Gideon.

No battle had marred Connecticut soil during the conflict, so Clara possessed only the imaginings conjured from Gideon's early letters. He wanted to spare her the worst of it—the sounds, stench, and sorrow. Once, he attempted to describe the cacophonous vibrations coursing through air and earth after an explosion. He did so only to demonstrate how thoughts of her were so powerful as to drown out the worst of such sounds.

While no doubt illustrating a blast much closer to his person, Gideon's description came to mind as the air beyond the walls and windows displaced long enough for her legs to buckle. Casey caught her about the waist before she lost her footing. "Casey. Was that an earthquake?"

"Can you stand?" At her nod, Casey released her. "Never had an earthquake here to my knowledge. It was an explosion, though not a large one and not in town." He, too, remembered well enough the sounds of cannon fire and muskets.

False hope filled her voice when she asked, "The lumber camp, wasn't it?"

"Wrong direction."

Her gloved fingers left imprints on Casey's coat, so tight was her grip. "Hattie went with Carson and Michael."

Casey gently unfolded her fingers from his arm and took her hand. "Come with me." A burst of unexpected warmth from the sun pressed upon Clara's face when they left the sheriff's office. Her eyes drifted upward and stared for a second into the sun, no longer hidden behind clouds, suspended in the center of miles of sky. Its rays danced across every snow-covered surface to create a blanket of ice crystals. Above the mountains, snarling gray clouds bided their time.

When next her gaze fell upon the ground in front of her, they were on the clinic's front porch, and Peyton stood half-in, half-out. He wasted no time in closing the door. In part she would soon realize, to keep out the cold, but also to keep ears inside from overhearing. "Clara, Alice is with Briley and occupied, but the noise has her asking for you. I'd feel better if you stayed here."

"Alice should stay, but I need to return to the inn. Susan and Elis will worry, and Augusta—"

"We'll move Augusta and Grace to Casey and Emma's house," Peyton said.

Three men on horseback, one of whom Clara recognized as the blacksmith, were already riding in the same direction as Michael, Carson, and Hattie had gone earlier. Shouts tinged with worry and question reached them from men and women blissfully unaware of recent events. Most, she hoped, likely suspected the lumber camp as the source of the blast.

Her narrowed eyes shifted to Peyton. "I don't understand. Why do they need to leave the inn? They are safe there." They had to be, because if Augusta and Grace weren't safe in the sanctuary she'd created for herself and Alice, were any of them?

"Trust me, please, Clara."

Peyton opened the door and whisked her inside. Emma waited within and took Clara into her charge. The door closed again before Clara could put herself back on the outside.

"Let them go, Clara." Emma gripped her friend's shoulders to hold her still. "If ever there is a woman on this earth who can survive whatever life puts in her path, it is Hattie. Carson will keep her safe."

Clara nodded, though the action lacked Emma's conviction. She recalled the story of how Hattie and Carson had met. Hattie nearly dead, almost drowned, and Carson keeping her alive long enough for Emma to do the rest.

Clara asked, "Does Briley know Michael went with them?"

"She does, and swears he will return alive, because he promised never to leave her again." Emma laughed on a sigh and her gaze bore into Clara's. "Have you ever known Briley to not get her way?"

"No." Calmer with each deep breath, Clara closed her eyes and soaked in Alice's unmistakable giggling from the other room. "I cannot go through it again. The loss. It is too much."

Emma did not pretend ignorance. "We all make such declarations, Clara. I did after I lost David. The heart, though, cannot be dissuaded."

"This time it can." Clara focused her mind on her daughter. "It has to be."

CHAPTER 15

"... and I should assure you, once more, we are safe and happy. Our existence is far from mundane, but truly, nothing extraordinary happens here, especially with winter heavy upon us. Of course, even the mundane, at times, can be exciting."

- Clara Stowe to her parents in a letter not yet sent

WAVES CRASHED AGAINST the ship's hull, a pleasant sound amid the darkness. Michael inhaled the cool, salt air as the rush of water filled his senses. Instead of exhaling on a fresh breeze, his lungs coughed up smoke and debris. Gone were the salt sea air and the harmonic waves. A discordant roar echoed in his ears, and his eyes, aching to open, did so briefly and closed again against the soot.

"Michael!"

His brain struggled to recognize the voice. No longer on the great ship crossing the Atlantic Ocean, Michael forced his mind away from the memory and into the present. With the pleasant surf gone, he returned to the battlefields. Cannon blasts, rifle fire, and sharp blades striking down the unsuspecting.

"Michael! Blast you, Briley will kill us if you die."

He wanted to smile, but his head pounded too much. Briley. Yes, he recalled now where he lay. Two shots had hit their marks. The third man never came out of the woods.

"Michael! Wake up!"

Hattie. Her voice took on Ireland's melody, and the sweet sound broke up the remaining roar in his ears enough for him to gain his bearings. "Hattie." Michael rasped her name and held his chest as his lungs expelled another hacking cough. The situation was too familiar, but he did not think death held a grip on him this time.

"Thank God. Hold still." Hattie poured water over Michael's eyes. "Don't rub them. Just let the water work." After a few seconds, she dabbed at his eyes with a cloth. "Can you open your eyes now?"

Michael's eyelids opened halfway, then shuttered. Hattie dabbed at them again, this time with a damp cloth. He opened them all the way and fought the urge to rub them clean. "Where's Carson?"

"He's fine." Hattie slouched in relief before straightening her back again. She knelt in the debris next to him—half snow, half pieces of cabin. "Carson's tracking the third man."

Michael closed his eyes, this time to concentrate on the minutes before the blast. "I never saw the third one come out of the trees."

"Neither did Carson. You got two of them as they approached. One man here went out to fetch their horses." Hattie gripped his arm. "We need to get you to Emma."

"No." He covered her hand, squeezed, and then released it so he could brace himself and focus on his body. "Nothing's broken." Michael wouldn't tell her about the bruised ribs he suspected or his probable concussion. He'd been through worse. Not too proud to accept her help, he pushed up with one arm and his legs, while Hattie helped hold him steady. Before he reached full height, Patrick Doyle was at Michael's other side.

"You have more lives than a man ought to, Michael Donaghue." Patrick slapped him lightly on the back, causing another round of coughs. "You'll live, won't you?"

Michael nodded as his lungs cleared. "That helped some, thanks. Yes, I'll live. What the hell happened?" His quick glance at Hattie apologized for the curse, but he returned his intent gaze to Patrick. "Or better question, how did it happen?"

The cabin in front of the one where Michael had perched not long ago lay as a shell of shambles. The roof where Michael had aimed from, fired, and took down two of the men no longer existed, and what remained of the small structure lay scattered around them.

"Was anyone still in the cabin?" He pointed to the one from which the explosion had to have originated.

Patrick shook his head. "We got them moved to the first cabin with my family."

"Is everyone accounted for?"

"Yes." Patrick's hesitation cost him, though Michael thought only he heard the catch in his old comrade's voice.

"You're sure no one is missing?" Hattie asked.

"One man went hunting, so not missing."

"He went alone?"

"Yes." Patrick hurried on. "Couldn't have been him,

though. He has a wife and son here. Traveled with us from Boston."

Michael knew the desperation of men. He'd also seen enough good men make choices in the name of hopelessness that they might not otherwise make under normal circumstances. Distant shouts drew their attention. "The sound of the explosion must have reached town. We'll have company soon, and the sheriff and marshal will want to speak with every adult here. Let's get everyone into the wagon and on horseback, women and children first. There's probably another sleigh coming."

Hattie nodded her agreement. "Casey and Peyton know we came out here. They'll bring transport and provisions."

"Very well." Michael whistled three times before his horse forged a path through the snow back to him.

"Where do you think you're going?" Hattie snatched Rian's reigns. "Never mind. You're going to find my husband. I'd encourage it if not for you almost dying a few minutes ago. You can barely move without holding your chest. Briley will blister you all right, and then Carson for not keeping you safe."

He almost laughed. "She won't scold you, though?"

"She knows well enough the hard heads of men. There will be no blame for me. You're close to dead, Michael. Be sensible."

Michael's muscles bunched in pain as he pulled himself into the saddle. He grinned down at Hattie. "But not dead yet. Tell whoever's coming we'll be back soon." Rian's thick muscles and powerful lungs carried Michael's weight through the snow, following the trail Carson had made. He imagined Rian's strong heart in sync with his own, for when his heart rate accelerated, Rian became more alert and his speed increased in gradual increments until snow scattered in the surrounding air.

"Steady, boy."

Rian responded to the gentle voice and light squeeze of Michael's thighs and knees, and slowed to a walk, then with another subtle press, stopped at the treeline on the other side of the first expanse of forest where a wide meadow stretched to the base of the mountains. Horse tracks, however, were not present.

"Slow, Rian." Man and horse walked along the edge of the trees where snow faded into fallen pine needles, and fifty feet into their walk, Michael spotted hoofprints, one set alongside another.

"*Go hifreann leat!*" The curse echoed, though whether the shooter was close enough to hear, Michael didn't care. He grasped his arm where the bullet grazed him enough to slice through his layers of thick coat and shirtsleeves. When he pulled his gloved hand away, a line of blood came with it. Rian pranced a little beneath Michael and pawed at the ground. Movement across the meadow caused Rian's ears to shift forward and drew Michael's focus. He sighted Carson's horse, heard two shots, and then . . . "Go!"

He wasn't certain how he made it across the meadow. Blood seeped from his arm wound and his head pounded. On they rode until Rian stopped a few feet from Carson, who slowly got to his feet.

"Are you hit?"

Carson shook his head. "Looks like you are, though. Good to see you alive. I wasn't sure when I saw the cabin explode."

"You did the right thing going after this one."

"I know." Carson walked the few yards to where the third man lay in the snow. "I'd swear I only hit his shoulder." He picked up the man's pistol and handed it to Michael before kneeling next to the man. "Looks like he hit his head on this rock when he fell. There's a scratch of blood on the stone."

Michael studied the terrain and saw nothing in the distance. "What's beyond this meadow?"

"The edge of my ranch."

"How far is the lumber camp from here?"

Carson stepped back. "Not far as the crow flies, but there are easier ways to get there. We've had a few problems of late with some of Harrigan's men crossing our land. Most are smart enough to go around. From here, they'd have to ride an extra three miles before they get to the nearest trail that connects to Harrigan's land."

"Let's get his horse and him back to town. If he lives long enough, then Emma can pull the bullet out before he's questioned." Michael dismounted, cursed his arm, and kicked the prone man's leg. "*D'anam don diabhal.*"

"You ought to be careful. Hattie knows a fair bit of Gaelic, and Briley, well . . ."

"Which is why I'm saying it now instead of around your wife." Michael led the third man's horse back to him.

Carson positioned himself at the man's head to take more of the weight while Michael lifted the legs. They tossed the man across his saddle with less effort than Michael expected, tied him in place for good measure, and gained their own mounts.

"What does it mean? What you said back there?"

Michael tossed the reins to Carson and took the lead. "I was damning his soul to the devil."

With a glance at the dead weight, Carson muttered, "Expect the devil's already waiting for him. What's really bothering you?"

"Patrick Doyle is a good man. I didn't know him long, but

well enough. They're poor, with nothing of value to tempt theft. If these men are from Harrigan, they don't need a few horses and a wagon."

"Then why are Harrigan's men attacking these people?"

Michael nodded. "Someone among them is hiding something."

They rode into the shattered camp, cabin bits strewn about, and half their number gone. Hattie stood talking with Peyton, her expression grim until she caught sight of Carson, then her features relaxed. Carson dismounted and pulled his wife close, ignoring the rest of them as he spoke to her in a voice too hushed to reach beyond their circle.

Michael approached Peyton with a small dose of caution. "Are you killing me with that look because Briley let into you, or is it something else I've done?"

Peyton's stern expression cracked into a smile. "Briley will let into you herself. She's still happy with me, thanks to our new daughter." He sobered. "How bad is your arm?"

"A graze. It's nothing. Where are the rest of them?"

Peyton waved in the direction of town. "Headed to town with a few men who rode out to help."

"You should be there, with Briley."

"I promised her I'd bring you home."

Apparently, Briley doesn't quite trust me to make it back there on my own. They had yet to get used to the idea the other was alive, and they were together. "You'll keep your promise." Michael gestured toward the man strewn over the saddle. "This one is still alive but needs doctoring if he's going to be of much help."

"I'll take him back now and you and Carson can escort the rest of these folks back to town. You'll meet up with a sleigh and wagon, but nightfall will be here soon, so you'll need to start back now. Only those who able to walk are still here."

"Fine." Michael ground his back teeth against the throbbing pain now circulating through his body. "Where's Patrick Doyle? He's—"

"I've met him before. He joined the first group into town. Why?"

"Because we need a few words with him. Did he mention one of their group went missing?"

Peyton shook his head. "Hattie did, though. Whoever he is, he won't last long out there without a horse."

"Yeah, maybe." Patrick knew he could trust Michael, so why hadn't he? Michael mentally listed questions to ask his old comrade, except the pain interfered with too much thinking. It wouldn't do for him to survive a war, only to die now. *Then again, not a bad place to wear out.*

"I CAN'T TAKE THOSE."

"Yes, you can." Clara folded three of her dresses carefully into one of her carpetbags. Two were simple everyday dresses, while the third was a nicer frock from two seasons ago. "I've no need for them, and we're close enough in size, so they should fit well enough. I'm still a novice seamstress, so I do not trust my ability to alter them for you, but there are a few women in town with the proper skills."

She added a second new nightgown. "I'll hear no argument."

"I have money."

"And you may need it." Clara rested her hands on her hips and studied Augusta's pinched expression. "This is not charity. When you get to wherever it is you want to go, you can send me money for the dresses if you wish, but I hope you'll accept them as a gift."

Augusta's mouth opened and closed a few times like a fish, yet no words came out. She lowered herself to the trunk at the foot of the bed and stared at the carpetbag. "Were it possible, we'd be halfway to the Carolinas. Grace is happy here, though, with Alice, and I'm not certain I can disrupt her fragile existence again so soon."

Clara sat on the trunk next to Augusta. "Peyton believes you'll be safer with the Latimers. No one will look for you there. They'll certainly come to the inn again. Casey Latimer is a U.S. Marshal and his wife is a doctor. There is nowhere safer for you and Grace than under their roof."

Augusta's gaze circled the room. "And if I choose not to go?"

"They, nor I, will force you." Clara stood and stared at her. "It may not feel like it, but the choice is yours, Augusta. The decision is entirely up to you. Everyone is only thinking of yours and Grace's safety, and hopefully it will not be for long."

"I don't mean to sound ungrateful. There is no emotion currently at my disposal to express the depth of my gratitude for all you have done—for everyone who has helped—I just . . ."

"I know." Clara's hearing cut through the quiet sounds of the inn to focus on the giggling in the room beyond. "Alice has grown quite fond of Grace, too."

Clara had no intention of contradicting Peyton's recommendation because her rational mind accepted it as truth. The inn was an obvious place for Augusta to seek refuge, and considering what happened to the last man who came looking, Lucas Harrigan likely knew where to find his wife and daughter.

She quickly sat next to Augusta again. "Why hasn't your husband come for you? If he truly wanted you back, why not lead his army of men down here himself?" When Augusta didn't answer, Clara prodded. "What more haven't you told us?"

Still, Augusta remained silent.

Clara could not prevent disappointment and anger from creeping into her next words. "Men have been injured protecting you, and they'll do it again and again. They take their responsibilities seriously to the town and the good people in it. Lives are at risk, by our choice, mind you, including Alice's. If there is more you are not saying—"

"It is more than Grace and me." Augusta choked on the words. "Lucas hasn't come because he can't. I don't know how long he'll be incapacitated, and I have been praying for a way to leave before he does, because if he's the one who comes for us . . ."

"Is it you or his daughter he wants more?"

Augusta gripped the fabric of her skirt into her fists. "It's not about us." She finally looked at Clara. "We'll go as your sheriff has asked, and I'll do whatever else he recommends to keep my daughter safe."

"I don't . . . understand. If none of this is about you, then what *does* your husband want?"

Augusta wiped away a few tears trickling down her cheeks and rose from the trunk. "I promised."

"Very well." Clara pointed to the bags. "When you're ready, Elis will carry those down. Emma will still be at her clinic, and Casey is helping at the cabin camp. One of them should return soon."

"You're angry."

Clara chose her words carefully. "Not angry. Sad and disappointed. When I said earlier that I knew, I didn't mean to imply I've been through the same situation. I know what it is to be tired, to question choices, and to wonder if those choices we make are the correct ones. The rest, well, it saddens me more that you can't—or won't—trust me."

Augusta hurried to Clara's side and hugged her fiercely before stepping back. "It is not about trust. What is the phrase? 'No more, where ignorance is bliss, 'Tis folly to be wise.'"

"Thomas Gray."

"Yes, that's right. Lucas wanted an obedient wife, not an uneducated one. He chose my reading material. Unfortunately for us, I did not remain ignorant of who he really is."

Clara grasped Augusta's hand and squeezed. "We are no longer youth untouched by the world's misfortunes. Ignorance of life's hardships has long not been an option. For them—Grace and Alice, and all the children it is in our power to protect—let them remain happy. You keep your promise because it's the right thing to do. However, the folly in this instance would be to remain blind to what may be coming."

CHAPTER 16

"I am certain Susan and Elis have an affection for one another, though neither has voiced intentions beyond friendship. It perplexes me how two people who so obviously care for each other say nothing to change their fate."

- Clara Stowe to her parents in a letter not yet sent

CLARA CHECKED ON the girls before making her way down the stairs through the quiet inn. Used to having people about, mostly family and those who worked in her parents' house, she missed the quiet bustle of guests coming and going. Though they were not plentiful, Clara enjoyed meeting the lodgers who ventured from far and near, who simply needed a soft bed and peaceful place to rest for a night or two before they journeyed toward their next or final destination.

Without Michael and Isaac under her roof, for the moment, the inn stood as silent as the first day she had arrived. Sometimes Clara thought her mother would faint if she saw how her only daughter chose to live so far removed from how she was raised.

A smile touched Clara's mouth as she passed through the hall and dining room into the kitchen. Every day came with its challenges, yet she could imagine nowhere on earth she'd rather be. The smile faded as reality encroached on her thoughts, drawing her away from the pleasant musings.

"Susan, there's been . . . oh, my it smells wonderful in here." A pot of soup simmered on the stove, and a fresh batch of herbed biscuits cooled on the counter. Susan cut strips of pie crust dough for the lattice top of her apple pecan pie. This close to the dinner hour, Elis could often be found enjoying a cup of coffee and sneaking the first taste of whatever Susan prepared for the evening meal. "Has Elis not come in yet?"

Susan laid the first strips over the apple filling and shook her head. "Haven't seen him. I asked earlier if he could coax a pail of milk from the cow since she wasn't keen on giving up too much this morning."

Clara smiled at Susan, who was focused on the pie and not on her. "He does like to please you."

Surprised eyes met Clara's. "Whatever do you mean?"

Her light shrug and wink were her response before she slipped her heaviest wool cloak over her shoulders, and opened the back door to the cold air. A hush of falling snow met her call for Elis, then she braved the frigid air head on. Dark clouds blocked the sun that had shined upon them most of the day, and she prayed Hattie, Carson, and Michael returned safely, and soon.

The barn door stood ajar only an inch, but it was an inch more than Elis would have allowed given the weather, especially with no one coming or going. With a misstep off the path Elis kept cleared, snow seeped into her ankle-high leather boots. Clara shrugged off the extra snow and called out for Elis again.

She pushed the barn door open enough to slip inside. Shafts of dull light came through the frosted glass panes but did not reach beyond a few feet. The horses moved about in their stalls, and one pawed at the boards beneath.

"Elis?"

"Was that his name?"

First, her feet became immobile as though someone had glued them to the floor. Next, her legs refused to follow orders. Inch by inch, fear inhibited her body's movement. She did not recognize the voice, and yet the whisper of it, the sinister nonchalance of its confession, stalled thought and motion. Clara begged her lungs to expel the air they held, and after what felt like far too much to survive, she breathed.

Only seconds had passed, for the man who emerged from the shadows was still a dozen feet away. She inhaled, breathed out again, and shook her hands to prove she could. "Was?"

"He's not sufferin' if that worries you." The man walked past a shaft of the meager light, slowly enough for Clara to make out general features: a few inches taller than herself, a thick, blond beard, and narrow eyes. *Elis. Elis. Elis cannot be gone.* Clara dared not close her eyes, but she wanted to so this man did not see the tears threatening to flow.

"Who are you?"

"Lady, you don't really expect me to say, do you?" Yellowed teeth appeared when he laughed. "The boss never said I couldn't have a little fun, and I reckon you're as close to fun as I'll get around here."

Two slow steps back put a little distance between them. He smiled again as though he could read her thoughts.

"Whatever you have come for, you won't find it here."

"I think I will." He advanced, stealing the precious ground she had gained. "I watched those men leave earlier. Figure it's just women here now that, what was his name? Elis? Yeah, now that Elis ain't no good to you anymore."

Her gaze darted around the dark interior of the barn for any means of escape, any way to fight the intruder back. "Do you work for Lucas Harrigan?"

The man scratched his thick beard and bobbed his head side to side. "Reckon I shouldn't say. You won't be able to repeat it, so . . ." He shrugged. "Don't matter who pays me. Figure we have our fun, then I take care of your pretty cook. There's the little yellow-haired girl . . . I'll promise to leave her alone if you stay quiet."

Clara's panic vanished at the mention of Alice and adrenaline propelled her into action. The pitchfork was so close, just by the door. She didn't know how she reached it before the man caught her, but there it was in her firm grip, aimed toward him. Her legs kept moving forward until she met resistance. A strange gurgle followed, and her hands let go. The thud brought her mind into focus and she spun away.

A firm grip wound her ankle and yanked her down. Her arms weren't fast enough to brace her rapid fall to the cold boards, and the impact jarred her long enough for the powerful hand to yank again.

She kicked with both legs, not caring what she hit, only to loosen the hold upon her. Another hard kick, and now free, Clara pulled herself across the boards, snagging the tie of her cloak in a crack. She wrestled it free, then sat upright.

Her attacker lay unmoving, blood draining from his mouth and staining his shirt around the pitchfork prongs. Rapid breaths in and out forced her to bend forward until she could control the nausea, and a low groan coming from the rear of the barn had her scrambling up. "Elis!"

Clara stumbled around the intruder and followed the next groan to the last stall, empty except for a fresh layer of hay. Her knees dropped to the floor, disturbing dust and straw. She waved the particulates away to see now that her eyes had adjusted to the semidarkness. "Elis, can you hear me?"

His low groan was one of the nicest sounds she'd ever heard. She couldn't see where he might be injured, and there was no way for her to move him on her own.

"Mrs. Stowe?"

She covered Elis's mouth to prevent another sound as she listened to the unknown voice.

"Mrs. Stowe!" Fevered concern marked her name. "You in here?"

Recognition penetrated her residual fear. "Isaac!"

He hurried to the back of the barn as quickly as his limp allowed. "Ma'am, you . . . Lord Almighty." Isaac dropped to one knee on the other side of Elis, slowly brought his other leg under, and felt around Elis's head, shoulders, chest, and farther down. "I think it's jest the wound on his head, but it's a bad one. Lots of blood."

"Can we move him?"

Isaac shook his head. "I figure it's best to bring the doc here."

"All right, can you stay with him? I'll get Emma."

"No, ma'am, you ought to stay here. I thought the banshees were on you when I heard your scream. Did that man hurt you?"

"Scream?" Clara didn't recall making any sound, though she must have if Isaac claimed to have heard one. "What? The man. Never mind him, Isaac. I'm fine, I'll go." She handed Isaac her wool shawl. "Do what you can for Elis, please." Without waiting for a response, Clara diverted her eyes away from their attacker who was long past the point of needing a doctor's help, and ran from the barn. Her boots slipped on the snow twice and twice she balanced her body to prevent a fall. The third time she took a tumble, near the edge of the inn's long front porch, she attributed to the tears now flowing freely from her eyes and blocking her vision.

"Clara!"

She made out the outline of a horse and rider, and several more people behind him. It was the voice she knew and welcomed. "Casey."

"My God, Clara, what happened?" He had to lift her, and when she couldn't stand on her legs any longer, Casey carried her to the porch and gently deposited her in one of the rocking chairs.

"Hattie, Michael, Cars—"

"They're coming." Casey rubbed her hands between his. "What happened, Clara?"

"Elis. The barn."

Casey motioned someone else to join them. Clara saw him clearly, but didn't recognize the man.

"Will your wife help her?"

The man nodded and called out a name Clara didn't catch. The Irish accent she recognized well enough, but she had no time to ask questions before Casey lifted her again and carried her inside while giving instructions to the woman who followed close behind.

"Mrs. Doyle, please stay with Clara. The kitchen is toward the back. It will help if you could get some water and warm tea into her. The rest of your party can come inside and warm themselves. Mr. Doyle, I need you to come with me."

Clara reached toward Casey, but he'd already left her side. She didn't know these people. Where was Susan?

"Mrs. Stowe? My name is Orla Doyle." The woman removed Clara's gloves from her hands and draped a quilt over her shoulders. "Is there anyone else here?"

She fought the lump in her throat. "My daughter, and another woman and child, upstairs. Susan." Had they heard the scream she didn't remember? Clara heard the sounds of footsteps—many of them—walk across the hardwood floors and rugs.

"Neasa, fetch some water, a cloth damp with cool water, and set a kettle for boiling. The marshal said the kitchen is down the hall past the dining room."

"What in heavens is going on?" Susan entered the parlor and rushed to Clara's side. "Clara?"

"I am unharmed." Clara attempted to stand and was gently pushed back down.

"You look near death. I come up from the cellar and . . . who are all these people?"

Clara remained silent, and she heard Orla answer Susan's question.

"Orla Doyle, and explaining all of this'll take more time than we have right now. I've seen the likes of this before. 'Tis shock she's in. It will pass. The marshal said we were to avail ourselves of the kitchen."

"Alice will wonder . . . she cannot see me like this."

Susan laid a comforting hand on Clara's shoulder. "Alice won't, I promise. All right then, explanations will have to wait. Which one were you about to send to my kitchen?"

Clara smiled despite her rattled condition.

Orla said, "Neasa."

"Very well. Neasa, come along with me. There's much to do."

Clara whispered Susan's name, drawing the other woman back.

"I won't leave you if—"

"Elis. He's been hurt."

The sudden paleness spreading across Susan's complexion helped break down part of the invisible wall Clara tried to chisel her way through.

"Where is he?"

"The barn." Clara squeezed her friend's hand. "Go to him, Susan."

Susan hesitated long enough for Orla to assure her Clara would be taken care of, and then she left at a run from the parlor.

"That's good, then. Keep breathing."

She listened to Orla's soothing voice tell her to breathe, which she thought she'd been doing all along, but something in how she breathed must have changed, for Orla continued praising her efforts.

A cool glass of water was encouraged into her hand, and she automatically drank deeply while a damp cloth was pressed to her forehead, then her cheeks. As though a fog encircling her lifted, Clara focused her eyes and mind on the woman beside her.

"There you are. Come back from it."

"Where . . . who . . . Orla is it?"

"Yes, Orla Doyle. You heard that much, so you weren't as far gone as I afeared. Your marshal brought us into town. My husband went with him. We ought to get you out of those clothes and—"

"With him . . . Elis. I sent Susan to Elis, and he's near . . ." Clara pushed away the quilt, the women, and rushed out the back door and out to the barn. She collided with the stranger who'd gone with Casey. "Is he alive?"

"He's alive. I'm fetching the doc now. You shouldn't go in there, Mrs. Stowe."

Feeling up to full strength again, Clara pushed him aside. "Go, please, now!" No body lay on the floor in her way, and she did not stop to wonder what had happened to the intruder. She found Casey and Isaac with an unconscious Elis, and Susan with Elis's head resting in her lap. "He hasn't awakened."

"Clara, damn it, you need to get out of here." Casey pulled her back enough so Isaac could try to get some water down Elis's throat.

"I'm well enough now, so save your curses for someone else." She used Casey's shoulder to help lower herself and gingerly lifted one of Elis's hands into her own. "Has he spoken or opened his eyes?"

"No. Isaac slowed the bleeding with some snow and your shawl. Emma will be here soon." Casey indicated Susan with a tilt of his head. "You shouldn't have told her."

"I wasn't thinking." Clara kept her voice low, though she needn't have worried about Susan overhearing. Elis held Susan's undivided concentration and care. "The man you sent for Emma is from the cabin camp, isn't he? What happened to the others? I thought there were more."

"Everyone is fine, Clara, and the rest are coming. There are a few injuries, but the camp—or some of it—was destroyed. Hattie explained most of the situation and Mr. Doyle even more on the trip in."

"What about Carson and Michael?"

Casey held Elis's leg when it twitched.

"Casey, where is Michael?"

"He's alive and with Carson. That's all I know."

Clara refused to succumb to shock again; now, having experienced it once, she never wanted to again.

"Had you seen that man before?" At her blank look, Casey added, "The man who attacked you, Clara. He's in the corner now and can't hurt you."

Clara was grateful her thoughts had been too scattered to notice. Even now, the face of the man she killed faded from her memory. "No, never."

Casey left the subject alone and when they heard Emma call out from the barn's entrance, Casey helped Clara to stand and moved her out of the way to make room for his wife. "She'll do what she can to save him, Clara. We've both seen Emma work miracles."

They'd need more than one.

A SOFT, VEILED gray tinged the early-evening sky when the second group from the cabins entered Crooked Creek. Clara stood on the front porch, bundled in enough clothes to assure Emma and Casey she would not freeze.

Emma had asked her to stay at the clinic for the night. When that failed, Emma suggested she and Alice stay with her and Casey along with Augusta and Grace. Again, she declined, but a warm hug and kiss to Emma's cheek accompanied her refusal. "You will have enough to worry about with Elis and the other injured. I will visit Briley tomorrow, and you can assure yourself of my well-being and good health."

Emma gently took Clara's hand. "No one is all right after what you've just experienced, Clara. You can let others be strong for you. Please let us help."

Even as she thought of Emma's words, she disagreed, at least with the part about strength. She had a daughter, people counting on her, and now a full inn that would soon overflow the rafters. Clara's return to the inn came with a flood of questions, and her simple explanation of venturing to the general store fell short of the truth or at least the whole of it.

She mindlessly estimated the number of newcomers, but it was not them she concerned herself with yet. Peyton tipped his hat to her and kept riding, leading another horse with a wrapped body over the saddle.

Hattie and Carson, who rode double on his horse, came into her eyeline next, and still she searched. Not until Michael's face became clear did she allow relief to flow freely. Tears wanted to follow; she held them at bay.

It was Hattie who dismounted first and walked to her. "I'd say all is well, except you don't look it. What's happened here?" Hattie looked past her to the front door.

"All is well. Everyone is eating, and I've put families together, so there should be enough rooms. Any bachelors will have to make do with cots in the parlor." Her gaze lifted to Michael's, who watched her from atop his horse.

Hattie shared a grin with Carson, though Clara missed it. They ushered the new and weary travelers into the inn while Michael dismounted. The fading light would have hidden his grimace if Clara had not been watching him so closely. She studied him as he walked toward her and she descended the steps. "You're hurt."

Michael drew her close to his body, wrapped both arms around her, and rested his brow against hers for a second before capturing her mouth in a kiss. The kiss was too brief for Clara's liking, and when she would have returned for more, Michael removed his right glove and cupped the side of her face against his palm. "For this moment, I only want to look at you and think of nothing else."

Clara had so many questions. Instead, she rested her head on his shoulder and wrapped her arms around him as he did with her. The cold barely touched them as night encroached.

Michael breathed deeply, and she felt the rise and fall of his chest. She also noticed a slight flinch when she pressed closer. "You *are* hurt."

He kissed her brow and leaned back to look at her. "Nothing a soft bed and some of Susan's apple pie won't fix."

She shuddered. "There are three of them freshly baked. One of the women, Neasa, has proven adept in the kitchen."

Michael tilted her chin up. "What's wrong, Clara?"

"Variations of that question have been asked a lot today, and it's all a little too exciting to be discussing out here. Let's get you inside. Casey is bringing Emma back soon to tend to anyone here in their rooms, and she can look you over, as well."

"Where's Isaac?"

"He is helping at the clinic. Your friend would make a good healer."

"What—"

Clara pressed a finger to his lips. "Not yet. Come inside, we'll get you tended to, and then we'll talk tomorrow after you've had a chance to rest."

He grabbed her hand and waited for her to face him again. "Tomorrow, Michael, please. Nothing can be done tonight."

He proved stubborn. "Done about what?"

"Elis is near to death and Susan is fraught with worry over him. Now, if you'll excuse me, I have a full inn. You still have your room."

Michael's hand circled her wrist, and she stopped not two feet from him. "I didn't set out to upset you."

She waited for him to walk up a step, and he let her keep the higher ground. Where she stood, they were at the same height. "It is too cold out here for important conversation, or any conversation, really. I'm freezing."

"You're right. We'll talk tomorrow."

Clara pressed her cheek to his and then rested her head briefly on his shoulder. "So many things upset me right now. Your protectiveness and concern aren't among them."

Michael held her away so he could look at her again, and this time their eyes were level with each other. "Is it Elis that has you so near tears?"

Her arms wrapped around his neck before her brain realized what she was doing. All of her strength, pain, and anger flowed into her fierce hold on Michael, and he accepted it. His hands crossed over the back of her neck and held her close.

"I took a life today, Michael." She whispered the confession, uncertain if she spoke loudly enough for him to hear, then she felt his arms tighten a little more, his body stiffen, and his breath come out on a soft curse when he nuzzled her hair.

CHAPTER 17

"Thank you for always filling our home with love. We did not show our affection openly, but I have always felt your love. I miss Gideon every day and I know he would be happy for us both . . . there is someone I want to tell you about . . ."

- Clara Stowe to her parents in a letter not yet sent

MICHAEL HELD FAST while he contemplated Clara's confession. More than once he thought it best if she returned to her parents' home. In Connecticut, she wouldn't have been forced to defend herself and kill a man. A dozen questions rested on the edge of his mind ready to be asked, yet instead, he held her close, drawing as much comfort from her as he hoped she did from him.

With extreme regret, he loosened his hold first but still kept her close enough to share his heat. "What happened to

Elis?" Tears dried on her cheeks, tempting Michael to kiss them away. Instead, he waited.

Clara's breath shuddered once before she answered. "The man must have been waiting in the barn for someone. Elis was in the barn and must have surprised the stranger or didn't see him. Emma said he'll be okay as long as he wakes up. Susan is with him at the clinic."

She spoke in a matter-of-fact voice, void of emotion. Michael was unsure whether she did so to hold herself together or if she was riding the edges of shock.

"As you've said, it's too cold to stay out here, and we both need to sleep."

Her head shook as she eased away. "I'm afraid. The altercation is too raw. When I close my eyes, I relive it. His face is a shadow now, but I still see him fall, and the blood."

"All right." Michael wrapped an around her waist and led her up the steps. "Then we'll talk over tea and pie after I'm patched up. The bleeding has stopped, so maybe pie first. I'd rather have coffee but eventually, we're both going to need to sleep tonight. Where's Alice?"

She leaned into him when they reached the top step. "Thank you for always thinking of her. She's asleep. Thank goodness for Grace because Alice barely knows what's been happening around here of late. They became fast friends and Grace will be missed."

"Augusta."

"Oh, she's with—"

"No." Michael tilted her chin up and toward the door. "Augusta is watching us."

They entered the inn to the low hum of voices carrying from the dining room. While none had appeared malnourished, he wondered how many hours or days had passed when one or more of them felt the hollow ache of hunger. He quietly and briefly wished them away, though guilt pushed the inclination for solitude aside. Michael let go of Clara to close and secure the front door. No one who shouldn't be there would have the chance to enter or catch any of them unawares. They'd have to take shifts on watch.

"Augusta, you're all nerves," Michael heard Clara say behind him. The fair-skinned woman's face was paler than usual with skirt fabric bunched in fists.

"Did they all come, from the camp, I mean?"

Michael stood beside Clara. "Almost. Four families, but one of the men is missing. You can trust them, and the young ones can be introduced to Alice and Grace tomorrow if you—"

"No. I mean, yes, I already know I can trust them. No, I don't want . . ." She breathed deeply and pressed a hand to her chest.

"Augusta?" Orla Doyle uttered the name when she entered the front hall from the dining room.

Clara shifted her gaze to Orla. "You have already met?"

Realizing her error, Orla kept silent, leaving it to Augusta to explain.

"It's all right, Orla. You have all done so much to protect our secret. Did they—"

Orla nodded. "With Sean. They were to come to town, but we've not seen them."

"Who are *they*?" Clara asked.

"Sean is my brother," Orla said.

Augusta asked, "Clara, Mr. Donahue, is there somewhere we can speak privately?"

"The parlor appears empty," Clara said. Of Michael, she asked in a murmur, "Do you know what's going on?"

"Guesses only, so no idea yet." Michael waited for the three ladies to precede him into the parlor. There weren't doors, so he walked to the fireplace and kept his voice low when they joined him. He gave Augusta and Orla a sharp look, unable to mask both it and his impatience. "I need to know what you didn't tell us when we first rode out to the camp. Patrick said one of your own was missing, and he was quick to assure me he couldn't have been the one to set the dynamite. Is that Sean?"

Augusta nodded. "I'm sorry I was not forthcoming before; the responsibility falls on me alone. I asked the group —well, Patrick and Orla, and the rest agreed—for their aid and protection. Endangering anyone was not my intention. I expected to leave Crooked Creek much sooner."

Clara, in her soft voice, encouraged Augusta to continue.

"I heard of a small group of Irish families who had come to the valley and my husband's lumber mill seeking work. Lucas mentioned that most of them left soon after they arrived. Patrick wouldn't say exactly what happened, but I have heard some of Lucas's men speak . . . unkindly about immigrants."

"Why the secrecy?" Michael asked. "I have tried to figure out Harrigan's motive since those first men came into the inn demanding you and your daughter." He glanced at Orla. "Then the men bothering everyone at the camp made no sense. They didn't need your horses, your food, and they knew who you were." Augusta received the brunt of his subsequent reproach. "And then another man shows up, lays Elis up at the clinic, and forced Clara into a situation where she killed a man, so when you say there is more to explain, it is an understatement. None of you may have intended for anyone else to get hurt, but did it never once occur to you that we could have been better prepared to protect all involved had we known?"

Clara's fingers closed around part of his arm. "They hear

you, Michael."

He tempered his apology. "Forgive me, ladies. My frustration is not directed at you, but the situation."

Augusta's eyes fixated on Clara. "I'm so very sorry."

Michael asked Augusta, "Who are you protecting, other than yourself and your daughter?"

"Grace is my everything."

"I believe you. However, earlier, you both mentioned 'they.' Who is with your brother?"

Orla rested an arm on Augusta's shoulder. "You need to tell them." She looked at Clara and Michael. "The intentions were honorable."

Michael knew about honor and how it too often came with a double-edged blade. "It is someone else your husband's after. Is that right, Augusta?"

"Yes."

He rubbed his tired eyes. "Ladies, it's late. Please, get some sleep, and we'll talk again tomorrow. I'll bring Sheriff Peyton and Marshal Latimer over in the morning. You'll need to tell us all the whole story."

Augusta hesitated while she gave Michael's demand consideration, then nodded.

Clara remained mostly silent until both women left the parlor, leaning on each other for comfort and support.

"You don't have to tell me I was rude. I'm already aware."

"If you want to think your behavior as rude, I won't stop you. However, concern is a more apt description, and well they know it." Clara stepped in front of him. "Somehow, your indignation on my behalf has cleared away some of the earlier shock."

"I'm sorry you ever had to make that choice, Clara." Undone by her calm, Michael pulled her close and rested his brow against hers. "Taking a life stays with a person, and the anger will consume you if you let it. You'll wonder if there was any other way, any other choice."

"Shh. It will stay with me for the rest of my life." She tilted her head back and cupped his face. "And never will I regret it. I can wish it away and pretend it never happened, and I can even berate myself for an infinitesimal amount of pride that under the worst of circumstances, I was able to protect myself." Clara lifted on her toes and pressed a kiss to Michael's mouth. "Tomorrow I will no doubt cry and possibly more days to come."

He drew her hands into his. "Tomorrow isn't going to be easy."

"I know."

"You should try to sleep," he said before he gave into temptation and invited her to his room. "Tomorrow is soon enough for what's coming next."

Her soft smile lightened his heavy heart. "I will try after we see to your arm." She plucked at his sleeve. "Your wound is bleeding again."

"It's not—"

"It is. Michael, I am not ready to put into words what is happening between us, but at the rate you are accumulating injuries, we won't have a chance to find out before too long. So if it all the same to you, I will see to your arm, and if it is more than my meager skills can handle—"

He cut her off with a heady kiss and left her speechless for several seconds after they parted. When she spoke again, it was to admonish him for his grin. That he should be able to smile so wide and with such honesty was a testament to her. "It's a graze."

Clara cleared her throat and tugged on his hand for him to follow. "Then come with me."

. . .

THIS TIME, SCREAMS awakened him. Not his own, but those that haunted him. The screams of men who lost limbs, women defending their homes, and children crying for the terror to end. A sheen of sweat coated his bare chest and soaked the sheets. At some point in the night, he had kicked away the top quilts.

"Michael?"

Then he felt her light touch on his arm. "Clara."

"You were having a nightmare. I didn't know what else to do except wake you."

It hadn't been the screams, then. He fumbled for the quilts to cover himself. "You heard me?"

"Not at first. I went to the kitchen to warm some milk for Alice. Isaac returned, and we both heard you when we came up the stairs." She pressed a glass of water into his hand, and he drank deeply. He counted silently to slow his racing heart. "Where's Isaac now?"

"Waiting in case he's needed. He keeps to himself."

"Has for as long as I've known him. Most days I don't know where he is, but he always shows up." Michael noticed now the thin shaft of light from the hallway. "I'm not decent." He couldn't see her blush in the darkness but would swear the color rose in her cheeks. "Sorry." He finished off the water, and she took back the glass and set it on the small table next to the bed.

"Would you like me to light a lamp?"

He thought of his state of undress. "Better not. What time is it?"

"Half-past eleven. I doubt you slept an hour."

"It happens that way sometimes." Michael desperately wanted to hold her, to feel life other than his own. He leaned back against the iron headboard instead and raised the quilts to mid-chest. "You should go back to your room now. I'll be all right."

Clara removed herself to the foot of the bed. He'd appreciate the distance she put between them better if she wasn't still within reach. The light in the hall drifted downward until the lamp was set on the floor, and Isaac's footsteps retreated to his own room.

Clara went into the hall, carried the lamp into the room, and set it on the table. She left the door ajar. "Do want to tell me?"

"There are images you shouldn't have in your head, stories best left behind with the horrors of war."

"Have you talked with anyone? Many of the men here did not go off to war, but Casey and Peyton did and know what you're going through."

Michael studied her in the lamplight's glow. The ribbon at her neck holding the thick robe together was a pale blue. Her shapeless nightgown did nothing to hide the beautiful woman beneath, and when she sat at the foot of the bed, she curled her legs and covered them with the generous fabric.

"Sometimes Alice likes me to sit with her until she falls asleep."

The edges of his mouth twitched. "You're going to watch me sleep?"

"Stay *until* you fall asleep."

He pushed the pillow into a better position behind his back and settled against it. Right now, a douse of cold water was what he thought he needed most and wished he had thought to open the window an inch before going to sleep. The sweat on his skin dried, and as much as he wanted a bath, he wasn't ready for her to leave. "You're glowing."

Clara smiled. "You mistake me for the lamp."

"I don't want you to ever again face the danger you had to earlier."

"The chances of that—"

"Are not improbable, Clara. This place—"

"Is home." Clara stretched her legs out so they hung over the sides. "Did you not tell me you didn't want me to leave?"

"I said it and meant it."

"Well then."

"I'd rather you live." Michael knew he shouldn't tempt himself and fought to ignore reason when he held out a hand to her. Without hesitation, Clara accepted and moved to the space next to his legs. "Screams and cannon fire. Sometimes it's just one, and other times both."

"Which was it tonight?"

"Screams, flowing together until I couldn't tell one from the next. Until tonight. Just before I woke, I heard you scream in my dreams, Clara. The one I wasn't there to hear in the barn. I should have been there."

"You cannot be everywhere, Michael."

"There were too many times I wasn't there. For my mother when she was sick, for Briley when she thought she was all alone, for innocent people who died before help arrived."

"Taking a life stays with a person, you said, and I know it well enough, but what of hope, faith, and love, Michael? Those are stronger than guilt and remorse. Not always easier to embrace, yet infinitely stronger. Let those emotions stay with you, if not to erase the anguish, then to overpower it." She shifted, leaned closer, and pressed a kiss to his mouth. "I have faith enough to share while you heal."

His hand circled the back of her neck and drew her closer for another kiss, to deepen it, prolong it. When he finally released her, he felt the curve to her mouth and the hand on his chest. "You should go now, while I'm strong enough to let you."

To his surprise, Clara did not rush away. She smoothed the damp hair from his brow and kissed him once before moving off the bed and walking softly from the room.

Michael eased his legs from beneath the quilts and sheet and let his head hang low to stretch the tight muscles in his back. He made do with a small towel soaked in cold water from the wash basin to wipe the dried sweat from his body. He found extra sheets in a trunk and changed the bedding before slipping back into bed. To his amazement and relief, he slept in peace.

The following morning, Michael slipped out of the inn, nodding to Patrick Doyle who had taken over the watch during the night. Patrick's apologetic expression told Michael that Orla had shared with her husband what had transpired the evening before. They'd talk it over later. For now, Michael wanted to breathe in cold air and bask in his new niece's unadulterated beauty and innocence.

Snow crunched beneath his boots as he trudged down the road toward town. Before the nightmare and Clara's visit to his room, they had both concluded his arm did not require stitching, so she cleaned and bandaged it, and sent him to bed after the promised tea and pie. She had added a bowl of soup and two biscuits to his meal and refused to budge until he finished every morsel.

He refrained from asking her when last she ate because he doubted she was over her earlier shock as she claimed. Michael contented himself to watch her finish a healthy slice of pie and a full cup of tea. The arm, stiff from lack of movement, did not otherwise pain him. His head no longer throbbed, which he gave thanks for because Emma did not need another patient.

His nightmares, blessedly, had left him alone the remainder of the night, perhaps knowing the depth of his exhaustion. Or maybe, it was Clara. Michael accepted Clara alone could not stave off demons, yet he liked to think she was somehow responsible. After her visit, neither dream nor nightmare had disturbed his peaceful slumber.

"Let hope, faith, and love stay with you," Clara had said.

Easier to hope they would than believe they could. Their troubles weren't over yet.

Lamplight glowed through the clinic windows, lighting his way through the new day's dawn. He opened the front door to warmth and the gentle cooing of his sister's voice. Michael entered, closed the door behind him, and removed his hat and gloves before crossing to the room where Briley whispered to baby Mariah.

"Ma always said you'd take naturally to motherhood."

Briley smiled before she even raised her head to look at him. "That is the nicest thing you'll ever say to me, brother." She waved him over. "Come and say good morning to your niece."

He needed no encouragement. Michael unbuttoned his coat, shrugged out of it, and accepted the baby into the cradle of his arms.

"You'd make a fine father yourself."

An image of Clara in bed holding a baby of her own—their own—invaded his imagination with such swiftness, Michael's response was a while coming. "Someday, I hope. You're both well?"

"Considering every person who walks through the door refuses to speak of little more than the weather. Peyton finally told me about yesterday after Elis was brought into the clinic."

Michael glanced up from the baby's cherub face. "Have you heard how he is?"

"Emma said there's no change. She put Susan up in a room last night. The poor woman won't even leave to eat, so Emma's had the café deliver an extra meal."

"Where's Peyton?"

"Clete Foster, my first friend in Crooked Creek as it happens, came over an hour ago to fetch Peyton. There was a disturbance behind the general store."

A rustling in a crib on the other side of the bed gained Michael's attention. "Did you have twins and not tell me?"

"What a beastly thing to say. One was difficult enough." She lowered her voice even more. "'Tis Gavin, Emma and Casey's son. Sadie Walker often watches him, but she's helping at the general store today. Gavin's just a year, and with the hours Emma and Casey have been keeping, I told her she may as well let him stay in here with us. They won't let me do much beyond lift the bairns anyway, though that one," she shook her head slightly, while smiling at the boy, "has to be watched whenever he's awake. He seems taken with Mariah."

Michael rocked Mariah in his arms and walked around the bed to get a peek at the boy. "I thought you might have also been asleep."

Briley sighed and leaned back against the pillows, allowing her body to relax. "I sleep when Mariah sleeps, mostly."

Michael's eyes narrowed. "Why won't Emma let you out of bed?"

She waved his concern away. "She's over-cautious."

"Briley," Michael said her name in the admonishing way only an older sibling or parent could.

His sister's heavy sigh and evasion of immediate eye contact sent his concern spiraling. "Briley!"

"Don't shout! You'll wake them both and then Emma'll have your head. There were complications with the birth." Before Michael could shout again, Briley hurried to reassure him. "I'm fine. Emma is a talented doctor and both the baby and I are well. She wants me to stay a few more days. Not everyone can be Ma, up and around not an hour after each birthing."

Michael willed his pounding heart to slow. "Why didn't you tell me?"

Briley circled the air to encompass him. "And send you into a fit of worry like you are now? Well, you know now, and Emma will tell you she's never seen a healthier new mother."

"I figured Peyton would get around to telling you what happened at the camp."

Her soft laughter filled the room. "Oh, a clever one you are, Michael Donaghue, thinking to get me as angry with you as you are with me. Yes, Peyton finally told me, and were it not for the sweet bundle you're holding I'd be angrier than Ma was when you pilfered one of her pies."

Michael smoothed a finger over Mariah's cheek. "I recall you helping me eat the pie."

"And you never told her." She patted the bed for him to sit. Michael obliged by returning to her side of the bed and returning her daughter before sitting on the quilt, mindful of his sister's legs and the sudden tears in her eyes. "I knew you'd keep your promise to not leave me again."

He leaned over and kissed her cheek. "Never again."

Briley chuckled. "You rogue, you're eager to leave now."

Michael offered her a quick smile. "You know me well. Listen, Briley—"

"Don't say anything you'll regret telling me. Peyton said

he may as well deputize you with as involved as you've become." She studied him carefully. "'Tis Clara, isn't it?"

Careful of his response, Michael merely nodded, then added, "It's a lot of things. I already know this town is where I will make my home, and the people who live in it are important and worth protecting."

"Peyton won't mind me sharing this, but he once said that as much he hated the war, leaving it behind and accepting peace was difficult. Becoming sheriff is how he coped."

Michael well understood what Peyton meant and felt it himself. The drive to be a part of the activity and the danger remained with him, and he hated the echo of longing as much as he had the seemingly never-ending battles. "I'd bet you helped settle him some, too."

"So he tells me," Briley said with a cheeky grin before her smile vanished. "There are things you should know about Clara, though it's not my place to discuss them."

Michael watched the rise and fall of Gavin's small chest as the toddler slept in the cradle and then turned his loving gaze on Mariah Rose. Precious new life, symbols of new beginnings, and what two people can make. Clara had made Alice with another man, and as much as he wanted to resent Alice's father, gratitude overwhelmed him for his part in Alice's life and Clara's happiness.

He looked sideways at his sister. "You haven't seen me with Clara beyond a few minutes. What has Peyton told you?"

"We don't have secrets, Peyton and me. Even what secrets he doesn't want to share, eventually he gets around to it."

"Briley."

"Observations, Michael, nothing more."

Michael stood and leaned over to kiss his sister's cheek and brush one over his niece's forehead. He slipped into his coat before facing Briley again. "We used to talk about finding love like Ma and Da shared. It makes me happier than I can say to know you've found it with Peyton."

Moisture beaded on Briley's eyelashes.

"A definition, at least one I can think of right now, doesn't exist for how I feel about Clara." He stopped at the door, aware of movement in the next room. "I love you, Briley."

Briley kissed her baby's cheek and smiled at her brother. "I love you, too."

Michael entered the clinic's outer room, surprised to find both Emma and Casey there. They murmured amongst themselves, unable to mask the strain visible on their faces.

"Elis?" Michael guessed.

Emma nodded. "He's not worse, but still unconscious." She measured a tablespoon of ground herbs into a tea strainer and poured hot water over them from the kettle heating on the wood stove. "Casey said you'd been injured. Why didn't you tell me?"

"You've had enough to do, and it wasn't too deep. Clara saw to it."

"And the head?"

"Sounds like you talked to Hattie as well."

Emma simply stared at him, and Casey shrugged as though to tell Michael he was on his own.

"I've had a concussion before, so I knew what to watch out for. I woke up this morning, and figure that's the best I can hope for given the state of things."

Casey coughed once to cover a chuckle when his wife raised her brow.

"Imbeciles, every one of you."

Casey translated his wife's statement for Michael's benefit. "You're not the first of us to avoid telling my wife about an injury." Casey returned the kettle to the stove for her. "Peyton is dealing with a drunk who tried to break into the mercantile this morning. I planned to go to the inn soon to get some answers from the new guests about why Harrigan's men might be after them."

Emma held the warm mug in her hands while the herbs steeped. "No one is interested in my solution."

Casey gently squeezed his wife's shoulder. "You suggested I haul Harrigan into jail and shoot him when he tries to escape. I recall you even suggested how to help him escape just so I could shoot him."

A soft rose hue colored Emma's cheek, yet she lifted her chin in defiance. "And I stand by it."

"I'd be tempted if I could find him."

Michael latched onto Casey's words. "Lucas Harrigan is missing?"

"Hiding more likely. Carson is the best tracker in this area. We're going out after I stop at the inn."

"About Harrigan. I have some information that could help fill in a few holes." Michael proceeded to tell them about his conversation the evening before with Augusta and Orla. "They hadn't come down yet when I left, and they're expecting at least you, Peyton, or Casey. Whatever, or whoever they're protecting must be valuable for them to go to so much trouble."

Emma leaned up and kissed her husband. "I have to get back to Elis, and Bess will send breakfast soon. You two be careful out there." She walked from the room, leaving the men on their own.

"Your wife is a wonder."

Casey nodded and secured his hat in place. "You don't know the half of it. Truth is, she and most of the women in this town are stronger than we are. They're just kind enough not to point it out."

CHAPTER 18

"One woman staying at the inn mentioned an Irish custom of placing a candle in the window on Christmas Eve as a symbol to welcome strangers and remember those who are far away. Alice has asked to light a candle for you this year."

- Clara Stowe to her parents in a letter not yet sent

CLARA'S KNOCK AT Michael's door went unanswered. Most of the previous day blurred in her memory, and what remained left her stomach muscles tense as she stared at the door for an extended time.

She remembered the kiss and Michael's embrace. It was impossible not to. She still felt the ghost of his warmth around her, and the palm she rubbed over her heart did little to diminish the longing.

Clara backed away from the door and made her way down the back staircase where she followed the aroma of ham sizzling in cast iron and something with cinnamon and cloves baking in the oven. Neasa scooped ladles of pancake batter into a skillet while Orla flipped the ham slices. The women laughed and talked in comfortable camaraderie and did not notice when Clara stepped under the threshold between the hall and kitchen.

"It smells wonderful."

The women quieted and their smiles grew hesitant, filling Clara with remorse. "Please do not stop on my account. I planned to ask Bess from the café if she could spare some time to cook here until Susan returns."

Orla set aside the fork she'd been using. "I hope you do not mind. We're of a mind to earn our keep. My husband had one of the men tend to the animals, and we'll be repaying you—"

"Excuse my ungracious words just then. It is a surprise and a blessing to find you hard at work so early. You would starve were it left to me to cook the meals. Please consider this your home while you are here."

Their smiles returned, and Orla stepped a little closer to Clara. "Patrick and I spoke last night, and we are sorry for any difficulty we have caused. None of us imagined how helping Augusta could lead to such tragedy, and whatever we can do to make it right, please tell us."

A small and frustrated part of Clara wanted to admonish the woman, until a louder voice of reason compelled her to say, "Your kindness does you credit, and the choices that led us here will work themselves out. I expect Michael will be here soon with either the marshal or sheriff and after the whole of it is explained, we can work together and formulate a plan." Clara accepted a teacup from Neasa, and before taking a sip, added, "It is Augusta's story we need to hear. Have you seen her?"

Each of the women replied they had not yet. Grace came to their room not fifteen minutes ago to walk with Alice to the dining room. She drew comfort knowing Augusta would not leave without her daughter. Clara drank half her tea before setting the cup on the long, center table. "Susan and Elis keep the stores well stocked, but if there is any item or ingredient you need, let me know and I'll see it's delivered from the general store or ordered."

"You've done so much already," Neasa said. "We were set to spend the winter out there in those cabins, and while we've surely lived in worse, though not through winters like this, it's grateful we are to have a warm place to rest. Had Harrigan's men not kept coming back, and if our men's pride . . . well, we're indebted to you, Mrs. Stowe."

It was not the first time her family's wealth caused Clara some embarrassment. Not a single second of her life had she gone without, nor would Alice ever experience the pinch of hunger or the lack of . . . anything. "My friends call me Clara." She smiled at both women and returned to the hall. "I will not be long."

She bundled herself into boots and her long, wool cape before leaving through the back door. The barn was secured, and Clara appreciated someone had seen to the animals. Her knowledge extended to providing food, water, and shelter, and never again would she take for granted how much Elis and Susan accomplished in a day. She whispered a silent prayer for Elis's recovery and to ease Susan's worry, though worry they would until Elis returned to them.

Pine trees burdened with snow and dormant bushes covered in red berries to nourish birds through winter dotted the landscape between the inn and the small cabin nestled fifty feet behind the barn. Clara walked through the cozy log structure once to ensure it was clean, furnished, and well-stocked for Elis. The whole of the structure would almost fit into the inn's generous parlor, and yet it seemed to suit the man who lovingly tended the property.

Smoke curled from the chimney and hastened Clara's walk. She stomped the snow off her boots and hesitated momentarily on the stamp-sized porch. She owned the property, but it was his space, and she silently promised to be away as soon as she found a spare set of clothes since the shirt and pants he had worn to the clinic had to be cut away.

To her surprise, the door did not budge when she rotated the handle, and to her knowledge, Elis never put a lock on the door. She pushed against the barrier again, this time gaining two inches. Society functions may not have prepared her for exertions, but working around the inn had . . . sort of. Clara shoved again, this time opening the door enough to squeeze through. The toe of a boot hit the corner of a trunk, the same trunk that seconds ago had kept her from an easy entry.

"Hello?"

A woman's touch came to Clara's mind, and she wondered how often Susan brought flowers or baked goods to the cabin. The furnishings appeared in as good condition as when she had them brought in. A crazy quilt was folded neatly over the back of a padded chair, and a festive vase of pine branches and twigs sat on the eating table. She should have been cold in the room but was saved that fate by the fire burning strong in the hearth.

"Whoever is here, show yourself now." Clara allayed her fears by telling herself that someone out to harm would not have bothered with a fire or to keep the room tidy. "It is far better to talk to me than to have the sheriff come and drag you out."

The last got her the desired, and unexpected, result.

"I can explain, Mrs. Stowe."

Tall and stalwart, Isaac stood before her, so it was without concern when she immediately shifted focus to the woman next to him. Swept-back curls of rich ebony framed a heart-shaped face with smooth almond-hued skin. Eyes of warm honey conveyed shared amounts of uncertainty and hopefulness. What Clara could see of her dark dress appeared in good condition and sufficiently warm. Nestled securely against her body, a blanketed bundle moved in the woman's arms.

"I reckoned, ma'am, we'd be gone before anyone was wise to us. I was just waitin' on Michael to explain why I'd be leaving."

Clara gave Isaac and the woman equal scrutiny. She already knew and trusted Isaac because Michael trusted him, and he'd given her no reason to change her mind. The woman had not arrived with Michael and Isaac, so how did Isaac meet her? And how did she end up in Elis's cabin? Questions mounted, and she brushed them aside to address Isaac's last statement.

"You will not be leaving, at least not anytime soon. It is literally freezing outside." To the woman, Clara asked, "Please, will you tell me your name?"

She remained silent until Isaac leaned closer to speak softly to her. "You can trust Mrs. Stowe." The woman steadied her stance and looked directly at Clara. Her soft voice held a hint of southern gentility, which had Clara studying her closer.

"Lela."

"And in your arms?"

She held the bundle closer to her breast. "He is Keldon, after my father."

"And your family name?"

To this, both Lela and Isaac said nothing.

"I suppose it does not matter. How did you come to be here, Lela?"

Isaac said, "I can explain it, ma'am, least what I've learned. Elis, he came to when we took him to the clinic. It was real quick like and I don't reckon anyone else heard. He said, 'Cabin behind the inn.' God's truth ma'am."

"I believe you, Isaac. Your integrity is not in question."

The man visibly relaxed.

"Lela, I know well enough the strength of a mother protecting her child, and yet to have come . . ." Like ice crystals slowly forming on a windowpane to create a pattern, answers to some questions manifested.

"Clara!"

All at once concerned and relieved, Clara held out a hand to stop Isaac and Lela from leaving the room. "You'll come to no harm from me or them, Lela." Over her shoulder, she called out to Michael. In seconds, he was inside with Casey directly behind him. Both breathed heavily, the air from their lungs visible as they exhaled.

Michael moved to Clara's side, sparing the other two occupants a cursory glance before asking her, "You all right?"

"Yes." She wanted to say more. Instead, she saved her words for a more prudent time.

Casey walked deeper into the room, his tall frame stopping three feet in front of Clara and Michael. He took in the room's layout before considering Isaac and the woman. He removed his hat long enough to slap it against his thigh and when he sighed, it filled the silence. "Isaac. This is unexpected."

"Isaac started to explain before you arrived. It seems Elis said something about this cabin during a brief moment of consciousness." She turned to Isaac. "I assume you found Lela here when you arrived?"

"Yes, ma'am. The man who—" Lela shook her head frantically at Isaac who told her it was all right. "The man who brought her to town, well, she says he told her to hide. She hasn't seen him since."

Casey asked, "Was this man Irish by chance?"

After a few seconds, Lela nodded.

"Sean? From the old cabin camp?"

Again, she confirmed.

"The broad view of things is becoming clear. Safe to guess why Harrigan wants you back, ma'am." Casey considered the baby in her arms, who yawned and then settled back into a contented sleep. "Is Lucas Harrigan the father?"

"The baby is mine."

"I do not doubt you, ma'am." Casey said to Clara, "There's the law and then there's what's going to happen. She and the baby will need a safe place to stay, and that's not in this cabin. It's too isolated back here. Augusta and Grace . . . Clara?" He followed her gaze back to Lela, whose eyes widened at the mention of Augusta. "All right then. You've confirmed you know Augusta, or at least know of her, and may I assume she knows of you?"

Isaac stepped a foot forward. "I reckon Mr. Elis planned to help her and I aim to see it through. They'll be safe here with me if it's okay with Mrs. Stowe."

No one mentioned Isaac's injured leg or asked how he planned to protect them on his own if any of Harrigan's men came upon the cabin. Smoke from the fire might pique someone's interest and place Lela and the baby in danger.

"I admire your convictions, and I don't aim to thwart them, but we need a solid plan because as long as Harrigan is looking for her, the townspeople aren't safe, either," Casey said, as he made a path to the door.

Casey's tone allowed for no argument or counter-suggestions, and neither did Clara's. "Wait. Casey, might we speak outside, please?"

No one came to Casey's defense, though Michael stifled a smile as he followed them outside. There was barely enough room for the three of them to stand comfortably, which proved beneficial since their combined heat made the cold tolerable. "It is not as convenient, but the main house is crowded and not conducive right now to the questioning you likely have in mind. I know you will treat her with the utmost care," she quickly added before continuing, "though I cannot help thinking more of the answers you seek, that we all seek, will come from Augusta at this juncture. She no longer has a reason to remain silent. If Lela is to Harrigan who we no doubt suspect, then subjecting her to so many people in yet another new environment—"

Casey's raised hand silenced her more effectively than words. His response was several seconds in the making. "You had me at 'wait,' though I appreciate your staunch defense."

Michael stepped closer to Clara when she shivered. "You're both right, but Clara, there's a good chance the man who brought Lela here is now dead. Harrigan seems willing to order the murder of anyone who stands between him and them. It's even more dangerous now that Harrigan can't be found."

Clara's eyebrows drew together as she turned wide eyes on Casey. "You can't find him?"

"For the time being. As soon as we talk to Augusta and get the rest of the story, Carson and I will head out to look for him. He could be missing, hiding, or making his way here to deal with Lela himself."

"Trust is difficult to grant, especially when a stranger asks, and we're asking a lot of Lela." Clara pleaded with each man in turn, first with her eyes, then her words. "You have both seen firsthand what Lela and her son might have endured, so tell me, is it truly better to force Lela into another unwanted or difficult situation? She has been through enough."

"You're not wrong, Clara, but we can't protect her out here."

Clara appealed to Casey with the only logic she had left. "Out here, she won't draw notice. Elis won't be using his cabin for at least a few days—God willing he'll wake up soon. The fewer people who know Lela and the baby are here, the better." When Casey did not argue, Clara rubbed her stiff hands together. Michael nudged her back inside ahead of him and left Casey to follow.

Michael carried the chairs from the eating table and placed them next to the fire. Casey invited Lela to sit in the cushioned chair while the rest of them took their seats.

Tension hovered between the cabin's occupants until Clara broke the initial unsettlement. "You may stay here for now, Lela. Elis takes more of his meals at the main house, so we'll send food out, and we have milk for the baby as you need it."

When Lela said nothing, Casey took over. "We can protect you better if you tell me what I need to know. Help us understand. I'll share whatever you tell us with the sheriff later, so you only have to explain it once, at least for now."

Lela rose, her hold on her son shaky. Isaac steadied them and coaxed her back to the sofa. "You don't know what you're asking, Marshal."

Casey removed his hat and propped it on his knee. Without the brim's shadow blocking his eyes, he waited for Lela to look his way. When she did, he offered her the only assurance he could. "I realize what I'm asking, and I promise no matter what happens next, no harm will come to you or your son."

After the seconds ticked by into a full minute, Lela dipped her head. "Ask."

"Is Lucas Harrigan the father?"

"Yes, sir."

"How did you come to be at the cabins?"

"I don't want no one else in trouble."

Casey pointed to the blanket on the back of the chair. "Isaac, would you mind unfolding that for Lela? It's still not warmed back up in here after we let some of the cold air in." While Isaac did as asked and covered Lela and the baby with the crazy quilt, Casey addressed Lela's concern. "As far as I can tell, no one who has provided you shelter has committed a crime. They seem like good, honest people."

"I put laudanum in his whiskey. He came around too quick so I hit him over the head. He should've died." Lela pressed her face against her bundled son. "He never dies."

CHAPTER 19

"After Alice was born and we learned of Gideon's death, you called me courageous. I denied it. Fear filled every waking hour, and were it not for my precious daughter, and your support, fear would have crippled me. Excitement shadowed my unease when I left home, but here, in Crooked Creek, I have found my courage because I see it every day in the women who call this place home."

Clara Stowe in a letter to her parents not yet sent

ALICE AND GRACE wore smiles and a dusting of flour when Clara, Michael, and Casey entered the inn through the back door. It was the doorway Clara considered the entrance to the home while the front was the entrance to the inn, and it seemed fitting to be greeted by such an inviting picture.

"Look, Mama! We're making cookies!" Alice held up one of her gingerbread men cutouts.

"And doing such a beautiful job of it, my love." Clara stepped into the kitchen to make room in the hallway for the men. Alice and Grace tilted their heads in unison and curiosity.

Orla encouraged the girls to finish cutting out their shapes before rounding the center table to speak with Clara. "Augusta is fetching an apron from the laundry." Orla looked at the faces beyond Clara. "What's happened?"

"We know about Lela and her son."

Orla sucked in a breath and pressed a hand to her stomach. "Sean explained?"

Clara said to Casey and Michael, "Please go ahead into the parlor. We can move to another part of the house if anyone is there."

"No one is in there." Orla wiped flour off her hands. "Three men are out looking for work, and my husband is with your sheriff. We want to help anywhere we can while we're here."

Casey thanked Orla for the information, nodded once to Clara, and walked down the hall with Michael. Once alone, Clara spoke quietly to Orla. "There is more to the telling than I can share right now. However, Sean was not with Lela. We are not sure where he is."

Tears filled Orla's eyes in a rush, and she swayed a little before Clara held her steady. "Casey will send men out to look for him."

In a stuttered whisper, Orla said, "He volunteered to go. The men from the lumber mill kept coming to the cabins. Sean and Patrick thought we'd be safer if Lela wasn't there, so Sean volunteered to sneak away with her."

Without hesitation, Clara wrapped her arms around Orla. "I am so very sorry." When she pulled back, she searched her pockets, produced a clean handkerchief, and handed it over. "Do not lose hope, or faith."

"He's alone out there, and it is so cold."

Clara did not contradict her. "Yes, and many survive. Sean and Lela, with her son, made it here alive, though how, in the snow with a baby, I cannot imagine."

"They rode out. Sean took a horse."

"He has a horse, then." Clara clutched Orla's arm. "Good. I will tell Casey. Whyever did you not come to town when it was offered so many times before? It cannot be charity as others have thought."

"That is part of it. The men are too proud sometimes and were told we could find no work in Crooked Creek."

Clara imagined Harrigan or one of his men spreading the falsehood. Though their small mountain village was not at risk of growing more than a few souls a year, and jobs were scarce, rewards existed for those willing to work hard.

Orla clutched at her apron, leaving fist-sized wrinkles in the fabric. "We took them in because our conscience required it of us. Augusta asked, and it is what God would have wanted us to do."

"But Augusta and Grace did not stay with you."

Orla shook her head. "Augusta left, hoping the men would follow her and lead them away from Lela and her baby."

"I understand. They followed her, but when they couldn't find what they wanted here, they returned to your camp."

"Yes."

"Your brother was right to take Lela and her son away. Good men, as your husband and brother surely are, wouldn't have handed a mother and child over, and they had to protect their own families." When Clara looked up again, Augusta stood in the kitchen entry. "Where are the rest of the children?" Augusta asked.

Orla wiped at her eyes and cheeks. "Sleeping or resting."

Clara doubted sleep came easily in the cold cabins with freezing night air creeping between gaps in the boards. "Did everyone have a chance to eat? There is plenty."

"Yes, and thank you. All the food and expense . . . we'll find a way to repay you."

She understood pride would not allow them to accept the food and lodging as a gift, so she agreed. "When you can. For now, why not finish the cookies with the girls? I'm sure the other children will enjoy them when they come downstairs again. Also, I need to ask another favor."

"Of course."

"Will you prepare two baskets of food? One with whatever was served at breakfast, and another with bread, preserves, and whatever else you find in the pantry and larder that will fit. The baskets can be left on the sideboard." Clara looked at Augusta. "It is time, Augusta."

"Where?"

"In the parlor. If you don't mind, I will join you."

"I'd be grateful." Augusta removed the clean apron, kissed her daughter's cheek, and followed Clara from the kitchen. When they entered the parlor, Casey and Michael were still standing, and only after Augusta lowered herself into a wingback chair next to the fire, did Casey sit across from her.

Michael remained standing, though moved closer to the chair Clara now occupied. Orla appeared minutes later carrying a tray weighted with a teapot, four mugs, and a tray of thin pound cake slices. Clara stood immediately. Michael lifted the burden from Orla and carried it to a small table.

Orla poured the first two mugs, while Clara filled the others and helped pass them around.

"I had hot water in the kettle and found the pound cake wrapped in the cupboard. I hope you don't mind."

"It was thoughtful, Orla, thank you."

Orla peered at Casey. "Marshal, my husband and I speak for my family and friends when I say we don't regret helping Augusta, Lela, and their children, and we would do it again."

"Thank you, Mrs. Doyle."

With an encouraging smile for Augusta, Orla left them to sit in silence.

"I will testify against my husband if necessary, if I'm allowed."

All eyes turned toward Augusta.

"We're not in England, so yes, but let's hope it doesn't come to that," Casey said. "Let's start with what events brought you here, and we'll go from there. First, you should know we've met and spoken with Lela."

Tea from the cup in Augusta's grip spilled over the rim. Clara quickly and gently took the cup from her and handed her the linen from the tea tray.

"She is safe, then? And the baby?"

"They are both well," Clara assured her.

With hands trembling, Augusta sagged into the chair. "I have one condition, Marshal Latimer, before I tell you anything."

"I'm listening."

"Grace hears none of this. No discussion of what I am going to tell you reaches her ears. If it is spoken of, and she enters a room, it stops. I will not have her knowing what her father has done. She's too young."

Casey nodded, as did Clara and Michael.

Augusta took in a fortifying breath as she struggled to find the right words. After a few starts and stops, she began with, "I learned of Lela three weeks ago when my husband brought her to live with us, after he returned from a trip to Georgia."

No one reacted, so Augusta continued. "My husband was not a man to own slaves, which always surprised me since he seemed to disdain their existence—their differences from us. When I asked him why she was there, he told me it was not my place to ask. I saw the baby, noticed Lucas's . . . lustful gazes for her, and I knew."

Augusta sat straighter and stared into the fire. "I also saw how much Lela hated him, how much she wanted to leave. She told me her former owner gave her as a gift to Lucas, and at the time, did not understand she was free."

Clara settled an arm around Augusta's shoulders. "You don't have to finish right now."

"Yes, I do. I need to say it so you understand why I had no choice."

GRAY CLOUDS BLENDED with the darkening sky like ink swirling into water. Two hours earlier, the faintest hint of snowflakes drifted from those angry clouds, masking the sunset and pushing anyone outdoors to shelter. The evening meal warmed bellies before weary bodies climbed the stairs to their rooms. Clara put her daughter to bed, and Michael stood in the hall while she read Alice passages from Hans Andersen's, *The Snow Queen.*

He returned to the lower floor, unable to find the will to seek sleep. Only a short time later did he sense Clara was not where she should be.

Michael found her on a window seat in the cozy library. Only a whisper of light filtered through the window, leaving her in shadows. Just as he'd known where to find her, drawn to her by an unseen force, she knew he was there, though he made no sound to warn of his presence. Her soft voice severed the silence when she spoke, though she continued to stare out the crystallized window.

"What demon possesses a man to whip his wife? The question won't leave my thoughts, and I cannot conjure an answer that makes sense save he is indeed possessed."

Michael crossed the rug, his boots muffled by the thick wool, and leaned against the wall next to the window. "She shouldn't have shown you her back."

"Have you ever seen whip scars healed over?"

"Yes." Michael filled the space on the seat next to her. Clara pulled her feet farther under her skirts to give him more room. "Once."

"Isaac?"

Michael gave his head a soft shake. "The doctor he was working with when he found me wounded treated Isaac like a man, not a possession. Freed Isaac soon after he purchased his papers. Isaac stayed on to learn about healing and because, at the time, he felt safe there, and the doctor had no other family. No, not Isaac. It was a younger man in North Carolina. A freed slave trying to make his way north. Another soldier and I were scouting and came across him hanging in a barn, his back stripped bare, flayed. We found a doctor willing to treat his wounds and nurse him back to health."

"Did you ever see him again after?"

Unshed moisture glistened in Clara's eyes, sympathy, deep and uncontrived. "No, he went underground with sympathizers who could help him get north." Michael leaned against the cold window to cool the anger from his memory. "That was a year before the war ended."

"Augusta showed me because she wanted evidence of her

husband's doings to be known." Clara lifted her face to look at Michael. "Twice she suffered from his whip trying to help Lela and her son escape, the second time too soon after for the first wounds to heal, and despite failing, she tried again."

"And succeeded in getting all of them out." Michael covered the hands she had rested on her knees with his own. Warmth from his skin transferred to hers. "They're alive and safe, and they'll stay as protected as we can make them."

"Augusta said her husband is obsessed with Lela. He will continue his search for her and send more men after her. He must know she is here." Clara twined her fingers with Michael's. "Even during four years of war, I never had cause to worry about Alice's safety, and now I fear if she leaves her room. Christmas will be here soon. She should be riding in a sleigh and helping to hang holly. In Connecticut, we would visit the sick at the hospital and deliver baskets of Christmas sweets to neighbors.

"My mother loved her balls and social gatherings, but every year in December since the war began, we packed up baskets with as much of the dried fruits and jams we could put together. Our cook baked for days ahead of our visit, and we spent hours reading to the wounded soldiers sent home from the war. Alice came with us last year, and she brought a smile of joy to every soldier's face." Clara pulled her hands from beneath his and hugged him close. "I want her to learn to be strong like Emma, Hattie, and Briley. I want her to learn to love this land and embrace the people."

Michael heard the struggle in her voice and saw it in her clutched hands and tightened muscles. She didn't see Alice already was all those things because of Clara.

"Alice can have any life she wants. You've shown her there's another world."

"A dangerous world, far more than I ever imagined it

would be." The tears she harbored, at last, slipped from her eyes and glided down her cheeks. "He whipped her, Michael. Hearing of such things is nothing compared to seeing the result. What will he do with Lela if he finds her?"

"Nothing." Michael slipped an arm beneath her legs and another around her back. Overlooking her shock, he lifted her onto his lap. "Harrigan will do nothing to her and the baby or to you or Alice." He tucked loose strands of hair behind her ear and kissed her lips. Her mouth tasted faintly of salt from her tears, and he kissed those away. "You didn't make a mistake coming here, Clara, or making a life for you and Alice in Crooked Creek. Whatever your original intentions, your inn has become a haven for many."

She relaxed against him, her head resting on his shoulder. He inhaled the woodsy floral scent of her hair and held her close.

"Arguments to convince my parents varied from the desire for adventure to fulfilling a promise to Gideon, but ultimately, too many people knew the truth."

"What truth?" When Clara lay against him saying nothing, he lifted her chin and tilted his head to the side to better see her. "What truth?"

"I am not a widow."

He allowed a few minutes to pass to process the impact of Clara's candor. His imagination did not lend itself to the goings-on of Clara's former life, of gentility and refinement, but he could imagine the whispers in private circles and the shame awaiting Alice if the truth of her birth became widespread. In Crooked Creek, Clara was simply a widow and Alice's father a soldier who died in battle.

"It is the only lie I have protected."

"Did you love him?"

"With all my heart."

Michael expected pain to manifest itself, yet none came, only gratitude for the man who gave her Alice. "Then there is no lie. Alice was born of your love as she deserved to be."

"Lela was not so lucky."

He wondered what had brought her to the confession, and now he understood. "Lela survived the worst of it, and now she and her son will have a chance." Michael kissed her brow and brought her close again. "Because you gave shelter to two women and their children, they will all have another chance at a life of their choosing."

Heavy snowflakes formed a curtain beyond the window, and each icy flake disappeared into the night. Michael estimated half an hour or more had passed since he had come upon Clara in her small library. The glow of a single oil lamp assured Michael that one of the men was on watch.

"Christmas was my mother's favorite time of year. The cottage would be cleaned: every corner, piece of furniture, and utensil. Afterwards, she sent us out to gather holly and evergreens for wreaths and to set around the house. Briley always made a new lace cloth for the table and knit us each a new sweater for Christmas. I remember every detail of our last Christmas in Ireland, and I can still picture my mother and father dancing in front of the fire after they thought we'd already gone to sleep."

"I am so sorry you lost them both."

"We didn't, not really. They live in us like Gideon will live on in Alice."

Clara tried to move off Michael's lap, and he let her only so far so he could still hold her. "Did I say something wrong?"

Her mouth curved into a beatific smile. "Something right. It does not bother you."

She said it as a statement rather than a question. Michael answered to erase any lingering doubt she might carry. "I am proud to know you, Clara Stowe." He stood and lifted her to her feet. "Traditions are important. Tomorrow, we'll take Alice to pick out a perfect tree. The clinic will have to work for a hospital, and Alice can share her smiles with Briley, Elis, and Susan. And you can still make up those Christmas baskets if you want. I'm sure plenty of folks around here would appreciate one."

Clara bit the inside of her cheek and the smooth skin on her forehead wrinkled. Michael wanted to kiss them away.

"With the inn full, Elis's condition uncertain, and—"

Michael touched a finger to her mouth. "Everything will keep. Alice deserves a peaceful Christmas and you need to remember the good things about living in Montana because I don't want you to leave. Selfish and presumptuous of me, and I'm okay with both."

He watched her digest his words and silently prayed she would accept them.

"Tomorrow then."

CHAPTER 20

"The foyer now smells like a forest. Fresh cut from nature this morning, our Christmas tree awaits the trimmings. I remember my fifth Christmas when Father lifted me high in the air to hang my first ornament almost by myself. Alice has asked to put the angel on the tree this year."

- Clara Stowe in a letter to her parents not yet sent

THEIR SMALL TREE-HUNTING party numbered seven by the time they left the inn. A sleigh from the livery carried Clara, Alice, Augusta, Grace, and Patrick's son, with Michael handling the reins and Patrick on horseback. Rian's lead was tied to the sleigh with enough length to allow the horse to walk comfortably alongside.

Stepping away from their troubles is what Michael planned for the outing, though he was not careless enough not to be prepared. Both he and Patrick carried rifles and sidearms, kept discreetly within easy reach and out of sight from the children, who snuggled beneath blankets and delighted in the jingle of small bells Michael had attached to the harnesses.

No more than one quarter mile away from the inn is what Michael promised, and with help from Peyton on where best to go, they rode the sleigh just shy of their mark. Several clusters of pine trees dotted the snow-covered landscape. A lone log cabin to the north stood tall in the center of a meadow. From its position, the occupants could see who was coming from all directions.

"Over there is Peyton and Briley's home."

"His suggestion makes sense now." Impressive, Michael mused and considered the commitment to build a fine house of its size in an unpredictable place. Not unlike Clara's inn. "Is this their land, too?"

"I think so. I've not been here in the winter, and the snow makes every structure or animal appear farther away. Somewhere east of the cabin, there is another road between town and their house."

Michael slowed the team and sleigh to a gentle stop close to the treeline. With a smile for the children, he pointed to the pines. "We need a good one for the inn. Do you think you three can find the perfect tree?"

In unison, the three children stood and waited to be helped from the sleigh. Augusta was content to remain under a blanket. Michael held out his hands for Clara, and when she leaned into him, he lifted her, held on for a few seconds longer than necessary, and set her on her feet.

"I saw a twinge."

"You don't weigh enough for me to twinge."

Clara poked lightly at his shoulder. "Your injured arm, Michael. You twinged. Twice."

His first instinct was to wave off her concern, yet he suspected an indifferent course of action would earn him no favor with her. "The muscle is still a little tight is all."

"Even with the liniment Emma gave you to use?"

"Well, now—"

"I found it!"

Michael was saved from finishing his response by Alice's excited shout. She waved to them from three yards away. Grace and Patrick's son flanked her, and all wore grins. "Well, let's see what they've found for you."

Patrick chuckled when they approached. "I talked them out of their first choice." He pointed over his shoulder at a tree almost as tall as the inn. "This is their second choice."

Eight feet tall, with full branches of pine needles, the tree stood proudly between two saplings and emitted a sweet and refreshing fragrance.

"It's perfect." Clara straightened the wool hat on Alice's head. "You've done a beautiful job. Now, you three need to stand away so it can be cut. Once it's set up at home, we can decide how to decorate it." Clara bent low and said to her daughter, "How about we find another tree, just a little smaller, for Elis's cabin. We can decorate it for him so his home looks like Christmas when he returns."

"Is Mr. Elis coming home soon, Mama?"

Clara tweaked Alice's little rosy nose. "We will keep praying he does, my love."

Alice raised both her arms above her head. "Time to cut the tree!"

"I'll fetch the axes," Patrick said with a laugh, and left them alone with the children who were already discussing what should go on the tree.

The children remained unaware as the soft breeze carried

raised voices from near the sleigh. Michael touched Clara's arm in passing. "Stay here with them."

When he approached the sleigh, Augusta and Patrick quieted in the middle of their argument. "Is there a problem?" Michael lifted the axes from beneath a canvas tarp in the sleigh.

Patrick shook his head, his gaze still on Augusta. "It can wait."

"Do I need to be worried?" This question he directed to Patrick.

"No."

He held out an axe to Patrick. "We're going to cut down this tree, and whatever is going on here, we'll deal with as soon as we get back. Not one word in front of the children. Understand?"

Augusta's heated face slowly softened. "Don't be cross with him. He is justified in his anger. Like he said, though, it can wait."

Michael returned with Patrick and at Clara's questioning glance, he whispered, "When we get back to the inn." Unwilling to spoil the outing, Michael kept the children talking while he and Patrick chopped at the trunk. It was not too thick, and the pine fell after a few well-placed blows.

"What about a tree for the baby?"

Clara peered down at her daughter. "You mean Briley's baby?" Alice remained ignorant of Lela and her son, and Clara hoped to keep it that way.

Alice bobbed her head. "The baby needs a tree."

"Darling, the baby will be home by Christmas and have a tree there."

"But what about a tree now?"

When Clara looked his way, Michael returned her question with a light shrug. "Arm's still working." He bent over to ask Alice, "Let's get Mariah Rose her first tree after we cut one down for Elis. Remember she's little, so she needs a little tree."

"A baby tree!" And so Alice and Grace dashed from sapling to sapling until they decided on a four-foot pine, its green a shade lighter than the larger tree.

"This one," Grace called out.

"And this one!" Alice hugged the branch of the one right next to it. "For Mr. Elis."

Clara moved closer until their arms touched, and while he liked to think it was just to be near him, the shivers coursing through her indicated otherwise. "Why don't you go back to the sleigh. We'll just be a few minutes."

"And miss more of those infectious smiles? Absolutely not." She tilted her head back to look at the top of another taller tree. "Wouldn't it be better to cut the top off of one rather than chop a little one? It's so adorable."

Michael choked back a laugh when he realized she was serious. "We're not going to chop it down. We're going to dig these two up."

"You didn't bring a shovel."

He held up the ax. "This will work. The roots aren't too deep, yet."

Michael walked to the tree and explained to Patrick what he wanted. It took longer to dig around the root ball of the two smaller pines than it had to cut down the first one. The children watched, asked questions, and Alice even asked if she could help. Thankfully, they had finished up by then, so Michael made it up to her by telling her she could help wrap the root balls. They quickly loaded the trees into the sleigh, and Alice insisted on sitting next to the baby tree.

Grace climbed under the blanket with her mother and Patrick lifted his son onto the saddle to sit in front of him.

The tension between Augusta and Patrick was obvious without the distraction of cutting down trees.

Clara sat as close to Michael as possible on the front bench and shared her blanket with him. "What happened between them, I wonder?" she whispered.

"I don't know yet. We'll find out once the trees are unloaded and the children occupied." He encouraged the team onward. "I had hoped we could forget the troubles for a little while at least."

Clara tapped his leg beneath the blanket. "Look at Alice."

He did, and at first was struck once again by how much she resembled her mother. Alice's rosy cheeks and flaxen hair heightened her radiant smile. "She's going to break every young man's heart in ten years' time."

"Twenty years, perhaps."

The fleeting image he'd had of Clara in bed holding a new baby of her own flitted through his mind once again. A child should have a sibling or two. Alice deserved a brother or sister who would love her as much as Michael and Briley loved each other. "Yeah, twenty sounds about right."

Stillness greeted them upon their return to the inn. In contrast, down the road, the midmorning sun had brought folks from the shelter of their houses. Smoke from the blacksmith's forge and various chimneys rose into the sky as people hurried from one place to the next, bundled against the cold. Word of events at the inn would have spread throughout the town, yet people moved through each day as though nothing in their mountain village had changed.

Michael took in the scene's peacefulness before turning back to study the inn and watch the front door. Each adult staying under Clara's roof had been assigned a task, at their request, as partial repayment for their food and lodging, and yet smoke curled up from only one chimney. The quiet matched the stillness of their silence.

"Where would everyone have gone?" The soft creak of the front door and Peyton's appearance on the porch answered Clara's question.

Michael stood up and jumped from the sleigh. "Briley?"

"She's fine, I promise. Emma said I can take her and the baby home today, but I'd rather keep her close to town for a few more days, until I can hire someone to help around the house and be there when I'm not. I'm not here about Briley, though. Clara, we need to talk."

Even before Michael saw the color fade from Clara's face, leaving no evidence even of the cold, the soft sympathy in Peyton's voice told him what he'd come to say.

Clara clutched Michael's arms when he lifted her to the ground, and she kept a tight hold.

Patrick said to Michael, "I'll take care of things here."

"Mama?"

Clara regained her senses enough to smile up at her daughter. "We will unload the tree soon, darling. I'll just make sure the space is cleared away."

"We have to take the baby tree to Briley and the other one to Mr. Elis."

"We will, just as soon as the big tree is set up inside," Michael assured her. He walked with Clara's arm looped through his to the front porch and into the house.

When the door closed behind them, Clara said to Peyton, "We don't have much time. It's Elis, isn't it?"

Peyton's hesitation gave her the answer she thought he came to deliver. "He's not dead." Clara nearly collapsed in her relief. She wound an arm over her stomach. "I'm so sorry, Clara. I should have assured you straight out."

"What's happened then?"

"He's still alive, but Emma thinks he's in a coma. Nothing she's done has brought him out of it."

She reached around to find a place to sit, and not finding one, gave the bulk of her weight temporarily over to Michael. "I should be there with him." Clara lifted tear-filled eyes to look at Peyton. "Susan?"

"Susan's mainly why I'm here. She won't leave him. Won't even let go of his hand, and Emma can't coax her away to rest or even to eat or drink."

"I need to go to her. I need to—"

The patter of children's shoes sounded on the porch before the door whooshed open.

Michael hurried her from the front hall into the parlor where Patrick's cousin was setting the fire.

"Oh, sorry these aren't done yet, Mrs. Stowe. The kitchen . . ." He noticed Clara's tears. "Are you okay, Mrs. Stowe?"

"What happened in the kitchen, Jack?" Clara asked.

"The water pump stopped working, ma'am. We got it fixed; just a bit frozen."

"Thank you."

He nodded. "I'll see to the other fires first and give you folks some privacy."

The cold room made Michael wish Jack had finished the fire before leaving. He sat Clara down in a soft chair and added kindling and wood himself to the glowing embers from the previous fire. Once the kindling caught flame, he knelt in front of her.

"Thank you." She wiped at her tears and searched for a handkerchief in her pockets. "I don't want Alice to see me like this. It won't be long before she seeks me out. If Elis doesn't awaken . . ."

Michael took over the search for the handkerchief when Clara's hands kept fumbling with the cloak. He withdrew it from her skirt pocket and dabbed at her eyes and cheeks before handing it over. "Patrick can see to the trees. I'll take you over to the clinic."

Clara shook her head and forced her breathing to slow. "Not yet. For Alice, we need to do this together. Susan will want to be alone with him for as long as possible."

"Is that how it was for you when Gideon died?"

"Elis isn't dead." The "yet" hung in the air between them. "Yes. Having people around made it worse somehow. Except Alice. Her existence was my only comfort in the early days."

Michael stood, pressed a kiss to her brow, and helped her to her feet.

"They never said it so I could hear, and Elis is a bit older, but I believe he and Susan care—no, care deeply—for each other. I hoped . . . her children will need to be told. They'll want to be here with her."

Michael glanced over Clara's shoulder when Alice called out for her mother. "Where are they?"

"Salt Lake City, with cousins."

He rubbed her arms then raised her chin. "Your tears are gone enough. We'll send a telegram after we go to Elis."

"The trees first."

He wondered if Clara would ever know the true measure of her own strength or the depth of her stubbornness. Considering both were for her daughter, he thought them admirable. "Trees first."

They selected a place in the front hall, near a wall and on the rug. From there, anyone coming inside and from parts of the front rooms and dining area would see the tree. After the larger tree was secured in a water bucket and stabilized with four pieces of wood nailed into the trunk, all the children old enough to walk participated in gathering pine cones and branches with winterberries, filling baskets and singing, "The Twelve Days of Christmas."

Augusta's absence was noted by both Clara and Michael, even though Grace had joined them.

Once back indoors and Alice was absorbed in stringing twine around pine cones and nibbling on a molasses cookie, did Clara allow herself to seek out Michael again. He stood nearby, waiting, and ready. Clara smoothed the single braid in Alice's pale flaxen hair and kissed the top of her head. "Be good for Mrs. Doyle, will you, darling? I am going to see Susan."

"And Mr. Elis, too?"

She did her best to hide the pain in her smile. "And Elis, too."

"I want to go, Mama."

"Not right now, darling." Clara lifted a dried apple from a bowl on one of the cloth-covered dining tables. "Perhaps you can make a few decorations for the baby's tree. We'll take it over before supper."

"Mama, what about Grandma's stars?"

Clara answered Michael's questioning look. "My parents sent a box of tree decorations, much earlier than needed. They seem to think it takes months for even a letter to reach us." She smiled at Alice. "The stars and other ornaments are upstairs, darling, so the box wouldn't be in anyone's way. We'll fetch them later."

"I'll get them now." Michael leaned close and whispered, "It will keep her occupied longer."

"Thank you," she whispered back. "The box is in our small sitting room on the third floor. The box isn't too big."

"I'll find it."

Five minutes later, Michael carried the wooden box into the dining room and placed in on the floor next to the decorating table. He removed the lid and set it aside where no one would trip over it.

"Sorry, it's bigger than I remembered. Your arm."

"Exercise is good for the arm." Michael nodded toward Alice, who was already kneeling next to the box. "And worth it."

Clara bent over again. "You be good now."

"All right, Mama." Alice accepted Clara's kiss, though her attention had already shifted to another child who held up a string of dried fruit for all to see.

Michael's hand rested at the small of Clara's back. It seemed she only managed to don her cloak and outdoor accoutrements with his guidance. The cold air kept her eyes from spilling tears. She sat close to Michael on the sleigh's bench, a calming silence between them. Sunlight continued to shine upon the valley and gave the illusion of a warmer day until one ventured outside.

When Michael stopped the horse in front of the clinic, Clara stared at the church in the meadow beyond. "Elis is a man of faith, if not religion. He once told me God was the voice in his head who talked him out of the best amusements."

Michael chuckled. "He said that to you?"

Clara's soft laughter joined his. "Yes, and turned as red as a winterberry after he realized he'd spoken the words aloud."

"I can sense you thinking, and you're wondering if I agree with Elis. You'll get no confirmation out of me."

"Yet you will not deny it."

Michael climbed out of the sleigh first, then lifted Clara down. "I'll not deny it." He secured the team to the hitching post and holding her hand, walked with Clara into the clinic. Emma pressed a finger to her lips in a request for them to be quiet and motioned them inside.

The lightheartedness from seconds ago vanished. Clara glanced at the closed doors. "Where is he?"

"Peyton and Casey relocated him to the last room down the hall for privacy."

"Is Susan still with him?"

Emma nodded. "I left her alone at first. It's what . . . well, what—"

"I understand." And Clara did. It is what they all would have wanted under the same circumstances.

"I'm glad you've come, Clara. Susan's been alone long enough now, and she won't come out."

Michael squeezed Clara's hand once then released her. "Go ahead. I'll look in on Briley and the baby."

She unwound her scarf and walked silently down the hall. Clara stopped outside the closed door. She raised her hand and knocked, and when not a sound came through from the other side, Clara turned the knob and eased open the door. The shield of strength she'd built around her heart since she heard the news that morning crumbled.

Susan's head rested on the bed next to Elis's shoulder, her eyes closed and breathing shallow. "Oh, Elis." His chest rose and fell—too slowly, she thought—and his skin was devoid of warmth and pale as the falling snow. She touched Susan's shoulder and whispered her friend's name. A faint whimper was her response.

Clara sat at the foot of the bed, careful not to disturb Elis, and waited.

CHAPTER 21

"I never expected life here to be so difficult. It certainly has many rewards, and my heart fills with gratitude whenever I see how well Alice flourishes. It is those moments when I remember why we've come."

- Clara Stowe in a letter to her parents not sent

A MINUTE OR two passed with Michael staring at the empty hall, wishing to be at Clara's side. It took Emma appearing before him to realize she'd been trying to get his attention.

"Clara's strong."

"More than she realizes." Michael rubbed his hands over his whole face and let them drop to his sides. "Lord, I don't know how you women do it."

Emma didn't pretend not to understand. "We choose this life, and in doing so, accept the challenges that come with it."

"Why choose it?"

Emma considered his question while she poured him a cup of coffee. "Here, you need this before you face your sister."

He wrapped his hands around the hot mug and inhaled the strong bitterness wafting from the dark liquid. "How is Briley?"

"She was arguing with her husband not an hour ago, so well, I expect." Emma's eyes brightened a little, like the sun first coming out from behind a dark cloud. "She and the baby are healthy and happy. Were it not for Peyton, they'd be in their own beds at home."

"I agree with him, but I'll let him draw fire a little longer before I say the same to her."

Emma's soft laugh eased a little of his tension, though not much. His mind and his heart traveled with Clara, and he knew hers burned with sorrow. "You don't have to tell me."

Emma leaned against the edge of the examining table and crossed her arms at her waist. "I'm not avoiding the question, just weighing my answer."

Michael sipped and drank deeply, allowing the coffee to warm him from the inside. "Is it that you don't know the answer or are too many?"

"Briley always said you were smart. The latter, I suppose. I came west hoping to find a place desperate enough for a doctor, they'd accept even a woman. My first husband served with Casey in the war. David wasn't much for a one-road wilderness town with a few trading posts between here and civilization, and no train to make the traveling easier. He stayed for me, though, until he went to fight, and eventually, a part of me stayed for Casey."

"Do you ever have any regrets?" Thinking again of Clara, he added, "Enough to make you want to return?"

"For women like me—like Clara—it is in our nature to

remember the easier lives we left behind, especially during trying times like these. We know how simple it would be to return to comfort."

Michael finished the coffee and placed the empty cup next to the hot stove. "Yet, you don't."

"A life of leisure offers no challenge, no opportunity to discover what we are capable of doing. Some of us need to know."

"I think I understand." He crossed the room and brushed a kiss on her cheek. "I haven't properly thanked for you the entirety of what you've done for my sister. Not just helping to bring Mariah Rose to us, but for everything you've no doubt done since she arrived in Crooked Creek. All of you were there for her when I couldn't be."

Emma hugged him as Briley would have, and for the first time since he set out to search for his sister, Michael realized he did have more family than he had hoped to again. She gave him a playful push and walked to the stove.

"What are your intentions toward Clara?"

His raised brow preceded his response. "Do you mean to test my worthiness?"

"Better me than Casey, Carson, or Peyton for that matter. They look on her as a dear sister and friend." Emma ceased her chiding. "No, your worthiness is not in question, and I've asked more than is my right. Still, I'm curious."

Michael didn't think she asked or said nearly enough. He let the matter rest, for now. "You mentioned before that Casey helped move Elis to the back room. What about Harrigan? I should go out there with the men hunting him."

"No, you are where you should be. We know the risks to Clara. You, maybe more than the rest of us, and she is not oblivious to them either." Emma poured more hot water from the kettle over a tea strainer into a cup. "Carson is still out there looking. Wind and fresh snow covers tracks and slows the search. Hattie would be with him if she had her way. Briley guilted her into staying with her soft, practical way of convincing a person to agree with her."

"You mean guilt."

Emma smiled. "Yes."

Michael pointed to Briley's door. "Hattie's in there now?"

"She is." Emma handed him the cup. "You can go in now. And see your sister drinks this."

His eyes narrowed. "Why don't you want to go in there?"

Emma responded with a straight face. "The tea is growing cold, Michael."

Duly ordered, Michael entered Briley's temporary bedroom in the clinic to be met with, "There you are. Were you shot again?"

Michael peered over his shoulder at Emma. "Thank you so much." He braved the room and handed Briley the tea. "Emma wants you to drink this."

Briley accepted the mug and sipped. "You'll not get out of explaining yourself, Michael Donaghue."

"Full name." Hattie leaned against the back of the chair and bit the inside of her cheek to keep from grinning. "Carson only uses my full name when he's cross with me."

"Happens often?" Michael asked.

She released her smile and a laugh with it. "Thankfully, no."

Hattie closed the book she'd been reading aloud when Michael came in. "Is Clara with you?"

Michael nodded. "She's in with Elis and Susan right now."

"I'll look in again while you sit with your sister."

"Hattie, you promised."

"I'm not breaking it." Hattie's sigh was exaggerated

enough to draw Michael's interest. "All right, so I was going to break it. Good saints you're a trial, Briley Sawyer."

Michael nudged his sister's shoulder. "Full name. Doesn't bode well for you." Briley's glare had Michael holding up his hands in surrender. "All yours, Mrs. White Eagle."

Hattie leaned over the cradle and ran a finger down Mariah Rose's soft cheek. "I'll stay close until Carson returns. I can't promise more."

Content to have gotten her way, Briley said, "Accepted."

Hattie exited the room, leaving brother and sister in temporary silence.

"Do you ever get out of bed?"

"Of course. I dress, bathe, eat, and walk about the rooms. I've taken a few turns outside with Peyton—he's fearful I'll fall on ice. Peyton joins us at night, with his feet hanging off the end of the bed, and still he doesn't want me home alone where we'd be more comfortable. I finished a new sweater this morning."

"You're bored."

"Am I ever." Briley smoothed a hand over the quilt. "I'm abed now because I was napping. Emma warned it's best to sleep whenever the baby does." Briley motioned to the chair Hattie left empty. "Sit and then tell me why you didn't let Emma treat you. Where were you shot?"

"It was a graze to my arm, and Clara saw to it. Emma has enough to do."

"I wish you wouldn't go out there again until this man and his ruffians are captured."

"You know I can't promise that, Briley."

"I know." She waved him toward the door. "I'm tired of resting, so leave me to dress and do what you must."

Michael lifted and kissed her hand. "By the way, I agree with your husband. You should stay here until the unrest is over." He departed quickly, closing the door on her muttered, "Michael Donaghue, get back——"

The outer room was empty, so he followed where Clara had disappeared to earlier and stopped at the last door. Slightly ajar, he did not have to push it inward to see Clara sitting at the foot of the bed, much like she had sat on his bed the night before. Upon noticing Michael, she moved to stand with him. "Briley?"

"Healthy and annoyed. We can probably expect a jailbreak any time now." He nodded toward Susan. "Is she awake?"

"Yes," Susan said, her voice heavy with exhaustion.

Michael and Clara joined Susan at Elis's bedside. "You need to sleep properly, Susan, and eat something," Clara said. "You'll be no good to him when he awakens."

"*If* he wakes. Emma won't tell me what's wrong."

"She doesn't know, dearest." Clara gathered her skirts and hunched next to Susan. "You need to stay strong for him, for your children. When they come home——"

"No. They are better off with their cousins." Susan shifted in her chair. "I hope you know how grateful I am for all you've done, and how happy I have been here."

"You speak as though you'll leave."

Susan swiped at a tear and nodded. "If he doesn't wake up."

Clara embraced Susan and held her fast as she cried. "I understand."

Michael left them alone and waited outside the room until Clara joined him ten minutes later.

"I wish it were in my power to find and destroy Lucas Harrigan for the damage he has caused."

"You have my faith in your ability to do that and much

more." Michael ran a finger down her cheek. "I need to help find Harrigan."

Clara leaned into him, relaxing into his embrace. "You should leave from here."

Michael tilted her face up. "Tomorrow. Alice wants to give her tree to the baby, and I need to speak with Isaac. I'll deliver more food to the cabin tonight so no one else needs go out there."

"What of Augusta and Patrick's argument?"

"I'll speak with Patrick later. Augusta has been through enough." Michael took her hand and led her down the hall. Voices he recognized as belonging to Emma and Hattie drifted from the front room. "Come. We have a tree to ready for Mariah Rose."

MICHAEL SLIPPED AWAY the following day before the sun rose above the highest mountain peaks. Clara watched him ride toward town from her bedroom window. They had not said goodbye or sought each other out before his departure.

Silent vibrations lay heavy in the air, a thick thrum of anticipation as everyone inside waited. The day progressed as any other. Clara checked on her daughter, and finding her abed at the early hour, descended the back stairs to the kitchen where already Orla labored on the morning meal. The makings of porridge were in a cast-iron pot waiting to be heated on the stove. Round loaves of fresh soda bread cooled on the counter, and sausage sizzled in a skillet.

"It smells wonderful."

"We've taken over your kitchen."

"I'm grateful." Clara leaned closer to the bread and inhaled. "Are you working alone?"

Orla turned the fat sausages over one by one. "Neasa's

been helping. She went to check on her children. They rise early."

"It is a day for it," Clara said, then helped herself to half a cup of coffee. "You are all welcome to stay for as long as you need."

Orla jerked her hand back when a hot splatter landed on her skin, and rubbed the sting away. She set aside the fork and wiped her hands on a towel. "We've talked amongst ourselves about where we'll go next, what we'll do. Work has been offered, though we know well enough there's little need for it this time of year."

Clara sipped at the coffee and wished for tea. "Do not be so certain. Peyton hopes to find someone to help at their house, especially with his wife wanting to return home with their baby. White Eagle Ranch is large and growing; any work offered there is not charity."

"Patrick and I think we'd like to stay in Crooked Creek. My brother is likely dead—I've accepted it—and I'd like to give him a proper burial when he's found. The others, including Sean's family, want to move on."

"Winter is still in its infancy, Orla. I'm assured it will last months. How will they travel?"

"There's talk of going with the supply wagon when it comes again."

Clara set her mug in the wash basin. "Please talk to them, ask them to wait until spring when the traveling is easier for everyone, especially the children."

Orla nodded. "We'll try again. Truth is, we would have stayed in those old cabins through winter if they hadn't blown two of them apart."

"It was one of Harrigan's men, who put the dynamite in the stove, wasn't it? I never heard."

"No one saw, but there is no other explanation. We hid in

the other cabins, and the gunfire and explosion happened so fast." Orla looked around the kitchen. "The cabins weren't much, but more than what we're used to than your inn. Not to sound ungrateful. I'm sorry, I did not mean . . . well . . . your inn is so lovely."

"I took no offense, and thank you."

"Would you like some of this porridge now? I can cook a bit up, and it goes well with the soda bread. Neasa makes the best I've ever tasted."

"I'll wait and eat with the others. May I be of help?"

"Heavens no. We have it well in hand, and Neasa will be back soon." Orla scooped some of the uncooked porridge into a smaller pot and set it on the stove. "Could be awhile yet before the others come downstairs, except Jack and Patrick. They'll have the fires going soon."

"I think they already do. It's warmer this morning than yesterday." Clara cut a thin slice of the bread and bit off one corner. "I'll take this with me."

They shared a smile and Orla went back to stirring the porridge. Clara passed through the dining room and parlor, found the fires lit in both, and continued to the front hall where Patrick stood near the front windows.

"Have you been here long?"

"A few hours. Jack will take over when he's done with the rest of the fires."

Believing it would do no good to explain to Patrick why such vigilance was unnecessary, Clara instead asked, "The cow needs milking. Will you join me in the barn when Jack relieves you?"

"We can see to that chore."

"I have to keep busy, Patrick, and my mind is not in a good place for reading as is my usual pastime at this hour."

"Then I'll join you." Patrick shifted his weight from one

foot to the other. "The argument between Augusta and me, well, I explained to Michael this morning before he left. I thought she'd confessed something, and she admitted she didn't."

"You're making no sense. What more could there be to tell?"

"Why, the gold, of course."

"What gold?"

Patrick's posture stiffened. "She didn't tell you? Michael wasn't surprised, and I thought——"

"Please, Patrick. What gold?"

"The gold Augusta took when she left Harrigan."

CHAPTER 22

"Christmas is but two weeks away now and the new year will be well upon us by the time this letter reaches you. I want you to know how Alice flourishes. She has Gideon's smile. For your son and for the daughter he would have cherished, I pray you may find it in your hearts to forgive us."

Clara Stowe to Gideon's parents in an unfinished letter

SINCE HIS YOUTH, Michael had craved adventure, though not the kind found on battlefields or the high seas. He longed for exploits closer to home, those that took him on long walks over the green hills of Ireland and along the soaring cliffs. He yearned to build, to create with his hands. His idea of adventure lay in building hearth and home and journeying through life with a wife and partner by his side and children to share their laughter and love.

Those dreams faltered when his family left Ireland and

fractured again when he and his father left mother, wife, daughter, and sister behind. He thought the dreams forever dead until he found his sister again and met Clara. Now, with dazzling rays bursting from the sun and blinding him every time he studied tracks in the snow, he vowed the future he once imagined would come true.

First, he had to ensure their safety.

Let Harrigan come to us. Carson was the first to agree when he said as much to the others. Peyton and Casey soon joined them, though not without reservations. Carson argued a pack of wolves obscured the last set of tracks he found, and there was no telling if the tracks would lead them to Harrigan when he picked up the trail again. He was content to let the wolves find the men first, and if any lived, they'd be easier to deal with.

Michael thought Carson's plan had merit. He didn't care how Harrigan disappeared, so long as he did.

On his last scouting assignment, Michael had hidden in shrubs not twenty feet from a confederate camp. He saw the men as brothers in arms, regardless of the color of uniforms they wore. Unfortunately, he couldn't always count on them to agree, and so he hid in the brush, studied the camp, and waited. Every so often the voice of instinct warned him to flatten his body to the ground and hold his breath lest he be heard. Twice, a patrol came within a few feet of his hiding place, and twice he evaded notice.

When his stomach roiled and the voice shouted in his head to leave, Michael listened, and crawled away as fast as he could. He counted one minute and a half before a soldier walked through the shrubs where he'd been hiding.

Instinct saved him then, so when the same voice repeated Clara's name, he listened again. Leaving his vantage point on a hill above the town, Michael rode Rian to the inn.

. . .

"WHAT'S THE BASKET FOR?" Patrick asked. He carried a rifle in one hand and an extra jug for milk in the other.

"Berries first. There's a variety growing near here that Emma told me about. We can't eat them raw but they make great syrups and jellies, and go well in pies, or so Susan tells me."

"I'm sorry about what happened to Elis."

"And I am sorry about your wife's brother. You've been out looking for him every day?"

Patrick nodded. "As much as we can. We don't know this land, the area, and shamed I am to admit, we aren't prepared for the elements when we do go out."

"Carson, Casey, and the others searching for Harrigan also look for Sean when they're out. They'll find him." Clara pointed to a stand of bushes along the treeline between the house and barn. "Over there." They cut through the snow, Clara holding the hem of her skirts up to the top of her boots. "None of it is your fault, nor is it Augusta's. Everyone has done what they need to survive."

"She should have—someone should have—told you about the gold. If it was given back, then maybe Harrigan would have left them alone."

Faint scars from the slash of Harrigan's whip across Augusta's back flitted into Clara's mind. "I am not so certain." They reached the berries and Clara picked up the pruning shears from inside the basket. "This won't take long."

"Longer than you think."

Clara's fingers tightened around the shears and her arm gripped the basket handle close to her side. She dared a glance over her shoulder. Where had he come from without them hearing his approach? He might have been any one of Harrigan's men, but in the face of their defeats, Clara suspicioned the man himself had exhausted his patience.

"Run, Clara." Patrick's voice was strained, yet firm.

"No, don't run, Clara. Drop the shears and walk into the trees before anyone sees us, or your friend dies now."

Clara walked a few feet to the right to get around the first bush. She moved deeper into the trees. "What do you hope to accomplish by taking us? There are men searching all over for you."

"That's far enough, just away from prying eyes."

Clara saw they had not ventured too deep into the woods and wondered at his motives. "You are Lucas Harrigan, I presume. Some suspect you are dead." *Or hoped you were.*

"That's because those whores tried to kill me."

"No, you do not consider Augusta and Lela as whores. Property, perhaps, your possessions. Things to command and destroy."

"This can be easy if you cooperate."

Clara sidestepped, hoping to gain a little more time to think. Harrigan's knife pressed too closely to Patrick's neck. If he tried to move, or even breath too deeply, he risked a slit throat. "Why do you think they're here? None of the men you sent ever found them, did they?"

"There's nowhere else for them to go except Crooked Creek, and you've already, in a way, admitted you know them. While your marshal and the men with him were tracking my men, I came here. I learned a thing or two fighting in the war with Mexico."

"You learned how to kill."

"I learned how not to die, how not to let them find me."

With hair the color of dark chestnuts and eyes of light brown, Harrigan stood only an inch taller than Patrick. A faint sprinkling of gray grew gracefully in his beard. He should have been handsome. Might have been if he were a different man. Wickedness and pain were the first words that came to Clara's mind when she thought to describe him. "You're a coward. Only a coward beats women and hides behind other men. I won't tell you where they are."

Harrigan's hand flashed from Patrick's throat to his back. "Last chance."

"Run!" Patrick twisted at the same time Harrigan thrust the blade upward. Patrick tumbled forward to the snow and needle-covered ground. He made no sound or movement as blood slowly turned the snow a dark shade of brick red.

Harrigan waved the bloody knife when Clara tried to reach for Patrick. "Leave him. You see, I think you will tell me, or every person in your house will suffer for it. I do not wish to kill more than necessary, but I will. No one takes what is mine."

How long had she and Patrick been gone? Would someone come looking for them? Clara tried to stall. "Soulless men do not care who they kill or how many, and that is what you are. You care only for your own self-preservation because you know with one scream, the men you fear will come, and you cannot fight them all."

Harrigan shrugged. "No, but I can kill you. I want what's mine, and all roads, as they say, lead to your inn. Should I go in there and ask the children? Your daughter, at least, will die. Or will you tell me where they are? Where is my son?"

Clara did not doubt his sincerity. Did she think "wicked"? No, she saw only insanity now. Her legs carried her only so far before she was yanked back. As Harrigan's hand rose and came down toward her face, Michael's name filled her thoughts, over and over. It was all she heard.

．　．　．

HIS HEART KEPT A STEADY BEAT, the same steadiness that prepared him to properly aim on a target and shoot. He held onto the calm as he guided Rian to the rear of the house and dismounted.

The barn door was closed ahead, and he heard laughter from inside the house. He walked in between trees until he reached the end of the barn. From there, he took shelter against the barn and searched the area. Silence met his perusal.

Clara's name repeated in his mind, over and over, each time growing louder. He raised his rifle, kept the sight steady, and nearly collapsed when Clara ran from the trees, her arms flailing, her lips bloody.

She wasn't fast enough. Harrigan yanked Clara backward against his hard chest, stifling her scream. Michael's gazed shifted to the man's face, took in the hard set of his mouth and narrow, wild eyes. He'd seen the look of men who took pleasure in a kill, who cared nothing for their prey except it be snuffed out.

He did not try to mask his presence. "Let her go, Harrigan."

Harrigan's eyes narrowed and then widened in recognition. "We've met, at the trading post."

"I remember. Let her go."

"Why? Because you said so? I think not." He growled low and ugly. "I want what's mine, and now, you're the only two in my way. This one stays with me until I'm out of the territory with my son."

Michael lowered his rifle, dropped it in the snow, and stepped one foot forward. "I spent four years learning how to kill men, and to my regret, it was a natural skill."

"You want her back, then we trade. Her for Lela and my

son, and no one else dies. I'll even agree to you following us to Wyoming, and she will be released there."

An owl's *coo* traveled through the air, telling Michael he wasn't alone. He'd be impressed with Carson's instincts later because he was sure it was Carson out of sight and ready. Right now, Harrigan held Clara too close for a clean shot. "No one else is going to die today, Harrigan, except maybe you."

He risked taking his eyes off Harrigan long enough to look at Clara. She winced in reaction to the pressure he had on her neck, and her hands instinctively pulled at Harrigan's severe grip.

Harrigan pressed his face against Clara's. "She wouldn't give them up, even to save everyone inside the inn. The man who was with her wouldn't, either. All of this for a couple of whores. They aren't worth it. You can even keep Lela, but you have no right to hide my son from me."

"Augusta no longer has the gold, if that's what you really want."

"I don't believe you."

"I have it."

Harrigan squeezed Clara's neck a little tighter.

"Your son or your gold. Which do you want more?" Michael gauged the distance now between Harrigan's head and Clara. He needed one more inch, maybe two for Carson to get a clean shot. The cabin door creaked open and Isaac stepped onto the small porch, rifle in hand, and closed the door behind him.

"Your freeman can't help her, either," Harrigan said through tight lips and pulled Clara closer to him. "Tell him to get back or I slice her throat."

Michael couldn't chance another look at Clara. "Kill her and you're dead. I'm betting that's a risk you're not willing to take." He advanced another step. "I'll take you now to the gold. Me for her."

Harrigan answered by yanking on Clara's hair. Her scream drew Michael's gaze to her face and the unmistakable anger he saw in her eyes.

Isaac advanced, drawing Harrigan's gaze.

"Stay there, Isaac," Michael called out without taking his focus off Harrigan. The owl's mimic *coo* sounded again. He couldn't see Carson, but knew he was there, waiting for his chance. Michael needed another inch, just one more inch between Harrigan and Clara.

The cabin door opened again, and this time Lela stepped outside. It proved the distraction needed to throw Harrigan momentarily off his target. Michael reached Clara in seconds and pulled her away a moment before a bullet hit Harrigan in the back of his head. "Don't look." He held her face against his chest. "Come away, Clara."

"Patrick is back there in the trees. I don't know if he's alive. I ran to keep Harrigan away from the cabin, but he caught me, and Patrick—"

"Shh. We'll help him."

"Who shot Harrigan?"

"Carson. I'll explain later." Michael lifted Clara into his arms. "Isaac, help will be here in a minute. Please, help Patrick, get him to the clinic." Neither Michael nor Clara spoke until he carried her into the house.

"Good, Lord." Orla rushed forward. "We heard the gunshot. Was she—"

"She wasn't hit. Can you bring fresh water, towels, and brandy to her room? And keep Alice down here." He didn't wait for an answer. Clara's silence escalated the terror in his rapid heartbeats, and her well-being consumed him. Michael carried her up the stairs to the top floor, located her bedroom, and laid her on the four-poster bed. Michael removed the torn cloak from her body and undid the first three buttons on her blouse before removing her boots.

"Clara, look at me." When he lifted his fingers from her face, the tips were colored red with the blood from the cut by her mouth.

Orla bore a tray of towels, a pitcher of water, and a bottle of brandy into the room.

"Set them on the table, please. I need a damp towel, and some of the brandy in a glass."

Orla passed him the damp cloth first, and he used it to wipe away the blood to examine the cut underneath. Another laceration trailed down the side of her neck. Michael gently wiped at it, relief passing through him upon finding it superficial.

"The brandy."

He took another cloth, dipped it into the golden liquid, and dabbed it over each wound. She flinched, and it was one of the sweetest things he'd ever seen. "That's right, feel the sting, Clara."

"I don't think . . ." A sharp look from Michael stopped Orla from sharing her opinion. "Everyone heard the gunshot. The children aren't sure exactly what it was, so they're all right, but Alice will ask about her mother. Augusta was with them, but I think she's gone to see what happened."

"Alice can't see me like this."

Michael heard the whisper. "Thank you, Orla. Can you send word to the clinic? Ask Emma and Hattie to both come."

Orla nodded and exited the room, leaving the door open.

Clara clasped the cloth in Michael's hand and lowered it to her lap. "How bad is it?"

"It probably hurts worse than it looks." He sat on the bed

and lifted her into his lap, like he had the evening in the
library.

She cuddled into him. "Where will they take Harrigan's
body?"

Michael didn't know or care. "He's gone. Nothing else
matters now." He buried his face in her hair and rocked her
gently.

"Harrigan wanted Lela and the baby, even more than the
gold, didn't he? His eyes, Michael. There was such obsession
in them, in the way he talked of her and the baby. Are they
safe?"

"They're safe. You could almost say that Lela saved your
life. Did you the hear the owl? Well, it wasn't an owl. It was
Carson. I wasn't sure he'd see me come for you." Michael
kissed her neck and tightened his hold. "Don't think about
any of it now. God, but I thought—"

"I'm alive." Clara eased away to look at him. "We're
alive."

Michael skimmed a hand over her back and glided his
fingers through the hair loosened by Harrigan. He separated
the tangles and watched the strands flow down her back,
erasing the memory of Harrigan's hands upon her. Michael
closed his eyes and doubted the fear or the memory would
leave him anytime soon.

ONE WEEK LATER, Augusta came upon Clara sitting on the
front porch, early in the morning. She'd returned to her
routine, as best she could. The mayhem of the week prior
haunted her slumber the first three nights, and then blessedly
on the fourth night, she slept.

Life, and the wonderfully mundane tasks that
accompanied it, kept Clara occupied from sunup until she

curled into bed, each night reflecting on what it was to be comforted in Michael's arms. He had not avoided her exactly. He joined her to visit Briley and the baby when they returned home. She appreciated his company on her daily calls upon Susan, who temporarily occupied Emma's spare room behind the clinic so she could stay close to Elis. They ate together in the mornings, though he was often absent at the noon meal without explanation.

Clara learned to adjust her expectations, even as she fought the impulse to ask him what had changed between them. For now, though, she thought of nothing save the fresh morning air and the chilly breeze caressing her skin.

Sunrise waited beyond the ridge, allowing dawn a few more precious minutes before the sun crested the mountains to give light to the valley. Augusta rocked in the chair next to Clara's for a time before speaking.

"We haven't had much of a chance to talk."

"It's over. We're all safe. Nothing more needs to be said."

Augusta stopped rocking. "Yes, it does, and I hope you'll give me a chance to explain."

Clara nodded.

"No one will talk about what happened in the last minutes with my husband. That's not what I want now. I need you to know that despite what he might have told you, it was always about Lela and her son. The way he watched her, obsessed over her, he was a different man with her around."

Clara slowed her rocking and continued to watch the early glow of the sun's ascent into the sky. "I believe you. He made clear what he wanted—Lela, her son, and the gold."

"I took the gold a little bit at a time, planning for the day when I would take Grace away from him, from these mountains. He thought one of his men was stealing, never suspected me." Augusta's heavy sigh was carried on the breeze. "I haven't cried. In truth, I feel relief, an acquittal from a life mired in misery and fear. We cannot ever thank you enough. You and your friends protected us when you didn't have to. Looking back on it, we should have kept going."

"The mother in me terrified for her child agrees. You should have kept going, never stopping in Crooked Creek, at my inn. But you were meant to come here." Clara pushed out of the chair, tugging the edges of a wool blanket tighter across her shoulders. "You saved yourselves, Augusta. Never doubt you saved each other." She leaned her back against one of the porch posts. "What will you do now?"

"I have Lucas Harrigan's money, more than Grace and I will ever need, and it is time it was used for good. I've settled some on Sean and his family, for what he sacrificed for Lela."

The greatest shock and joy of the past week was Casey's arrival at the inn to share the news with Sean's family that he'd been found, wounded and weakened from exposure to the elements, having found a cave to hide in after leading more of Harrigan's men away from Lela. But he was alive and now under Emma's care. Clara doubted the town's doctor had ever been kept so busy.

"You're leaving Crooked Creek, after all."

Augusta nodded. "There are too many unpleasant memories here, and other than meeting all of you, none are good. I'll return home to the Carolinas. Lela and the baby will go with me and I'll see they do not want for anything. Isaac has asked to join us, as well. Emma gave him the name of a surgeon from one of her medical journals who can mend his leg, and I'll see to it he's looked after."

Clara had not heard of Isaac's desire to leave and wondered if Michael knew. "Isaac is his own man, and I've noticed his affection for Lela and her son. He mentioned a time or two about his fondness for a warmer climate. Spring is a long way off. Some say half the year is winter."

"We won't be waiting until spring. It's time to move on and start anew, now." Augusta stood. "Two of the Irish families also wish to leave. Sean and his family will remain here with his sister and Patrick. Orla forgave me, even after what happened to her husband."

"Despite Lucas's efforts, Patrick lived."

"He lost the use of an arm, Clara."

"Lucas, and he alone, is to blame. You could not have stopped him."

"I know, but I can't help feeling responsible." Augusta released a heavy sigh. "I'm selling the lumber mill. There are two large supply sleighs at the mill. It won't be easy, but we'll use those to get as far as Fort Benton where we'll wait for passage on a steamboat to St. Louis. From there, the train will get us home."

"It will be an arduous journey, especially for the children."

"Yes, but we have the resources now, and I truly believe it's for the best."

Clara had no argument to disabuse Augusta of the notion. In her heart she agreed, and her silence said what she could not voice aloud. "It sounds as though your late husband's money will do a lot of good. Have you already sold the mill?"

"Not yet. I thought to do so when I reached St. Louis."

"Please, will you wait to leave? A few more weeks, until after Christmas."

"Of course. For you, I will do whatever you ask." Augusta embraced her briefly. "Thank you, Clara. We'll never forget how you invited us in from the cold and for gifting us with your friendship."

She turned back toward the sunrise before the door closed behind Augusta.

Two hours later, after breakfast was served and Alice spent an hour with her lessons before begging to play with the other children, Clara readied herself for the familiar walk to town. Since she'd grown accustomed to it, walking in the snow became enjoyable when the winds ceased and the sun shone brightly above.

A flock of black-headed geese honked and passed. Moments later, an eagle soared overhead, its chirping whistle drawing a smile from Clara as she imagined what beautiful wonders it must see so high above. Her gaze drifted to the church and the small school beyond it, closed since the teacher married in autumn and left before the first snowfall.

Clara enjoyed lessons with her daughter, though she fretted over what Alice would do when Grace left and hoped the next few weeks would give her daughter time to grow closer with the other children staying behind with their parents. She rapped on the clinic door before entering. Greeted with warmth from the large stove in the front room, she removed her outer clothes, and set them on the bench. "Emma?"

"Be right there."

Without Briley and the baby in residence, the clinic was quieter. Susan would be with Elis, reading to him or telling him stories from her own childhood. Except to eat, finally, and sleep, she rarely left his bedside.

Emma entered the room, wisps of hair flying about her smiling face. "I was about to send for you."

"What is it?"

"Come, see for yourself."

Clara followed her back to Elis's room and rushed past Emma. Elis's head was propped up with two thick pillows, and his lips closed around the spoon Susan held to his mouth. She scooped up more broth and repeated the process.

"Guess the good Lord wasn't ready for me just yet." Elis's smile was faint, his voice weak, and his spirits high.

"He knew we weren't ready to let you go. Welcome back to us, Elis." Clara held onto her tears and left the room. She stumbled into Michael. As hard as she tried to hold them at bay, tears fell unbidden and unwanted. Once again, Michael lifted her into his arms and carried her into the room where Briley had brought Mariah Rose into the world.

He held her close and whispered words she barely heard. His voice soothed as his body comforted. "You've held it in long enough."

Sobs of joy, sorrow, hope, and fear dissolved into each tear. Clara clutched at his shirt, and every so often pounded his chest, releasing the anger she'd penned within for too long.

She fell asleep in his arms.

Michael breathed in the floral scent lingering on her skin and smoothed a hand over the silky softness of her golden hair. When Emma ventured in to check on them, Michael merely held Clara closer and waited for Emma to leave them alone again.

Half an hour passed before Clara stirred in his arms. Her eyelids fluttered open. "You're still here."

He nodded. "When you're ready, will you go somewhere with me?"

Clara stifled a yawn and smiled up at him. "I'm ready now."

She rode behind him on Rian past the church to the hill overlooking town. She'd often walked up to this spot during the summer to gaze upon the place she chose to call home. It was no less beautiful covered in snow. He helped her down, untied a blanket from the saddle, and enveloped her within its warmth.

"The first time I fancied myself in love with a girl, I was twelve years old and her name was Hannah. She had bright red curls and was never without a smile. She died a month later from fever, and I swore I'd never love again."

"And did you?"

Michael stepped around Clara so they faced each other. "I love my family deeply, this land, my home country." He brushed his lips over hers. "Love alone doesn't explain what I feel with you. I've spent this past week convincing myself you weren't lost to me, and then thought of every reason I couldn't make you happy."

A tear dropped to her cheek. "How many did you come up with?"

"Too many, then realized none of them mattered." Michael withdrew a folded sheet of paper from his pocket and handed it to the Clara. "Instead, I wrote a letter to Gideon."

Speechless, Clara unfolded the letter and read.

I'M the man who cherishes the woman you love and the daughter you created together. You and I fought the same battles, each struggling to survive long enough to get home again. Only God knows why I should have lived when you had so much waiting for you. Alice is everything a father could hope for in a child, and Clara is the most beautiful mother whose strength will live on in your daughter.

I don't deserve them, but I vow to become worthy of their love, to make this world better for them. By God's good grace, we won't meet for many years. Until then, I promise to give all I am to make them happy, to treasure them every day, and to never give them a reason to lose faith in me.

MOISTURE BLURRED her vision before she reached the end.

"I thought the war destroyed every ounce of hope left in me, Clara. Your light filled me from the beginning, and I began to believe again, to trust there was more to life than merely existing." Michael traced her damp cheeks and smiling lips with a gentle touch. "Will you let me love you for the rest of our days?"

"We both know how quickly life and love can be taken away, how unpredictable our tomorrows." Clara held the letter to her heart and then replaced it with Michael's hand. "Yes!"

"Will it be too much if I ask for forever?"

Her lyrical laughter got lost in the kiss. Michael accepted it, drew it out, and held her close until survival demanded they breathe.

"Yes, Michael, forever sounds like just enough time."

EPILOGUE

"I never expected to love again. Michael is all things you would want for me—that Gideon would want for his daughter. The greatest adventures of our lives are only just beginning."

- Clara Stowe to her parents in a letter finished the week before Christmas

ALL THEIR NEW friends stayed for Christmas and filled the inn with laughter, love, and joyful song. Lela and Isaac planned to marry on their arrival in North Carolina, though Michael doubted Isaac's fortitude would last that long with so much time between here and there.

Evergreen boughs intertwined with winterberries graced the mantels and tabletops. Hot apple cider warmed their bellies in preparation for the feast ahead. Augusta and Grace sang "Silent Night," their voices a melody all their own, and then everyone else joined in for "We Wish You a Merry Christmas."

Peyton held Briley close to his side, with their precious Mariah Rose cradled in her mother's arms. Casey lifted his son onto his shoulders, making Emma's heart lurch and eyes close until she heard young Gavin's boisterous laughter. Hattie, her countenance so filled with happiness as she cradled the flat of her stomach, Carson's hands covering hers. Emma had confirmed they'd become parents in the spring.

Susan and Elis married two days earlier in the small church near the hill overlooking Crooked Creek, surrounded by dear friends. The telegram they sent to Susan's children promised a big celebration when they returned.

Together, Clara and Michael bought the lumber mill from Augusta, the purchase to be paid for quarterly for a percentage of the profits, which Augusta intended to set aside for Grace. They wanted to buy the mill on their own, without asking for financial help from Clara's father, even though she believed he would consider it a wise investment. Jobs would again be available for honest, hard-working men.

Their lives would shift like the seasons and deliver surprises as unexpected as a winter storm in June. Clara welcomed the challenge of every wonder awaiting them, and the promise of every miracle yet to come.

Alice lit the candle in the window to guide anyone lost to their door, and should anyone knock and seek refuge, they would find a room for them out of the cold and into the warmth of their home and hearts, for love is all Clara had room for now that she'd found Michael.

Later the same evening, when the lamps were dimmed and after Michael finished reading *A Christmas Carol* to Alice, Clara tucked quilts around her sleeping daughter. Once assured she would not awaken, Michael and Clara retreated to the cozy library to watch a light snowfall through the window.

He grabbed a blanket, leaned against the window seat's backrest, and left room at his side for Clara to rest against his chest, her legs spread alongside his. Michael unfolded the blanket and laid it over them before embracing her.

"Four hours left until Christmas day ends."

Clara's head bumped his chin when she looked at him. "Are you going to spend those last four hours at the window?"

Michael tugged her closer. "Until our wedding next week, then I will think of someplace warmer."

"Next week? Briley and I planned for next month."

He kissed her soundly. "I heard next week. So did Peyton. Hattie and Emma probably did, too. And I'm sure Carson and Casey—ow."

She smoothed over where she had pinched his arm. "Next week, is it?"

"Unless you think sooner is better?"

"My parents?"

Michael's sigh was heavy with regret. When Clara tilted her head back to peek at him, she saw his eyes closed and a smile played on his lips. "Spring?"

Clara shifted, slipped from his embrace, and knelt in the narrow space between his legs and the window. "You would wait until spring?"

"For you, anything," Michael said, and meant it. Clara had transformed his life with her strength and love and captured his whole heart and soul.

Clara's beatific grin came in degrees until the joy of it overwhelmed them both. "I have been told winters are quite long here."

He groaned, and meant that, too. "Unbearably long."

"My parents will understand."

"Are you sure?" Michael's entire countenance brightened.

She braced her hands on his chest and leaned close. "We can invite them to join us in the spring, when the journey is less arduous."

"Or we could travel to them."

Clara loved him all the more for offering. "True. However, I want them to see the life Alice and I have been blessed with here in Crooked Creek. The letters I send cannot do justice to its beauty."

"Avoiding, of course, mention of the danger you encountered these past weeks."

"Of course." Clara kissed him soundly, then adjusted her position so she once again lay in his embrace, her head resting against his shoulder, hand placed over his heart. "No matter how many Christmases we are fortunate to share, I will always cherish this first one."

Michael lazily brushed a hand over her hair and kissed the top of her head. "So will I. After all, you gave me the greatest Christmas gift I'll ever receive."

She smiled, though privately she desired to gift him with a son, God willing, next Christmas. "I noticed you lit a candle tonight, the one on the mantel in the parlor."

He nodded. "For Gideon." Michael raised his shoulders in a soft shrug. "His sacrifice gave me you and Alice."

Clara's eyes welled with tears. "Thank you, Michael Donaghue, for being our Christmas miracle."

Thank you for reading
Christmas in Crooked Creek

Hungry for more historical adventure, romance, and mystery? Explore MK's other exciting and heartwarming books at her website.

Want to keep up with MK's news? Sign up at www. mkmcclintock.com/subscribe

ALSO BY MK MCCLINTOCK

Montana Gallagher Series

Gallagher's Pride

Gallagher's Hope

Gallagher's Choice

An Angel Called Gallagher

Journey to Hawk's Peak

Wild Montana Winds

The Healer of Briarwood

Christmas in Briarwood

British Agent Series

Alaina Claiborne

Blackwood Crossing

Clayton's Honor

Short Story Collections

A Home for Christmas

The Women of Crooked Creek

Hopes and Dreams in Whitcomb Springs

You may find all these and more and see what's coming next at
www.mkmcclintock.com.

ABOUT THE AUTHOR

MK McClintock is an award-winning author of more than twenty works of historical romantic fiction. Her novels and short stories of adventure, romance, and mystery sweep across the American West to the Victorian British Isles, with places and times between and beyond. MK enjoys a quiet life in the northern Rocky Mountains.

Discover more at www.mkmcclintock.com.

"The four interconnected short stories will have powerful appeal to readers who like an author who can cut to the chase quickly, get to the meat of the story quickly, without a lot of fluff and padding. MK McClintock knows what readers want. A good collection of short stories." — Readers' Favorite on *The Women of Crooked Creek*

"Ms. McClintock succeeds in masterfully weaving both genres meticulously together until mystery lovers are sold on romance and romance lovers love the mystery!" — InD'tale Magazine on *Alaina Claiborne*

"*Journey to Hawk's Peak* by MK McClintock is one of the most gripping and thrilling western novels that anyone will ever

read. This is probably the best novel that I have yet read as a reviewer. It clicks on all cylinders—grammar, punctuation, plot, characterization, everything. This novel is a serious page-turner, and for fans of western fiction, it is a must-read."
— *Readers' Favorite*

"The Montana Gallagher Collection is adventurous and romantic with scenes that transport you into the wild west."
— *InD'tale Magazine*

"I just finished a six-book series by MK McClintock, the Montana Gallaghers. It is honestly the best series I have ever read. Each person is developed into a star and given their own book, but all the other characters are given their own time and investment in that book. Wow! What a series. I guarantee you won't be able to stop reading. Well done MK!"
— *Pioneer Hearts Reader*

"Ms. McClintock has a true genius when writing beauty to touch the heart. This holiday treat is a gift any time one needs to remember the true meaning of love!" — InD'tale Magazine on *A Home for Christmas*

Made in the USA
Las Vegas, NV
26 April 2023

71123696R00173